The Dead Man in the Tree

CAROL PRIOR

All characters appearing in this work are fictitious. Any resemblance to people, living or dead is purely coincidental.

Cover designed & created by Zara Prior

Copyright Carol Prior 2019
Winchelsea Publications

To my husband Ollie, with love…

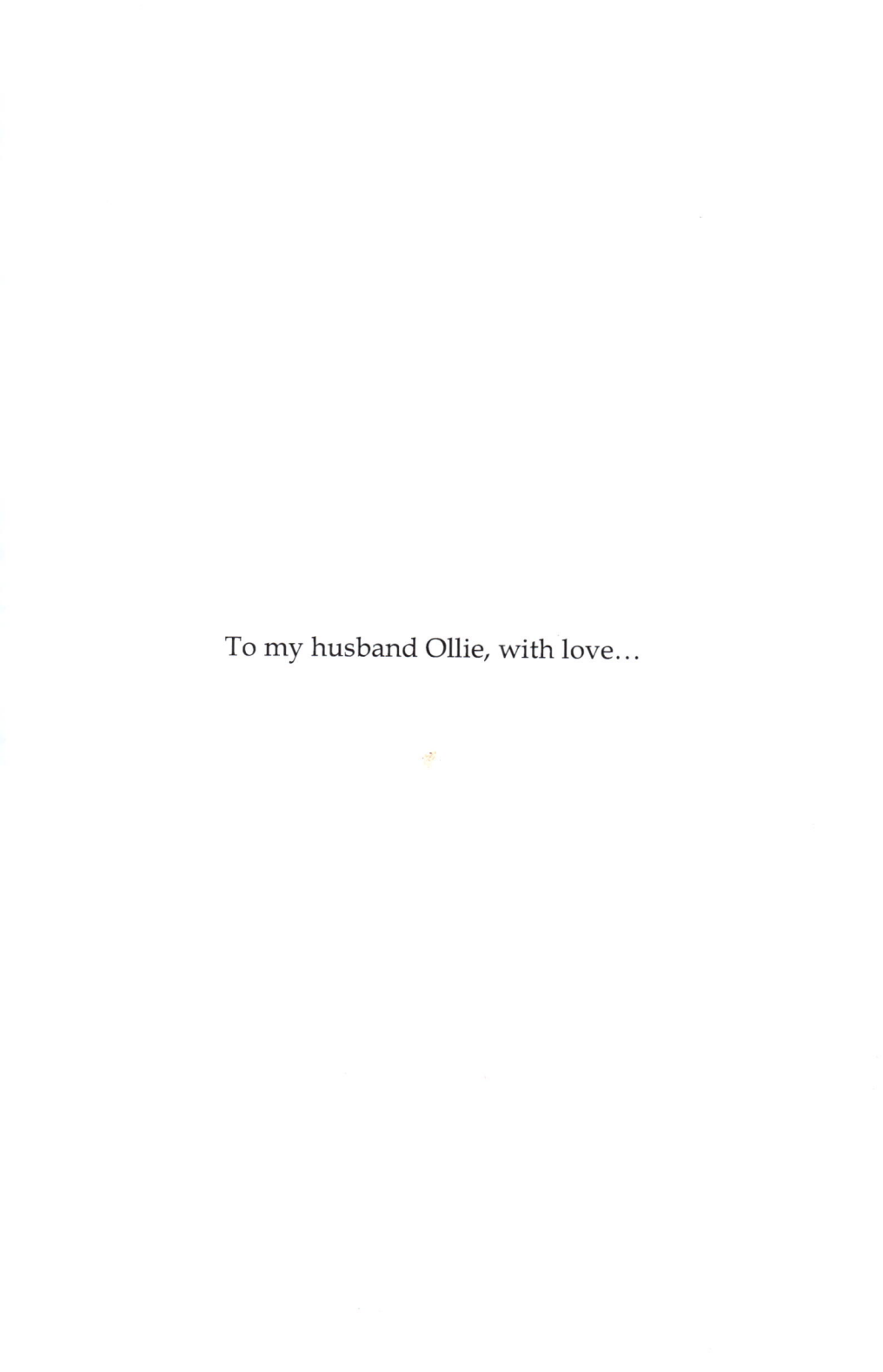

The Dead Man
1994

He watched from the trees, silent and still, hardly daring to breathe for fear of drawing their attention to him and away from the man lying dead at their feet.

There were three women; two were young and unkempt, with faces prematurely lined, and hair scrunched back, revealing pale, careworn foreheads. He noticed the younger of the two was the prettiest by far, but she frightened him the most; her grey eyes were full of pain and resentment, like the eyes of an animal caught in a trap. The third woman was much older, rake-thin, and pale; she sobbed quietly into a large handkerchief, occasionally raising her eyes to stare in horrified silence at the dead man, before being overcome by waves of emotion and further weeping. He watched, transfixed, as one of the women began to dig a hole in the wet soil, lifting the turf carefully and piling it into a heap at the edge of the clearing. Then the second woman took over, the younger one with the beautiful eyes; she hacked at the earth, muttering fiercely to herself all the while, 'Bury the bastard... I hope he rots in hell for what he's done to us!' and she gave a hefty kick to the side of his head, and he turned to stare, with open, sightless eyes, at the hidden boy who couldn't look away.

'Bit late for that, Iris,' said the first woman, 'too bad you didn't stand up for yourself when he was alive! Here give me the shovel, it needs to be deep or the foxes will dig him up.'

The old woman snivelled into her handkerchief, 'It's my fault, it was me. I did it! We should have called the police, not waited till it was too late... He deserved to die, but it's still not right, we should have called for help.'

Iris stopped to catch her breath, 'They never helped us, we tried to tell them before, but no one wanted to know. No one cared, we thought we'd be safe here, but he found us again. Let me get on with this, the sooner he's dealt with the better!'

She began to dig again with renewed energy, making tiny, dusty swirls with the shovel in the bright sunlight, and showering the body of the man with powdery earth that glinted in the air.

The old woman stared into the trees and, for one dreadful moment, the boy thought she had spotted him, and he edged around the thick trunk of a beech tree, pressing his face into the rough bark until it cut into his cheeks.

Clouds drifted overhead, heavy, and black with

rain, casting deep shadows over the sunlit clearing; then the sky opened, drenching the women in their thin, cotton dresses and turning the soil into mud. Still they continued to dig, until the hole was deep enough for the large man, then they fell to their knees and rolled him in, without preamble, or ceremony, wiping their hands on their muddy clothes, before filling in the hole.

Mary replaced the turf, stamping it down over the hastily dug grave, 'He won't bother us again!' she cried; and Iris laughed, and punched the air, while their mother bowed her head and made the sign of the cross over her bony chest.

The boy wondered if he'd been missed. He should have stayed next door, in his own garden; his mother was always warning him not to stray, and she would be angry if she found out where he'd been. He puzzled over what he had seen, but he couldn't quite make up his mind if it was real. After all, he recognised one of the women, the larger one whose name was Mary; she'd been at chapel, but she looked different then, smarter, and more normal. Maybe they were playing some make-believe game? Yes, that was all it was; of course, it was just a game, no one was dead, not really, and he made up his mind not to mention it to anyone; and anyway, who would believe him if he did?

So the man, who was buried where the wood met the end of the garden, remained a secret known only to the three women and the small boy, and it would have remained so until they were all dead and gone, had it not been for the storm.

It came one dark night in November, clothed in a warm wind from the west, almost tropical in its ferocity, howling, and wild, ripping the trees from the ground, while the rain poured in torrents from the hills into the valley, until the ground was sodden and the sheep confined to islands of muddied grass surrounded by vast lakes of rainwater.

Later, when the sky was a watery blue and the air was fresh and fragrant, a small crowd of onlookers gathered in the copse behind the house, where a giant beech had blown down, felling the smaller trees around it. It was strange to see such a large tree upended, but stranger still was the scarecrow-like figure that hung from the topmost roots, almost like a man hanging from the gallows but, in reality, just a series of bones, rattling in the breeze. One trouser leg was empty, and the skull looked about to drop from his chalk-white, brittle vertebrae, but oddly, after so many years, all of it still held together by a fragile shroud of ragged clothing.

CHAPTER 1
WALES
2018

The small house was spotless, and the women who lived there middle-aged and quite respectable, if a little odd by normal standards. Their mother had always described Mary as portly, even when she was a teenager, but now, to be honest, she was rather fat. Iris, on the other hand, was still slender and beautiful, though her eyes had lost their sparkle on the day that Mary mislaid Angelica.

Their garden was anything but tidy; small saplings had grown into tall trees, throwing leafy, dancing shadows into the rooms when the sun shone, and casting a deep, depressing gloom when it didn't. Honeysuckle, and a rampant Virginia-creeper, hung insolently from the chimney tops and gutters; 'Cut me back; if you dare!' they sneered, while pigeons, nesting in the roof, cooed in agreement.

Mary and Iris rarely ventured into the garden, preferring to imagine it wasn't there at all; that way they never had to dwell on the fact that Finbar Delaney's body was slowly rotting beneath the earth, where their overgrown lawn met the trees. They'd considered moving many times, but Kathleen was in the churchyard on the other side of the village and they didn't want to leave her, and anyway, they felt safe there now, in spite of the fact that Iris's common-law husband was buried in the shadow of the tall, beech tree in the copse. There were others, who might still be searching for them, asking what had become of Fin, and Angelica, but it seemed unlikely, after so many years

The thunder came in the night; a low rumble at first, gradually increasing to an ear-splitting crescendo with a menace that seemed almost pre-meditated, and flashes of lightning, splitting the heavens into jagged pieces like broken glass. It even scared Iris, who usually loved storms, and the sweet aftermath, when the air freshened, and the sky cleared.

Drawn out into the field by the commotion, they made their way to the back of the crowd and gazed in horrified silence at the skeletal remains of a man hanging from the roots of the tree.

'Fin...!' moaned Iris, and Mary seized her and pulled her away. 'Hush... it could be anyone...'

'Is she okay?' asked one of their neighbours; he didn't know them well, though he'd seen them go in and out of the house often enough.

'Don't worry, David, she will be fine, it's just that since our mother died, she's become less able to cope with…' Mary paused, unsure of what to say next.
'Of course,' he smiled gently, 'I understand, best take her away; give her a shot of brandy, maybe?'
He watched as the two women walked back down the overgrown path, and the memory of an incident long forgotten began to clamour at his consciousness.

'Iris, what were you thinking?' scolded Mary, when they were safely back in the kitchen, 'You mustn't let anyone know who he is; you do know that, don't you?'
'We murdered him…' wailed Iris, and Mary glanced around anxiously, making sure the windows were shut. 'We didn't murder him, we just buried him!'
'So, we just buried him, well, that's fine, nothing to worry about at all! We only buried him…!' and her voice echoed around the room, and up into the stairwell. 'Enough, Iris, try to be calm, it was so many years ago, and there's nothing to connect us to this man…' Mary refused to utter his name, 'and they won't know how long he's been there, or who put him there.'
'I hate my life,' moaned Iris, 'it's been a failure from start to finish; I'll be glad when it's over.' She started to sob, and Mary eventually gave up trying to console her and went out of the room. Mary was certain that all the bad things that had happened to Iris were because of her interference. There was no getting away from it, she, and she alone, had ruined her life.

CHAPTER 2
DUBLIN
2018

My name is Angelica, it's what my mother called me, my real mother that is; my other mother just calls me Angela and, for now, that's who I am, just Angela.

The night seemed long, as it always does when sleep refuses to come, when you turn from one side to the other, willing your brain to stop thinking, and your heartbeat to slow. I'd given up hope of ever dropping-off when the light came, seeping around the blinds, chasing away the smothering darkness. I pulled the covers up to my neck, stretching my legs until my feet met the bottom of the bed and poked out into the chilly room, holding my breath to listen as birdsong started up in the trees. A single, solitary blackbird first, trilling notes as pure and liquid as water spilling from a spring, and a siren call to all the other birds that immediately started to chirrup and warble, regardless of the early hour. The sound was enchanting, and almost unearthly in its purity. No one else was awake, I was sure of that. Carolyn hadn't got in until two, slamming the front door and evoking a yell from Jono, 'For pity's sake, some of us are trying to sleep!' I dozed briefly after that, but only until a dog in the street began to howl as if the world were ending. Still it wasn't too bad, lying awake, listening to the birds, and enjoying some solitude before the day began.

I hadn't slept well since my father passed away, less than a month before. It seemed so unfair; he was only sixty-five when he keeled over and died from a heart attack. He wasn't overweight, and he didn't smoke, or drink too much; in fact, he'd been cycling to work when it happened. In my mind I pictured him falling, clutching frantically at his chest, cars screeching to a halt, doors slamming as drivers got out, some already on their mobiles calling for help, while others meandered, reluctantly, to investigate the man with the upturned bicycle, who was lying flat on his back in the middle of the road. I tried to dispel this imaginary scenario from my mind; after all, I hadn't been there when it happened, so it was pure conjecture. Maybe he would have lived if I had, or maybe not; I just knew it would have been a comfort to us both if I'd held him in my arms.

'You should get yourself checked out,' said Carolyn, 'these things are usually hereditary. You might think you're fine, Angela, and then, suddenly, it's last orders, and that's it, the Grim Reaper turns up with his sickle,

and, before you know it, it's all over!'
We were sitting at the table having breakfast when she said it, and I could see Jono's right leg moving as if he were trying to nudge her into silence, but either he'd missed, or she hadn't noticed.
'Don't worry, Jono,' I murmured, 'it was just one of those things.'
Carolyn suddenly realised her mistake, 'Oh no...! I'm sorry, I didn't mean to sound so... so flippant.'
That had been two weeks earlier when I was still reeling from the shock, and perhaps I should have told them then that Patrick wasn't my real father, but if I had, it might somehow have lessened his importance in their eyes, and that was the last thing I wanted.

Not my real father? Of course, he was real, because he was the person who had known me since I was a tiny baby, the one who nurtured me, and made me laugh, and put up with my tantrums, and my teenage years when home sometimes felt like a battleground. Maybe, I should tell them that Aileen wasn't my real mother, just in case something should happen to her; after all, I wouldn't want to embarrass them. No, that would be unkind; they weren't to know because I hadn't told them that I was adopted, or that my name had been Angelica; I knew that because Aileen told me so. She said it was embroidered along the edge of the pink shawl I was wrapped in when they handed me over. She'd decided to change it, though only slightly, out of respect for the woman who gave birth to me; and it had the added advantage of being the name of a saint, which was always a bonus to someone as devout a Catholic as Aileen.

I got out of bed and pulled up the blinds. The grass had grown long; it stretched to the end of the wide garden, dark green, and lush, because of the constant rain. Jono complained that it rained all the time in Ireland. He'd done nothing but moan about it since his return from England, where he'd studied for five years to become a vet; an occupation that made him very popular in Dublin and the surrounding area, treating farm animals and horses as well as the usual cats and dogs. Maybe he'd be able to find a goat to keep the grass down, an unwanted goat, like the two abandoned cats and the rabbit he'd brought home; though the rabbit died when the fox turned up one night and broke into its run. People were always acquiring animals as if they were just lifeless objects, like stuffed toys that could be disposed of whenever you fancied a change, or just got bored with them.

He was already in the kitchen, 'Why are you up so early?' he asked, 'Are you still waking in the night? It will get better, Angela, I know it will. Have you seen your mother this week?'

I shook my head, 'No, but I'll call round tomorrow, I'll have more time. I know things will get easier, Jono, I just have to be patient, I suppose.'

He put his arms around me and gave me a hug, 'I've got to dash; I'm up to my eyes this morning, just downing a coffee before the chaos begins. Try to be happy, Angela, your dad wouldn't want you to mourn, not for too long.'

I envied Jono, he was only four years older than me, yet he seemed to have his whole life sorted. He was from a large family in Wicklow, and his mother was always begging him to return. 'There are plenty of animals here', she'd tell him, 'and your father is missing you, and so are your sisters and brothers. Please come home, Jono.'

I couldn't imagine why anyone would object to being showered with so much affection, but he said he found it stifling, and he needed to forge ahead on his own; and big families weren't all they were cracked up to be. There was too much responsibility for a start, always having to worry about someone or other.

'Don't forget to feed the cats,' he said, as he was leaving, 'Carolyn came in late, so she won't be up for a while.'

I opened the kitchen door and walked through the long, wet grass to the end of the garden. My jeans were soon soaking wet, and I knew I would have to change before work, but it was worth it as the earth had such a fragrant smell. The rain had turned to drizzle, but it was refreshing rather than cold, and the sky was starting to brighten over the rooftops. 'Enough blue to make a pair of sailor's trousers!' Dad would say, and it made me feel melancholy when I remembered his smiling face. I went back indoors to boil the kettle; it was already gone seven, time passed so quickly, apart from when you were trying to sleep, or when you were stuck at work with the whole, boring day ahead of you; then it seemed interminable. The grey tabby brushed against my legs, he always slept on Carolyn's bed which meant she was up and in the bathroom.

Carolyn and I met when we both got a job at the run-down travel agency on Cory Street; run-down because there wasn't the same demand for travel agents as there once was. Now, nearly everyone used travel sites and made their own bookings. At the time, she was already house sharing with Jono and a friend who was moving out, so I leapt at the opportunity to leave home when they asked me if I'd like to take her place. It had worked out well, the house share, not the job, as I very quickly reached the conclusion that I was useless at it, not to mention bored half to death.

Just the week before, Mr O'Donnell had put an envelope up on the shelf, and his last words before he went off to lunch were, 'Now Angela, old Mr Kennedy is coming in on the train to pick up those tickets. He says he's no way of printing them himself; be sure to give them to him when he arrives, now. He's already paid.'

I hadn't heard a word he'd said, or if I did, it didn't

register in my brain; it made me blush with shame every time I thought of it!

'No, Mr Kennedy, he didn't mention any tickets. I'm really sorry but I wouldn't know where to find them!' He'd looked so disappointed.

'But I've come all this way to pick them up, and Michael promised me they'd be here.'

Mr O'Donnell returned soon after. 'But I told you, Angela. Look, they're here on the shelf, just like I said. Well, you'd better put them in the post, and we'll say nothing more about it.'

'He felt sorry for you, losing your da an' all...' explained Carolyn. She laughed, 'and he's mellow when he's had a few. He's a nice man, one of the few, as you'll no doubt find out.'

I didn't need to find out, I already knew, and preferred not to be reminded.

I was eighteen, and just out of school, when I met Conor. Aileen and Patrick had insisted I spend time 'in the real world' instead of going to university, or travelling with my cousin, Roisin, who was taking a year out before coming back to study at Trinity. I'd been desperate to join her, but they said that traipsing around Asia wasn't being in the real world either. I had to find a job first, so that I'd have a better idea of the direction my life would take; as if it would be easier to decide at nineteen, or twenty-six, or even thirty for that matter.

Conor claimed me from the off. I'd found a position as a 'minor clerical assistant', in a one of the larger banks, which turned out to be double-speak for, 'tea maker for the senior clerical assistant', or, more specifically, Conor, already well into his thirties, although everyone agreed he looked much younger.

To begin with, he showered me with romantic gifts, like bunches of roses, and cheap jewellery, and he'd send me badly written poems, and little notes telling me how wonderful I was. Aileen would wait up when he walked me home in the evening, peeping around the frilly, lace curtains, and rushing to open the front door, just to make sure that 'nothing untoward' was happening on the doorstep. 'Is he serious?' she'd ask, but she didn't seem to mind, and I forgot how indignant I was about her spying, and told her, yes, he was. He seemed like a kind man, they decided, even if he was a bit old, but caring and responsible nevertheless; and wasn't it strange how he'd managed to escape marriage for so long. He must just have been waiting for me, and neither of them objected when I decided to put off university indefinitely, to move in with Conor.

That was when I discovered what living in the real world really meant.

It was soon obvious that Conor had another side to him, not so much caring as controlling, and that wanting to keep me safe was more like keeping an animal in a cage; though I didn't have any inclination to escape. I'd already begun to feel disheartened, and intimidated, and certain that I needed him, because I was hopeless on my own. He dictated where I should go, and whom I could see, including when I was allowed to visit Aileen and Patrick, and then he would accompany me everywhere, watching, and listening, for every word, or movement, that could be interpreted as flirtatious, or wayward, or disobedient.

It was two years before I had the courage to leave, and that was from sheer terror that he might hit me again. He'd raised his fists many times, but the last time was the worst, punching me until I fell onto the hard, kitchen floor, and kicking me, over, and over… The memory stayed with me, as if it were yesterday; the fear as I lay motionless, listening for his footfall, and his nervous cough, or anything that might indicate he was anywhere near my prone, bruised body. It felt like an eternity, and I still recalled the relief when I heard the door slam behind him, and the frantic beating of my heart, making me breathless and light-headed, because I was terrified it was merely a way of tormenting me further and that he was hiding, just waiting for me to raise my head from the floor before attacking me again. I'd waited for ten or fifteen long minutes, until I was sure he was gone, and then, terrified that he might return, slowly pulled myself to my feet and left, shoeless and coatless, at last certain that I'd suffered enough.

I went back home after that, and I'd probably still be there if it hadn't been for Carolyn and Jono.

CHAPTER 3

My mother, whom I shall refer to as Aileen, in order to avoid confusion, was sweeping the front step when I turned the corner. It was the only home I could remember, a two bed-roomed terrace in a tiny back street, with a small strip of grass along the front, and a backyard just long enough for a line of washing. My parents had never been well-off, but they always made sure I had everything I wanted, and it wasn't so bad being an only child. For a start, I'd never had to share, unlike my cousins who were useful for company, but only when you wanted it. I could think of nothing worse than having a house full of noisy, quarrelsome brothers and sisters. Roisin was just a few months older than me and we'd always got on well, even though I hadn't known her for the first five years of my life because her father had decided that life would be better in Canada. As it turned out it was worse, and they were homesick, so they'd come back. Roisin met a local boy at university who proposed the moment they got their degrees, and now she was working on the checkout at the supermarket, when she wasn't caring for her baby daughter.

'Forget Conor,' she'd say, 'it's been ages, and there are

lots of men out there; you're just not looking hard enough!' If only things were that simple, for all I knew, I could have numerous brothers and sisters; and what if they were living just down the road in Dublin? There was always the possibility that I could end up dating my brother without even realising.

Aileen waved as I came down the street. She'd lost weight since Patrick died; deep lines furrowed their way between her mouth and nose, and her cheeks, once pink and round, now looked hollow, and sunken, so that anyone might think she was at least ten years older than she really was.

She called out to me before I'd even reached the gate.

'Roisin's little one is due soon, a baby brother for Chloe; it will give us all something to live for, something to celebrate.'

I forced a smile to my lips, 'I know, and I can't wait,' I replied, and then turned away so that she couldn't see how envious I was. A husband, two babies, and a degree, surely a measure of success, and what had I learned in the real world? Only how unfair life could be. It was alright for Roisin, she could trace her roots back across several generations, but mine were a mystery and I knew that I'd never be happy till I found out who I really was.

I wondered if it would be inconsiderate of me to question her so soon after Dad had gone. I'd tried to ask him on more than one occasion, but he always avoided any issues that might lead to emotional outbursts or embarrassment. 'Ask your Mam,' he'd say, and he'd hide behind a newspaper, though he was never a great reader, except when I was asking awkward questions, 'I can't remember anything that happened that long ago.'

It always struck me as odd; there are some memories surely that defy the passage of time, like adopting a child, for instance. I followed her into the house, it enclosed me like a shell, warm and secure, yet there was something suffocating about it now that Dad had gone. It was no longer a family home, a place to live, but rather a place to hide away until life had finished with you, rejoicing in other peoples' babies. I wasn't sure why it felt that way because Aileen was only in her sixties, she could marry again if she felt like it, and she seemed to be taking her loss better than I was. I sat in silence while she bustled around putting away dishes.

'You're very quiet today, Angela,' she said eventually.

'Have you got a birth certificate for me, Mam?' The question shot from my mouth unbidden and it surprised me that I could be so insensitive, but I continued anyway, '...Or something from when I was born that would indicate who my birth mother might be?' I felt ashamed of myself for asking, but she was calm when she answered.

'I'm your mother, Angela,' said Aileen, and she pulled

out a kitchen chair and sat down, 'I'm the only true mother you've ever had. The woman who gave birth to you didn't w....' I knew she was about to say, 'didn't want you,' but she changed her mind at the last moment.

'She couldn't care for you, not properly, not in the way that we could,' she said instead.

I nodded, 'Yes, I know that, but you must have a birth certificate for me, what if I need a passport, wouldn't I need to prove who I am?'

'We've put all that stuff away,' said Aileen, 'for safe keeping, we didn't want to lose any of it.'

'But I'm an adult now, I don't live here anymore!' I watched as her face crumpled, and I blinked several times to hold back the tears, wishing that I'd held my tongue, 'I'm not being unkind, Mam, it's just that I might need it, what if I want to go travelling? I've always done what you, and Dad, wanted but he's gone now and it's time I knew…' a sudden dreadful thought went through my mind, 'you never wanted me to go travelling with Roisin, did you? Was it because you didn't want me to see my birth certificate?'

'We weren't given one,' murmured Aileen, 'it was a private arrangement, a young girl we knew who kept her pregnancy a secret. We helped her, even her parents didn't know. They were very religious and…'

She stood up, 'Let me make us some tea, there's no need for any of this.'

'Then who am I?' I asked, 'Leave the tea, Mam, I need you to tell me what happened.'

Aileen turned off the tap and came back to sit at the table next to me.

'If I tell you the truth, you'll be angry...'

'I won't be angry, I promise, and anyway, why would I be angry if you were helping someone? We can fix this, there's sure to be some kind of a record... or did she give birth in secret?'

There was a long silence while she considered what to say next.

'You want to know? Alright I'll tell you!' She stopped and fell silent again while I waited impatiently, listening to the dripping of the tap, and the clock ticking away on the shelf like a death-watch beetle.

'If you must know, I found you, under a hedge of sloes, where you could easily have died of the cold, God forbid...' She spoke slowly and quietly as if she knew that once spoken the words could never be retrieved, 'so, there you have it, you were abandoned, like Moses in his basket waiting for someone to love you and care for you, but I doubt you're any happier now you know. I'll make the tea.' She got up and crossed to the stove, 'Sometimes it's better not to know these things, everyone has their secrets and some things are best left hidden.'

I stood up, tipping over the chair in my haste and it crashed onto the floor behind me. How could she be so calm, complacent even, after what she had just told me? 'Secrets, how did you ever hope to keep this a secret? Did you think I was going to spend the rest of my life here? And how many people know about this? Did you tell Kitty, and Roisin? And the boys, do they know? How could you do this?' Tears, I'd frantically blinked away, welled up in my eyes and overflowed, 'How could Dad do this to me?'

'Sit down, Angela, and I'll tell you the whole story,' said Aileen calmly, and I wondered why she wasn't crying too. 'I've wept too many tears in the past,' she said, as if she'd somehow guessed what I was thinking, 'too many nights crying for the mother who left you and wondering where she was; and what had driven her to abandon you. Your da said she'd be around to fetch you, he went straight back to the fields to see if anyone was about, but the place was deserted, apart from a herd of cows. He went again the next morning, but he saw no one; whoever left you there was content to move on. We wondered if you were the child of travellers, but there was no sign of horses, or fires. By then I didn't want to lose you, and you were hungry, so we had no choice but to get you a bottle of milk formula from the town. I persuaded your father to pack everything we owned, and we moved on that afternoon. He realised how depressed I'd been, and he blamed himself for our infertility, though I'm sure now that it wasn't him and he might have had a dozen babies with someone else. We told no one we were going, and we kept ourselves to ourselves for a while, a low-profile you'd say these days. It was easy to find a small place to rent, and your da could always get work; we were happy, and any qualms that we might have had were swept away every time we looked at you. We'd been living miles away, out in the country, so when we came back to Dublin with a baby, everyone just thought you were a lovely surprise, but I told them all we'd adopted you, and people didn't ask too many questions. Kitty and her husband were in Canada, luckily, or she could have been more difficult to convince; we were always close, Kitty and me. Maybe I should just have lied and said I'd given birth to you; it would have been easier on reflection.' She smiled, 'You've given us so much pleasure, darlin', try not to be too hard on us...'

Stolen... I was stolen! Stolen, the word echoed around in my brain. How could she be so duplicitous? This woman who had always seemed so kind, so caring? And how could I have been taken in so readily, fobbed off with gentle good humour whenever I asked? I even remembered Patrick's words when I'd become too curious, 'Sure you were found under a gooseberry bush, Angela, just like all the other babies in the world', and I had been so trusting, and so afraid of hurting his feelings, I'd let it go.

The room suddenly seemed too bright, it hurt my eyes,

and for a moment I thought I was going to faint, but instead, I wrenched open the front door and ran out into the darkening street on legs that were threatening to collapse under the weight of my despair. I stopped and looked back when I reached the corner and caught a glimpse of the woman I'd always thought of as my mother. She stared back at me anxiously; baffled by my reaction, as if I were the one who'd committed some dreadful misdemeanour, like the theft of a child.

I ran down the main road, oblivious to the rush-hour traffic, stopping and starting as the lights went from red to amber, to green. Then the rain started, it ran down my back in rivulets and plastered my fringe onto my forehead, dripping into my eyes until I could barely see where I was going, not that it mattered. Wheels screeched, and a horn beeped, when I suddenly changed direction and lost my footing, stepping into the wet gutter, barely aware of the rainwater splashing around inside my shoes, running on and on, with little concern for my safety, knowing only that I had to escape, to become someone normal, not someone who was 'stolen'.

A crowd of lads was gathered in the doorway outside Grogans, they brushed against me as I ran and one reached out his arm, but I pushed it aside, 'Can I buy y' a drink darlin', he called after me. My breath was coming in ragged gasps and I turned and looked back at him, half tempted by the offer. Tears welled up in my eyes and began to pour down my face, salting the rain on my lips. I took a step in his direction, and I could see him moving slowing towards me, pulling his coat collar up over his head to keep off the rain, stumbling slightly... He smiled and beckoned, but I backed away and waved a little half wave that said sorry, but no.

I was soaked to the bone, and overcome with weariness, when I turned into a side street and sat down on a low wall to shelter under a laurel. It was quiet, the distant traffic muffled to a soft hum; drips splattered through the leaves but at least it offered some shelter. I wasn't sure how long I sat there, but when I eventually stood up my legs felt stiff in my wet jeans and they chafed the backs of my knees when I walked.

I reached home eventually; all the lights were on and it looked warm and welcoming, and through the window I could see Jono fetching plates from the dresser in the front room. The rich aroma of spicy food drifted down the front steps and I suddenly realised I was hungry. I banged on the front door and Carolyn came out into the hall and peered through the glass, 'Is that you, Angie?' she called, 'Where are your keys?' She opened the door and stared at me, her face deathly pale in the light from the streetlamps, 'Holy, Mother, Angela, you look like shite! And did you forget your coat? Come into the warm, before you catch the pneumonia.'

'Did you get caught in the rain, Angela?' asked Jono, and he grinned at me, a friendly teasing grin, and I noticed his teeth were incredibly white and his blue eyes crinkled when he laughed. 'Will you have some Korma, there's a load left? I can put it in the microwave?'

'I'd love some,' I replied, 'but I need a shower first.'

My jeans clung to my legs like an icy, second skin and the effort required to peel them away from my thighs nearly exhausted me, but the water revived my frozen limbs and I turned up the tap until it was almost too hot, pummelling my head and frozen shoulders, and warming my numb hands and feet. I felt unexpectedly calm as if a crisis had passed, as if something I had suspected all along had been brought to the fore, exposed, no longer a secret but important information that would allow me to get on with my life. Carolyn laughed when I walked into the kitchen, 'You look a bit better, though, actually, there's no way you could have looked worse. I'll get you a beer, go sit by the fire and dry off your hair.'

I'll get the beer,' said Jono. He looked at me, 'Well, d' you want to tell us about it, Angela? I'm a good listener, not sure about her though, she just likes to gab.'

'Sure, I am a good listener, Jono; the cheek of it!' She smiled at him and he smiled back and, despite

everything, it was impossible to ignore the look that passed between them.
'Come on Angie, tell us about your day,' she added, 'are you sad because of your da?'
'Of course, I am...' I murmured softly, 'but it's a lot more complicated.' There was silence while they waited for the rest because it was obvious there was more.
'I was stolen...' I murmured.
I was stolen. Just three little words, but they gazed at me, disbelievingly, as if I'd gone mad, Carolyn, mouth agape, and Jono with the beer bottle poised over the glass. Then the microwave pinged, and the spell was broken.
'Who stole you, Angie?' asked Carolyn as Jono handed me the glass and went to dish out the curry, slowly and quietly, so as not to miss any important revelations from the mad woman sitting by the fire.
'My Mother stole me, that is to say, Aileen stole me. She's not my Mother; she's a... a kidnapper, a baby thief!' It was true, I knew that, but I still felt I was betraying her by vocalising the indisputable horror of it all; and once I'd started there was no stopping me, the words tumbled out of my mouth as if they were anxious to escape, keen to weigh heavily on someone other than me. I drank the beer too quickly and Jono poured me another. I was starting to feel hysterical, even slightly amused.

'She said she found me under a hedge of sloes, and she thought I might die of cold if I was left there.' It was starting to sound logical, rational even, as if it were quite normal to take a baby and pretend it was yours, just because you wanted one; and she'd had all those years to convince herself that she had done the best for me... that it wasn't just about her and her need of a child.

'I haven't even got a birth certificate! It's why I haven't got a passport, and it explains why I was never allowed to go travelling with Roisin!' I was starting to feel ridiculous, how could I have been so easily deceived, so undemanding, and compliant? It was as if I'd been unwittingly complicit in the crime, and the thought terrified me.

Jono shook his head, 'You're twenty-five years old, for God's sake, and you've never left Ireland?'

'And why would she?' asked Carolyn, 'I've never left, and I won't care if I never do; sure, it's grand here.' She smiled at him, and I noticed the look pass between them again.

'You can find out now though,' she added, 'there must be a record somewhere, a missing baby, it doesn't happen that often, does it? The newspapers will have the story somewhere, and you know the year so it will be easy, plus there were sloes in the hedgerows so it must have been autumn. You'll be able to get a birth certificate, and a passport; you'll know who you really are. Perhaps Aileen was right, you could have died if she'd left you there, and she really did save you. See Angie, all will be well,' and she added, 'so long as she doesn't get put away... though maybe she deserves to be.'

I was warm by the fire, but a shiver ran down my back at her words. I didn't want her to be arrested; she was still the woman who'd lovingly raised me; and anyway, it had been me who'd always just accepted everything without question. And I immediately felt guilty because I knew why I was asking now, it was because Patrick had gone and, while he was alive, I would never have hurt him, not for all the world.

CHAPTER 4

I went back to see her, Aileen, my adoptive mother, because, in spite of the unconventional way she'd come by me, I still felt responsible for her wellbeing. Two days had passed, and the weather had changed from icy rain to cold, bright sunshine, giving everything a startling clarity. It mirrored precisely the way I was feeling, elucidated, as if a blindfold had been removed, making everything clearer, more precise. I looked for her as I turned the corner, half expecting her to be out sweeping the step, or polishing the windows; after all, she'd always told me that cleanliness was next to godliness, but I couldn't see her and I wondered if maybe she wasn't home, and for some reason that concerned me. I wasn't sure why, after all, no one spends all their time lingering on the front step; perhaps I'd driven her away completely? She had certainly raised me well for I was constantly consumed by guilt, even when I knew, deep down, that I wasn't to blame.

I let myself in, and for the first time I noticed how shabby the place was. It was tidy; there were no newspapers scattering the floor, or unwashed dishes in the sink, but then there was no one to make a mess, not anymore. Rays of sunshine fell across the floor in dusty stripes, I glanced out of the window and there she was, in the yard, chatting with old Mrs Gaffney over the fence.

I was about to bang on the glass, but I changed my mind at the last minute and sat down at the table to wait for her to come in. She smiled when she saw me, a funny half smile. 'Are y'feeling better, chicken?' she asked, as if I'd had a cold, or a funny turn.

I smiled back, 'I just wanted to say sorry; I overreacted.' It was a lie, but I said it anyway.

Her face fell, 'No, I should be the one saying sorry, I was too... forthright... too blunt. I've changed since your da went, and, yes, I know we should have told you before, but we didn't know how. I just didn't expect to be left alone... so soon...' Tears flooded her eyes and overflowed down her cheeks, 'so much joy, yet so much regret; time has flown away with us, it just goes by without us noticing and it's not until we've nearly run out that we realise how little we have. It was for the best, Angela; we thought we were doing the right thing, though your da took some convincing, so we mustn't blame him, it was my fault, my selfish desire for a child of my own.'

It was the Catholic guilt again, she was taking all the blame and I wondered if men were judged in the same way, or if they were, irrationally and unfairly, considered less accountable for their actions.

She pulled out a chair and sat down opposite me. 'He would have told you, but I always begged him not to, it wouldn't have helped if we'd been put away. True, they could have given you back, but you weren't the baby they'd lost, you'd turned into a lovely girl and it would have reminded them of all that they'd missed.'

'Would that have mattered?' I asked quietly, 'They might just have been relieved to know that I was alive.'

'I've often thought of that, but they could well have gone on to have many more children, and I couldn't; we only had you.'

We sat in silence for a while, both unsure what to say next, to make everything alright, to make it all go away, but there was no going back, nothing could be changed, or righted. She got up after a few minutes and went to fill the kettle.

'He wanted you to go to university, and to go travelling, but we were afraid. And when you wanted to go off with Roisin it was hard to dissuade you, you had your heart set on it, and it hurt him when he saw how desperate you were to go. We were so happy when you met Conor; it seemed as if our prayers had been answered, though God knows how it would have solved anything, even if he'd been a decent man. We were in denial, thinking it could be kept a secret, but you'd always have found out, sooner or later. We encouraged you to move in with him, and I'm so sorry for the way it ended. I just thank the Lord that you never married the bastard.'

I'd never heard her use such language before and it shocked me. 'It wasn't your fault, Mam,' I murmured, 'I was smitten, completely taken in by him.' We were arguing now over who should take the most blame. She gave a wry smile, 'Typical of a man isn't it, just leaving everything for a woman to sort out? But you're still young, you can do all those things now, better now than in twenty years' time. He left you money, you know... thirty thousand; he did you a favour going early.'

I gazed at her in disbelief, certain that she was mistaken; how could Patrick have saved so much money? 'I have to find her first,' I said at last, 'before I do any of those things.

There was a long silence while she fussed around pouring tea from the old china pot. She seemed to be considering something.

'Iris,' she murmured when she'd finished adding the milk, 'Her name is Iris.'

'Iris...? You mean... you know her name?'

'Yes, I've always known her name. She was little more than a child when she lost you, too much responsibility for one so young; young enough to have many more. I've still got the newspaper upstairs; it was old news in under a week. She was only a girl, twenty years old and unmarried at that, it would have been taken more seriously if they'd been a respectable couple. Only a few years back she would have been taken in by the nuns and her child given away. Would you like me to go and get it?'

I nodded, words were beyond me, two days before I had been angry, but now I felt only pity, for Aileen, for myself, but most of all for Iris.

She returned almost straightaway, carrying a cardboard box wrapped in a little pink shawl and tied with a ribbon, and began to empty the contents onto the table.

'Look, Angela, it's your first school report, and this is the first card you ever made me, see, it's a Christmas card. And here's a photograph of your first day at school, and weren't you precious in your little uniform? Now where's that newspaper, it was here the last time I looked?'

I could barely contain my impatience, 'Here, let me, I'll find it; I have to go home soon.'

'This is your home, Angela, it's where you belong. Please stay with me; I get so lonely on my own.'

I took the photo out of her hand; it was smeared with fingerprints and torn at the edges, where she'd held it over the years.

'I can't stay Mam; I have to go to work.' I was lying again, but it was better than explaining to her how I wanted to live my own life, that would have been far too harsh. She needed help; the death of my father had obviously affected her mind and brought all the years of guilt and deceit to the fore, and, worryingly, she seemed blissfully unaware that she could still be called to account. I rifled through the box until I found a tattered, yellow newspaper dated October 1993.

"Where is Angelica Mary?" asked the headline, then, just beneath, "The three-month-old daughter of Iris Malone and Finbar Delaney is still missing, four days after disappearing from a field in Kilkenny where they were staying in a rented farmhouse with her sister, Mary, and her mother, Kathleen. A basket found nearby is believed to belong to the person who abducted her, turn to page two..."

'I have a middle name...' I murmured. I didn't know what else to say. I picked up the newspaper and the shawl, 'can I have these, just as a keepsake?'

She nodded, then stood up and kissed me on the cheek.

'You'll be off now, I expect? You don't want to be late for work.'

I hugged her tight, 'I'd better,' I said, 'and thank you for telling me... all this.'

She nodded again and went to open the front door for me to leave. My tea still sat on the table untouched, but she hadn't noticed; she seemed to be barely present, as if she were just going through the movements that make up a day until it was over. I hoped she'd go into the garden to resume her chat with Mrs Gaffney, but when I looked back from the gate she'd returned to her seat at the table. I watched for a while, but she just sat there, immobile as a wax figure, staring at the cardboard box as if she were afraid of its contents.

I didn't want to speak to anyone. I needed somewhere quiet to sit, to get everything into perspective, and I wanted to read the rest of my story on page two, without Aileen peering at me, making me feel that I was being unreasonable. I walked down to the river, it was blowing a gale and the wind tied knots in my hair, but I managed to find a bench in a sheltered spot, and I sat down and took out the newspaper. My keepsake I had called it, though really it was a record of my history and a true account of where I had come from. Inside was a picture of Iris, she was holding a tiny bundle in a shawl, clutching it to her, as if she somehow knew that our time together would be short, and I noticed that her fingers were bandaged and claw-like, and her left eye was swollen and bruised. Apart from that she looked very similar to me, perhaps a sixteen-year-old me; she didn't look anything like twenty and I wondered if maybe she'd been younger. The picture took up most of the page, but just below was a smaller snapshot of a man, my father, Finbar Delaney. It was slightly blurred, though I could see that he had a handsome face and a strong jaw, yet there was something about him that I instinctively disliked; maybe the set of his mouth, or the harshness in his eyes, that made me think of Conor; Finbar Delaney from Coolock, North Dublin.

Just like that, I had two parents and two last known locations. I would be able to find them, or, at least, people who might still remember them; I would be able to prove my identity, and become a real person, but at what price? What would become of Aileen if I found my real family? She could still be charged with abduction; on the other hand, if I decided to continue the way things were, she might live for thirty years, or more, while I lived my entire life in Ireland pretending to be Angela Sullivan. It wasn't fair that I'd been put in this position; none of it was my fault. I watched the swooping gulls blown in from the Irish Sea, wild and uncaring, and for a moment I wished I could join them. Why was my life so complicated?

Carolyn had been working a Saturday morning shift, but she was there when I got back.
'I've got a middle name!' I told her as soon as I was in the door.
She was peeling potatoes, but she looked up and grinned, 'So, what is it? Is it as exotic as Angelica?'
'No, it's just Mary,' I said, 'I'm Angelica Mary Molone.'
'That's a perfectly fine name, and the same as mine. I'm Carolyn Mary Kavanagh. And, where did the Malone bit come from?'
'My mother was Iris Malone and I've got a newspaper to prove it. My other mother, Aileen, gave it to me, as a keepsake. I've got two mothers!' it seemed strangely

frivolous put like that, 'I'll show you when you've finished peeling the potatoes.'
She dried her hands. 'You'll show me now, Angelica Mary. You can't expect me to go on peeling spuds, not after news like that!'
I handed her the pink shawl, and she took it and held it to her cheeks, then she pored over the newspaper for ages.
'It's tragic,' she said at last, 'your poor mother, she's like you, but she looks like she's taken a beating, and she's so young. My heart bleeds for her, for what she went through, can you imagine? She probably thinks you're dead, though there'll always be a part of her that hopes you're still alive, and that you've had a good life, but I doubt she'll find any peace, not till she knows for sure.' She looked up at me, flicking her long, red hair behind her ears, Irish hair, wild and untamed, like the seagulls. 'Perhaps she's still hoping that you'll find her one day.'
I just nodded, maybe later I'd tell her and Jono about my dilemma and ask their opinion, I was sure they'd tell me to go to the police, but I needed to think it through first, not be rushed into decisions that I might later regret.
'Your father has a cruel face,' she added, 'he's an attractive man, but there's something about him. You should stay away from him, Angie.'
'Maybe it's a bad photograph,' I said, 'or he was angry

because his child had been taken. Anyway, Iris wasn't married to Fin, the church could have taken me in; I could have been placed in an orphanage. Perhaps Aileen is right, she did me a favour; she rescued me. Pregnancy is always the fault of the woman, we're just too attractive, too tempting and the poor souls can't resist us!'

Carolyn didn't look convinced by my arguments, she laughed, 'Not sure about the 'poor souls', it's almost, but not quite, what I'd call them. Still, I suppose we must be grateful for small mercies, after all, what would we do without them? At least you'll get a birth certificate, now that you've got a name and parents, and a birth date.'

'Yes, perhaps I will, but by my reckoning I'm a month older than I thought I was.'

She laughed again, 'Ah, and me only twenty-three, you poor auld thing!'

I left the shawl and the newspaper on the table; Jono would want to see them when he got in. We were like a family; except we were more tolerant and good humoured than many of the 'real' families I'd known. I went upstairs and sat on my bed. It was hard to get my head around everything that had happened since Patrick's unexpected departure; apart from anything else, I had an inheritance. How had he managed to scrape together such a vast amount of money? They were always short when I was growing up. I'd be able to leave my job at the agency, where I was the very definition of a square peg in a round hole. I could study, or travel, everything I'd ever wanted was within my grasp, but would it be at the cost of Aileen's liberty? I had to decide, or my way forward would be forever barred by the lack of genuine proof that I existed. However, one thing was certain, regardless of my predicament, my first task was to find my real mother, to hold her close and tell her that I was fine, and that now I'd found her I'd always be there for her.

CHAPTER 5

I'm not sure why, but I slept better than I had for a while. It was exhaustion, I decided; emotional, physical, and mental exhaustion, all competing to sap away at my energy levels. The house was quiet when I woke, and Fluffy, the tabby, aptly named by Jono's vet nurses after they'd brushed all the tats out of his fur, was prowling around looking for company. Carolyn's door was open, but she wasn't about, and I knew straightaway that she'd moved up to Jono's room, on the top floor. Lucky Carolyn, he was a good catch, hardworking and ambitious, not to mention, easy on the eye! I'd missed an opportunity there, but I'd been wary of men since Conor, and everything that had happened recently only confirmed that they were a lying, cheating bunch. Even dear Patrick, whom I had trusted implicitly, had been privy to a secret that had left me floundering when I discovered the truth. As for my, so called, real father, Fin, well, we hadn't met yet, but it seemed highly likely that he was as selfish and violent as Conor. Of course, there was dear old Mr O'Donnell down at the agency; he was a very nice man according to Carolyn, and it was true, he was, but he had a wife of about forty years standing, and an age to

match; not that I found Mr O'Donnell attractive in any way! Still it seemed a good idea to get down there; I'd be early to work, for a change, and I could grab a coffee on the way. Carolyn would turn up eventually; I knew Jono was far too responsible to be late for work. I wrote her a quick note.
'Carolyn... have gone to work, I've fed the cats. Angie xx'

It felt almost like spring when I stepped out onto the street. The wind was still gusting, but it had lost the ferocity of yesterday and become refreshing and 'blowy', as Dad used to say, 'Patrick dad' that is, not the other one. I still smiled every time I thought of Patrick, and I made up my mind to concentrate on the happy times, rather than allow recent revelations to destroy my childhood memories. What was the point of dwelling on the past anyway? I had to stay in the here and now, rather than inside my befuddled brain. What was it called? Oh yes, mindfulness; I could do that! I skipped down the road, stopping briefly to grab a takeaway coffee and an almond croissant. Live today, diet tomorrow, I told myself; be in the moment, enjoy the fruits of the earth, and the occasional almond croissant, half of which had already disappeared down my throat when I reached my place of work, O'Donnell and Henry Travel. I had no idea what had happened to Henry, I'd have to ask one day; the way things were going he had probably just disappeared without trace or been stolen! The aforementioned, Mr O'Donnell, was already there.

'Well hello, Angela,' he cried, with an unmistakeable note of surprise in his voice, 'you're bright and early, for a change. Will y'turn around the sign on the door?'

I obliged, we were now **'OPEN FOR BUSINESS'**, which I'd always thought was a strange thing to have on the door, and maybe more suited to a betting shop, or an estate agent. It didn't reflect the glamorous image we were trying to convey, with our exotic posters of Kenyan Safaris, that no one ever bought, or the, slightly more successful, Spanish Package Tours; not to mention our shiny computer screens. I poodled around, switching things on and wiping dust from the counters; then I sat down at my desk to finish my coffee and croissant. I could hear Mr O'Donnell shuffling paper in the back room, but the street was quiet, and no one came in. It was too early for the sort of people who came into O'Donnell and Henry to book their travels.

It was still quiet when Carolyn showed up about an hour later. She looked rosy in the face and slightly blurry around the eyes, as if she hadn't slept all night; which she probably hadn't.

'You've got bed hair...' I whispered as she crept in and sat down, in an attempt to look as if she'd been there for some time.

'What? Sure, I haven't, it's just the breeze!'

I reached across and plucked a tiny, white feather from the rat's nest at the back. 'Oh... and however did that get there? Did it come from a little bird?' I queried, and I pulled my hairbrush out of my bag and gave it to her.

'Ah, so you've decided to come to work after all, Miss Kavanagh,' said Mr O'Donnell, without the slightest hint of sarcasm in his voice, 'and when Padraig arrives, we'll have the full compliment.'

Personally, I couldn't understand why we needed Padraig at all; he was useless, drifting in when he felt like it, and then spending most of the day copying recipes from the net. One theory was that he was Mr O'Donnell's lovechild; there was no other explanation as to why his presence was tolerated.

People were starting to drift in and out, picking up brochures that were sure to finish up as landfill, since most of them never ventured further than Donegal or County Clare. It suited me when they came and went, because it meant I didn't have to move from my desk, and I'd begun to sink back into my state of depression. The manic euphoria I'd felt earlier had dissipated and I wondered briefly if I was becoming bipolar.

I was watching Carolyn as she tried to deal with a particularly difficult customer and completely oblivious to the woman standing in front of me, until she announced in a loud voice, 'Well if you won't be attending to me then I'll go elsewhere!' and she turned and marched out, slamming the door behind her, making the **'OPEN FOR BUSINESS'** sign fly up and swing around to **'CLOSED'**, which was more apt so far as I was concerned. Mr O'Donnell came out of the back office at a run with the intention of rescuing the situation, but he was too late, she was already hot footing-it in the direction of O'Donahue and Kavanagh, no relation to Carolyn, who were more advantageously situated in the High Street.

'Angela...!' he yelled, in a tone that was unmistakeably threatening, 'Will y' come into the office? I've been wanting a word with you; I know you were early this morning, and that was commendable, but overall...'

My bottom lip had started to tremble but there was nothing I could do to stop it.

'...and I know that your father passed away only recently, and I've been very patient because of it, but I think we have both come to the conclusion that you're not really suited to this kind of work, so...'

And that was it, he didn't have to say any more, I was on my way, and suddenly my lower wobbling lip, joined by the traitorous tears pricking my eyes, took over completely, and I sank down onto the nearest chair and began to bawl. Everything had become just too much, all the resentment, and shock, and despair, had suddenly come to the fore at the most inconvenient moment. I couldn't blame Mr O'Donnell, nice Mr O'Donnell; I knew I was useless, but I'd managed, more or less, up till now. He looked down at me with not inconsiderable alarm, obviously floundering and full of remorse, and without a clue as to how he should handle the blubbering wreck that I'd become. He hovered next to me, a too large presence, patting me on the back like I was a child who had swallowed a crumb gone down the wrong way.

'Carolyn…! Carolyn get in here!' he bellowed, 'I'll take over out there.'

Carolyn didn't need to be asked twice, I glimpsed her face through watery eyes as she shot through the door with a startled, though relieved, look on her face. 'Oh good,' it seemed to say, 'you can deal with the miserable auld biddy'. It changed to shock as soon as she saw me.

'Oh Angie, what's wrong?' she murmured, and she grabbed a box of tissues from the shelf and gave me a clump. I mopped and sobbed; bone shaking, heaving sobs that refused to heed any suggestion from my brain that now might be a good idea to stop, and that I should take control over my breathing, and the stream of water that was coming out of my eyes, not to mention the noise I was making.

'Ahhh, you poor thing, it's all been too much! And did Mr O'Donnell tell you to be gone?'

'Yes…' I gurgled, 'he did, and I don't blame him…' and I started to blub anew.

'I'll tell him, about your mam and all, he'll understand, sure he will.'

'No...' I wailed, 'You can't tell him; no one must know! I told you why.'
I suddenly felt calm, as if I'd reached fever-pitch, and now the only way was down. 'No one, Carolyn,' I sniffed, 'promise me you'll tell no one.'
'Fine, I won't tell anyone, I promise. Now, blow your nose, you look like a pink hippopotamus.'
A pink hippopotamus...? I glared at her and blew my nose.
'I only mean that your face is all pink, and puffy, and watery,' she grinned, 'the rest of you is nothing like a hippo.'
I managed a watery smile, 'Thanks Carolyn, for being here. I'm off home; I'll just get my bag.'
'You're not going anywhere like that! I'll get my concealer, it's brilliant for blotches, and I'll make us a cuppa. I could do with it; I didn't get much sleep last night.'
'I know,' I said, 'that's to say, I guessed; I hope he'll be good to you Carolyn.'
'Angie, you've got to stop this, of course he'll be grand; not all men are like Conor, you've just been unlucky. Be angry, not sad, and find your ma, your real ma; we'll help you if we can, Jono and me. There are lots of ways to find people, you can decide what to do after that.'
She was right; I had to be angry, well not exactly angry, just strong, and positive. I should see it as a quest, one that would be fine in the end. All I had to do was take

charge and stop being a victim. I had money, and my whole life ahead of me.

'You have to gird your loins and go for it!' she added.

Yes, I could; I would 'gird my loins', and it suddenly felt like an adventure.

Mr O'Donnell popped his head around the door as we were downing our tea. 'Has normal service been resumed, ladies?' he asked, 'I've just closed up and I'm off out for a bit of lunch and a bevy. Padraig will be in at eleven. Can I give y' one more chance, Angela? I'm sorry; I didn't mean to upset you like I did.'

'No, you're alright, Mr O'Donnell. I'll be off when we've washed the cups. Thank you for everything.'

He hesitated for a moment, as if about to add something, but then changed his mind and went back into the shop and out through the front door that was still displaying the **'CLOSED'** sign. He was probably relieved I hadn't taken him up on his offer of 'one more chance', and I didn't blame him. I followed soon after.

'See you later,' I said to Carolyn, and I gave her a hug, 'I'll get the spuds on.'

The house was empty when I got back. According to Carolyn, Jono was off in the wilds, checking on a horse he'd been treating for laminitis. I slumped in an armchair feeling totally drained. The cats sat either side of me like bookends, gazing at me as if they understood and felt sorry for me. I was touched by their concern.

Cat lives were so uncomplicated compared to mine, or that of any other human, come to that. I wanted to make a sandwich, and turn on the television, but I somehow couldn't find the will to even stand up. I could hear my mobile buzzing from my bag on the other side of the room, where I'd dropped it when I came in. It seemed a vast distance away, equal to the Gulf of Mexico, at least. Someone was anxious to get in touch with me; I knew because every time it stopped and went to voice mail, it began again just a few moments later.

Eventually, I dragged myself to my feet and staggered over to my bag just as it stopped for good. Seven missed calls, from Aileen, I almost dropped the phone. Was I about to be subjected to new and dreadful revelations? I wasn't sure I could take any more; I might lose it completely and career off to the nearest bridge to drown myself in the river. Should I call her back? I wavered, weighing up all the possibilities. Perhaps she was going to tell me that it was all some practical joke; no, even she wasn't that mad, and anyway, I had proof in the form of a newspaper, and a little knitted blanket with my real name, Angelica, embroidered along the edge. So, what else then? Was she after getting me round there, cajoling and begging, until I agreed to move back in? That was a battle she'd never win. On the other hand, what if she was ill, and would I ever forgive myself is something had happened to her? She could be lying on the kitchen floor, or at the bottom of her narrow staircase. I called her.

'Angela, darlin', it's your cousin, Roisin, she's gone into labour and she's down at the hospital. We should get down there; we don't want to miss it!'

'And how will that help exactly?' I asked crossly. She'd made me stand up and walk across the room just to tell me this!

She paused, 'Are you still angry with me, Angela?' She sounded peeved, like I was the one being unreasonable. 'Do you never answer your telephone, Angela?'

'You can't call me when I'm working, Mam,' It wasn't exactly a lie, more of a fact, but I was still starting to feel guilty, 'and we'll only get in the way if we barge in. Leave them to it, let Sean and Kitty do the worrying.'

'When are you going to settle down, darlin'? It will be good to have a little one running around the house again.'

'I'll have to call you back, I'm really busy. I'll talk to you later.'

'Do y' promise Angela?'

'Yes, I promise, Mam, we'll speak later, okay?'

She rang off reluctantly, and I resumed my armchair slump. Fluffy soon gave up on me and cleared off to play in the garden, but Bagpuss remained, perched on the arm of the chair, gazing at me with sympathetic, golden eyes. Perhaps he'd been through something similar in a previous life; or maybe he was just really depressed because they'd named him Bagpuss.

I was still there when Jono came in. He wasn't surprised to see me, so I assumed that Carolyn had already called to warn him of the state I was in. I could just imagine their conversation, it would be full of words like 'nervous breakdown', and 'bawling fit to wake the dead', and 'lost her job', and, worst of all, 'be careful what you say, or she'll be off on one again'.

He looked at me nervously, 'Are you well, Angela? Can I make you a cup of tea?'

'I nodded, 'Yes, please, Jono. Did you speak to Carolyn?'

'Yes, she told me that Mr O'Donnell had given you your cards. Look, I'll bring you some tea and you can tell me all about it.'

'I didn't like the job, anyway,' I said, when he returned, 'and I need to find out what I really want to do with my life. I've got some money now, so I can take my time deciding. I might go to university; I never got the chance before, even though my grades were good.'

What was I going on about? Did I really care about my career moves, or grades? Those things had been superceded by far greater issues, and Jono knew that, he was anything but stupid.

'Drink your tea, Angela, and then we'll talk,' he said quietly, 'I've finished for today, and Carolyn won't be in for a while yet.'

'I have to peel the potatoes,' I told him, 'I promised.'
I could tell that he was trying not to laugh, but then he gave up and started to chuckle. 'I'm sorry, Angie, I didn't mean to laugh, it's just that you look so serious. Forget the peeling, and the job, you hated it anyway. None of that matters; not anymore, you've got to focus on the real issues here. Would you not consider asking the police for help? They'd probably find Iris in no time at all, and I know it's hard, but have you considered that Aileen deserves to face justice for what she did? She persuaded herself you'd been abandoned, and she didn't even consider the possibility that your mother might be close at hand, maybe here in Dublin; you could have passed her in the street, or stood next to her at a bus stop. And Patrick, you talk as if he were blameless, but he could have done more to make her give you up. Instead, it's taken his death before it's come out, and you a grown woman, not a child anymore. You can't go on like this, Angela, pretending you can cope with it when it's obvious to us that you can't. Let's face it, how many of us could, after everything you've had to deal with in the last few days?'

It was true; I couldn't go on pretending that I was strong and resilient enough to resolve this on my own. I needed help, not only to find my real parents, but also for emotional support, someone to lean on; someone like Jono.

'We can help you, Angie,' he added after a moment, 'Carolyn is here for you, and so am I.'

He squeezed my hand, and his kindness made me feel fragile and weepy all over again, and I thought I was going to cry, but instead I blew my nose and smiled at him.

'Thanks, Jono, I really appreciate your support. You're right; I do need help because I haven't a clue where to begin.'

'We'll start with the Delaneys from the area around Coolock. I'll get my laptop. Now what did you say his name was?'

'It's Finbar Delaney,' I said, I didn't need to check because now I knew it, I'd never forget.

'Not a one…' he said, after a few minutes of searching, 'lots with the different spelling, but none in Dublin, not on here anyway. It doesn't mean a thing, not everyone is into social networking, and there's nothing on Google either. What about Iris?'

'She's Iris Malone, not a common name, is it, not in Ireland? The 'Iris' I mean, not Malone.'

He looked again, 'No, nothing, we need more information. Anyway, they could be anywhere in the world. Perhaps it's easier to forget what's gone before if you leave and start over. Are you sure you won't go to the Garda? They have ways of finding people that we can only dream about.'

I shook my head; how would I ever live with myself? I

had to protect my 'mother', regardless of my situation. Everyone had to be kept happy, even if I wasn't.

'Carolyn will be back soon,' I said, 'she's sure to have some ideas.'

Carolyn breezed in not long after. 'Mr O'Donnell said I was to go home,' she announced cheerily, 'he said I was as much use as a chocolate arse, well, not exactly in those words, but almost. He was gone two hours down the pub and when he came back, he was three-sheets to the wind, hardly upright he was, and there was nothing doing, and Padraig didn't turn up at all.' She stopped to draw breath, 'How are y', Angie? Are y' feeling any better now? And what's so funny?'

'You are,' said Jono, but with obvious affection, and she began to laugh too. It was the best I'd felt since my euphoria, earlier that morning; my moods were swinging between hysteria and despair, and I wondered again if I was becoming bipolar.

'Why don't you just look in the telephone directory?' she said when we'd explained the lack of suitable Delaneys and Malones.

'Worth a go,' said Jono, 'it's online. We'll try the Delaneys, first.'

CHAPTER 6

There were surprisingly few Delaneys in the area around Coolock, perhaps they were ex-directory, or, as Carolyn suggested, without landlines, now that everyone had mobiles, but I decided to try anyway, after all, there were only four on my list. The first rang and rang, and, after a dozen, or so, rings, I gave up; ditto the second, and I was just about to give up on the third when a man answered. He sounded out of breath and when he spoke, he apologised for not answering straight away.

'I'm sorry,' he puffed, 'I was coming down the street when the phone went and the old woman won't pick it up; it worries her, everything worries her now.'

'No... I'm really sorry for disturbing you both!' I cringed, feeling embarrassed for all the trouble I was causing, but I had to ask, 'I'm trying to trace a Finbar Delaney, it's very important; I know he lived in Coolock at one time.'

There was a long pause and I thought he'd rung off, and then, when he replied, his voice was so quiet I could barely hear him.

'Finbar Delaney? That would be my brother! We haven't seen him for many years, I'm sure my mother would be pleased if you were to find him, but I'd rather not get her hopes up.'

'Who is it, Donny?' enquired a voice in the background. 'Just a friend, Ma, it's for me, there's no need for you to get up.'

'Is that you,' I asked, 'Donny? And you're Fin's brother?'

'Yes, that's me, sure enough; and who might you be?'

I hesitated, suddenly unsure of what to say, 'I'm his daughter, Angelica.'

There was a sharp intake of breath at the other end of the line, 'She's gone,' he said, 'disappeared many years back, and never found!'

'Who is it, Donny?' asked the old woman again. The 'old woman', that would be my grandmother. My heart skipped several beats.

'It's me, really it is. I can prove it. Can we meet, Donny? I'll come around to see you if that's okay. Would tomorrow be too soon, at four?'

'I found him,' I gasped, as soon as he put down the phone, 'Fin's brother... and my grandmother!'

'You've found your uncle but not your da,' said Carolyn, 'though it's a start, isn't it, Jono? Just like that! And here, in Dublin; it's hard to believe.'

'No, not my father, they don't know where he is; apparently he's been gone for a while. I think the old woman is still grieving for him.'

'Well, and is he missing, or dead?' she asked, 'Still, I

suppose either way she'd fret.'

'Are you sure he was telling the truth, Angie?' asked Jono, 'there are some funny people about, they'll say anything if they want something out of you.'

'No one would get much out of me,' I said, 'I have nothing.'

'So, what about your inheritance, have you forgotten about that? Just be careful, Angela, that's all I'll say. We'll drive you there; surgery finishes early tomorrow, then at least we'll know where you've gone.'

Carolyn and Jono dropped me at the end of the street, a long line of weathered, grey terraces stretching off into the far distance. There was a perilous looking playground to one side, consisting of a few lop-sided swings hanging from knotted chains, and a rusty climbing-frame, sitting slightly askew and sinking crookedly into the muddy grass.

'Will you be alright if we leave you here, Angie?' asked Carolyn, she looked around anxiously, seeming reluctant to let me out of the car. 'We don't know for sure that this Don is really Fin's brother. What if he's a serial killer?'

I laughed, 'I'll be fine, Carolyn, you can't believe all you hear about a place. It looks grand to me.'

'Call when you're done and I'll come back,' said Jono, 'we might just take a little drive; not too far away,' he glanced at Carolyn, 'are you sure we can't walk you to the door, Angela?'

'No, really I'm okay, don't worry about me,' I replied, 'and yes, I'll call you. Thanks Jono, for driving me.'

Number nineteen was where the road began to curve towards the shops, and I wound my way between randomly parked cars, broken pavements, and discarded bicycles. The house looked neglected, paint was peeling from the front door and the curtains were only part drawn. I tried to ring the bell, but it didn't work, it didn't matter though because it opened anyway. Don was waiting for me and, as I stepped inside, I realised that I had no proof, whatsoever, that the person I had spoken to on the phone was any relation to me. For all I knew he could be the mass murderer that Carolyn had feared, and I was entering his house voluntarily. Inside, a heavy lace-panel hung between the curtains, making the room dark and full of shadows. Shelves lined the walls on either side of the fire-place, crammed full to bursting with a variety of dusty, china ornaments and frames displaying age-faded photographs, and at least a dozen statues of the Virgin Mary, all looking almost identical in the dim light filtering through the off-white lace. There was a distinct whiff of old tobacco. I couldn't see her at first, sitting by the unlit fire, a blanket wrapped tightly around her shoulders. Her face peeped out over the top, an ancient, wrinkled face that seemed to be folding in on itself. She was surprisingly fat for such an old woman.

He put his arm around my shoulders, 'Mam, I've brought Fin's girl, Angelica, missing near thirty years and now back with us! Isn't it grand, Mam?'

She blinked up at me as if she couldn't quite understand so I bent down next to her chair and took her hand.

'I'm so pleased to meet you at last!' I said, and she looked back at me with faded blue eyes, almost clouded over with cataracts.

'Can she see me?' I asked when she didn't respond.

'Sure, she can, but she probably can't believe you're here, we thought you were gone for good.'

I knelt down and leaned in closer, 'I'm your granddaughter, Angelica,' I explained again.

'Murdered...!' I jumped back; her voice was loud and guttural, and heavily accented.

'We thought you were dead and gone. Where have you been all this time, child? Your da came looking for you; he never came back either. Did y' see him, darlin'? Did y' bring him back with you? Will y' tell me where I can find him?'

Her voice softened to a murmur, 'He's never come back to me, not once. I want to see him before I die, I just need to find him first, my little boy. Why can't you find him, Donny?'

'Where is he, Donny?' I asked him, 'Where is Fin?'

He shook his head, 'I'll tell y' later,' he said quietly, 'for the moment she's happy just to see you so she may as well make the most of it; she has few enough pleasures.'

'It's good to have y' back, child, did they treat y' right?'

Oh, you mean Aileen, and Patrick, my abductors? I nearly said it, but I stopped myself just in time. 'Yes, Grandma, they did,' I said instead, 'they looked after me well enough. You're cold; can I light the fire for you?'

'There's no reason, it burns too fast and I'm colder when it goes out. I can't carry the coal anymore, and I was such a strong woman... when I was young...'

'She doesn't move much now,' explained Donny, 'but she's done well; she was eighty-nine years old, last Tuesday.'

'Donny will y' stop talking about me like I'm already gone...! Come back and see me, child. And if y' find your da, tell him I miss him; he was my last, the youngest of six that lived and all I've left is my Donny, he's just like his da, he was a good man, the best; no one else bothers about me now. Get me another blanket, boy; then off y' go, leave me to my own devices.'

Donny caught my eye, 'Wait a bit, I'll get my coat.' He went through a door in the corner of the room and I could hear his feet crossing the floor upstairs. He came back straightaway, wearing a black overcoat and cap, and carrying a thick, red blanket that he wrapped tightly around the old woman. She reminded me of a Russian doll and the thought made me smile, then I kissed her goodbye and promised to come back soon.

He seemed different out on the street, he looked taller and younger, and I could see that he'd once been a very attractive man.

'Can I buy y' a drink, there's a place on the corner?'

I nodded, 'Do you live here, Donny,' I asked, 'with your mother?'

'First of all, will y' stop calling me Donny; only she does that. I'm Don to everyone else, and yes, I do live here, there's no one else to care for her, and I'm retired now so people think I've nothing else to do.' He grinned, 'You must be getting on a bit y'self now, Angelica, almost thirty years gone.'

'Actually, it's only twenty-five years, and you can call me Angie. I've always hated it, but I'm not used to Angelica, it's a bit of a mouthful. Maybe one day I'll change it to something completely different.'

'Fine, Angie it will be, for now.' He grinned at me and I wondered if he and my father were similar. I hoped so, but he must have read my mind because he added, 'Fin and me, we were never alike, he could be... difficult. I don't mean it unkindly, he was my brother, but he liked his own way, and he thought the world owed him a living.'

I noticed he was referring to Fin in the past tense, as if he'd already made up his mind that he was dead, but

I let it pass, I still hoped to find him, I suppose. I thought of the photo of my mother, and the bruises on her face, and her bandaged fingers, and I had to ask. 'Was he a violent man, Don?'

He nodded, 'True, he could be short tempered. Our sister took off when she was young; she was older than him, but he made her life a misery, he always managed to hide it though. He could do no wrong in Mam's eyes; it was always someone else's fault. Here we are, take a seat, I'll fetch you a drink; what'll it be?'

'Gin and tonic, please; I'll sit over there, in the corner.'

It was quiet in the corner I'd chosen, away from the clamour of the bar, but I could still hear them discussing me, the barman who looked too young to be serving drinks in a public house, and Don; his voice was strong, just like his mother's.

'So where did you find her, Don?' asked the young lad behind the bar, 'she's an improvement on your usual ladies. Will she be wanting ice and lemon?'

'Yes, Mick, all the trimmings; and she's my niece, back after thirty years, or thereabouts.'

He laughed, 'I thought she looked a bit young for you, Don; and a bit too good-looking. I've a mind to ask her out m'self.'

Missing thirty years? It was more than a slight exaggeration; I laughed quietly, but I didn't know why. And my father, Fin, was missing too; surely, he hadn't been stolen; and was he 'short-tempered'? Don said he was, so perhaps I'd had a lucky escape, but what of Iris? I had so many questions I needed to ask him, but I didn't know where to start; I wished I'd written them down.

He was whispering now, no doubt telling the whole sorry story to anyone who would listen; I began to worry, did I really want everyone to know? I stood up and walked over. 'Come and sit, Don,' I said, 'I need to talk to you.' They looked at me curiously, the two ruddy-faced old fellas propping up the bar, and the young barman, who raised his eyebrows; he might just as well have said, 'Watch out, Don, typical woman, giving her orders already!'

Don picked up the drinks and carried them back to my hideaway in the corner.

'Here's to you, Angie,' he said, and he lifted his glass and downed a good third, 'now what can I tell you, darlin'?'

It was hard to concentrate. There were at least six people at the bar now, and I could tell by the expressions on their faces that my life story was being repeated to all and sundry.

'I wish you hadn't mentioned it, Don,' I said, 'I don't want the police to find out, not yet at least. My mother is still alive.'

'You mean Iris? Surely, it's your intention to find her, and Fin?'

'Yes, I want to find them, of course I do, but Aileen is

still alive, and she might be arrested for abduction, and I don't want that, my father has just died.'

He scratched his head, 'You'll need to start at the beginning, Angie; for a start, who in God's name is Aileen?'

'You must promise not to tell them,' I nodded towards the bar, 'I mean it, Don, no one can know if I'm to tell you.'

'Of course, Angie, you should have said before, I won't repeat another word, unless you give me full permission,' and he drew his fingers across his lips, 'there, zipped!' he added.

I was starting to wish we'd gone to the park instead of the pub, but he would probably have told them anyway, sooner or later, and at least now I'd had the chance to warn him to keep the rest to himself. The rest, the bit about me wanting to protect the people who'd snatched me from my real mother, and who'd made me feel complicit for not demanding to know more. It didn't make any difference because I still loved them and they'd shown me nothing but kindness, a quality entirely lacking in Fin, according to Don.

'Aileen and Patrick brought me up. I thought I'd been adopted legally, but I've just discovered that they found me, in a field, or rather Aileen did. She found me lying there, and it was late in the day, and in October,' I was still making excuses for her, 'and she took me home so that I didn't die of the cold. It said in the paper that I was three months old,' I smiled, 'that's a month older than I thought I was.'

He didn't smile back. 'It's like a fairy tale, sure it is; did she think you'd slid down the rainbow on y' arse? You were taken, and it tore the family apart; she should be punished for it, even now, no matter what!'

I decided to change the subject, 'Tell me about your family, Don.'

'That'd be your family, Angie, your real family,' he paused, 'there's not a great deal to tell. Fin went missing not long after you'd gone, though maybe a year or so. We searched for him, but he'd disappeared, some said he'd gone to England, taken the boat; he thought Iris had you, that it was all a ruse to keep him away, but I didn't blame her if she had, and neither did Maura.'

'Who's Maura, Don?'

'Our sister; she worried that Fin would turn up on her doorstep, but he never did. We've three more brothers, all younger than me, all still in Dublin, off living their own lives with no concern for anyone else. Maura keeps in touch, women are better at that sort of thing; I can give you her address in England, she'll be glad to hear you're alive. I couldn't believe that Iris could fake so much grief, and to begin with we all thought that Fin had you; the truth was that neither of them trusted the other, mostly none of us trusted Fin. He was cruel to her; I never knew a day when she wasn't covered in bruises, I hoped she'd somehow fooled him and taken you, and so did Maura, but Iris didn't have the cunning for that. She was a beautiful girl, and bright, but not manipulative, and God only knows why she took up with Fin in the first place. You have her eyes, grey-blue and soft as mist; she could have had anyone, certainly me, but our Fin could charm the birds from the trees; sure, never a truer word was spoken.'

'I want to find Iris, Don, but I don't know how. I hoped that if I found Fin then someone would be able to tell me where she is, but I'm no nearer to knowing where either of them went.'

He shook his head, 'I've searched high and low for him, not for me, y' understand, for the old woman, so I doubt you'll find him either. To be honest, you've been better off without him in your life, and if Iris has managed to hide from him for all these years, then good luck to her!'

'I have to find her, Don; I need to find her, to tell her I'm fine, that I'm alive. And there's another problem…' I paused, wondering if I should confide in him, I took a deep breath, 'I have no birth-certificate, or anything else to prove that I exist…' I suddenly felt depressed, it descended on me, a heavy blanket of depression, wrapping and constricting me, like the blankets covering my ancient grandmother. The ice had melted in my glass, and the tonic water was flat, but I picked it up and downed it anyway.

'Then you've no option, Angie, you must go to the Garda, it's the only way. They won't arrest Aileen, surely, after all these years.'

'I can't risk it, Don, I just can't. Don't concern yourself; I'll work it out, somehow. Thank you for the drink, and for listening. I'll be over again to see my grandmother; I still can't believe I've found her.'

I looked back as I was leaving; he was off to order another drink. I really hoped he wasn't about to relate the rest of my life story to Mick, and the ruddy-faced old guys at the bar. I wandered back down the street trying to decide whether to call Carolyn and Jono; they'd promised to pick me up, but I was reluctant to bother them. They'd already been so kind and were content in each other's company, at least, for the moment; and I didn't want to feel like a gooseberry, the unattached friend, who was always wanting a lift, or a shoulder to cry on. I walked back to the corner; the playground was occupied now by a crowd of teenagers. Two girls, done up in high-heels and shiny lipstick, were draped around the swings exchanging cheeky remarks with the five or six boys who balanced precariously on the top of the climbing frame. They were all smoking and paid no attention to me at all. I took out my phone and sent a text to Carolyn.

'Finding my own way home; thanks. All well, details later... Love, Angelica. xxx'

CHAPTER 7

My mobile rang just two days later; it was a journalist. He'd discovered that I was Angelica Malone, the baby who'd gone missing twenty-five years earlier and he wanted to interview me about my life in general, and most particularly, about where I'd been all these years. He said it would be 'a scoop' and he'd make sure I was 'well paid.'

I pressed the off button and hid the phone under a cushion, but it rang relentlessly, stopping only to start again a few moments later. I turned off the sound, but I could still hear it vibrating so I retrieved it and put it in a drawer in the hall, then came back into the living room and turned up the television.

How had they found out that I was Angelica? And how had they got my number? There was only one person who could have betrayed me, and I'd specifically begged him not to tell anyone… Don Delaney!

Carolyn came in at five, she was holding my mobile. 'I found this in the drawer,' she said, 'it was vibrating like a giant bumble-bee, so I answered it. It's the press, Angie, they're on to you!'

'That's why I left it there,' I groaned, 'so that I couldn't hear it. I wish you hadn't answered it, Carolyn.'

'You could have turned it off! Still, that wouldn't have mattered; look you've got about a hundred messages and missed calls. They'll make it up if you don't tell them; you know that, don't you? Call them, Angie, tell your story, you never know, Iris might read it.'

She was right, Iris might read it, and just maybe I could make things right for Aileen. I'd been about to call Don, to ask him for Maura's address, but now I just wanted to kill him. I called him anyway.

He couldn't stop apologising. 'I'm really sorry, Angelica. It wasn't me, I swear to God. I left it on the bar, someone must have stolen your number!'

'It wouldn't have happened, Don, if you'd not gone around shooting your mouth off. And are you saying that someone took your mobile, copied my number, and then put it back. Why wouldn't they just keep it?'

'My friends aren't thieves, Angie. Why would they steal it when they only wanted information?'

Was this man mad? 'For money, Don, that's why, maybe this person is being paid anyway, by the gutter press? Isn't that just as bad as thieving?'

'Well, sure, but it's not my fault, and I've said I'm sorry, and…' he paused,

'And what, Don…?'

'I want to find Fin; for Ma.'

Was that it, not some anonymous 'friend' of his at the bar, but a loyal son, desperate to please his mother in her few remaining years? I softened my reply.

'I can understand that, but...' I struggled for words, 'but he's been gone a long time, and he's never contacted you... he might be dead, Don. Have you considered that?'

'It wasn't me, Angie,' he insisted, 'but I'm hoping that some good might come of it. I've a feeling they're out there somewhere, Iris and Fin, not together, I grant you, but it might be your only chance to put your life in order, you'll become a real person in the eyes of the law.'

I still didn't believe him, but there was no point in persisting with my accusations. Maybe he was right, and I'd be back where I belonged, I'd be me, the person I was supposed to be all along, with the right identity and all the stuff that went along with it. I wondered how it was that the taxman was still able to take a good percentage of my wage every week. Surely a non-person should go tax free.

'It's not the paparazzi, Angie,' he added, 'you'll not warrant that, they'll want a few photos, and a bit of a story, then it'll be over in a week or so. You'll have to control it, or they'll control you!'

I said goodbye and rang off, and it wasn't until then that I remembered, I still hadn't asked him for Maura's address, his sister who lived in England.

The paparazzi turned up the next morning, in the shape of a thin, greying man in a shabby jacket, with wispy hair hanging out of his nostrils, and eyebrows that joined in the middle. I checked his identity before inviting him in, Carolyn had got me nearly as obsessed with serial killers as she was.

'My name is Martin Fitzgerald, but you can call me Marty,' he murmured, in one of those soft Irish voices that are barely audible, and he held out his hand for me to shake. It felt cold and flabby.

I sat on the couch in the living room and he sat next to me, brushing his legs against mine a little too cosily, so I got up and moved to the chair opposite, but I could still smell the whisky on his breath from a metre away. He stared at me earnestly, 'Tell me about yourself, Angela, or do you prefer Angelica?'

I stared back at him, trying to avoid looking at his mono-brow and nasal whiskers. 'What have you heard already?' I asked him.

'I spoke to your Uncle Don,' he replied softly, and I waited for him to elaborate but he didn't.

'Did Don call you?' I asked.

'No, it was some old fella in the bar. Don especially asked me to tell y' that. He said you were worried about your adoptive mother, but that's the part I'm interested in, Angie. Is it alright for me to call y' Angie?'

He was worried about calling me Angie when he was about to expose my entire life to the whole of Dublin and beyond! I nodded reluctantly.

'There's no record of you ever being found,' he said after a short pause, 'the question is…' he paused again as if he wasn't quite sure how to word it, 'the question is, where were you for all those years? And, why was no one informed that you'd been found, and adopted? Who adopted you, Angie?'

'That's three questions…' I said. I didn't know what else to say, I suddenly felt light-headed and my hands had started to shake. I held them clenched together but it didn't help. 'I have to get some water,' I murmured, 'can I get you something, er… Marty?'

'No thanks, but you go ahead.'

I left the room; he was scribbling on a notepad when I looked back. Why did I feel as if I'd been caught breaking the law?

I glugged a glass of water and took several deep breaths to compose myself, then I went back to my interrogator.

'There are certain things I can't tell you,' I said, 'but my mother is called Iris Malone, and my father is Finbar Delaney. And I don't know where they are, but if they read this, I'd be really happy to hear from them.'

'But where have you been, Angie? Were you imprisoned somewhere? Did you escape?' He leaned towards me across the rug, his eyes wide with curiosity, and… anticipation. He licked his lips, 'Were you… mistreated? You may as well tell me, Angelica. I will find out!'

It sounded like a threat.

'And I'm sure the police will want to know that you're safe. A lot of people still remember that poor, missing child, never found and presumed dead, and her grieving parents. They combed the fields for you, Angie, and now, look at you, fit and well; and grown into a good-looking girl, if y' don't mind me saying!'

Help... where was Carolyn in my hour of need?

'I've been grand, well cared for and loved,' I replied, 'and my adoptive father has just passed away, and I don't want to worry my mother. She's been unwell since he died.'

He leaned closer, 'Ah, yes, and they would be Aileen and Patrick Sullivan?'

I felt sick, he obviously knew everything. Don, or one of his 'good friends', had repeated everything I'd told him and, whether or not, he was the one who had actually informed the Press, the result was the same and he was responsible. Or was it my fault for telling him so much, but then how could I avoid it if I wanted to find Iris? I was no longer sure I wanted to find Fin, after what Don had told me.

'I think you know as much as me, Marty,' I said at last, 'but I'm begging you, please don't pursue Aileen, she's been good to me. I only want to find Iris. Promise me that you'll be kind?'

He stood up to go, 'I'll bear that in mind, Angie, but this is a big story, everyone will take an interest, they'll be glad you've been found. We'll pay for any photographs you have of Aileen and Patrick, and you as a tiny tot, and growing up,' he paused to leer, 'I don't doubt you'll need the money?'

'I'll show you out now,' I said, 'I'll try to find some photos, I wouldn't want people to think I've been unhappy.'

I escorted him to the front door and watched as he went down the steps; I'm not sure why, out of politeness, I suppose. When he reached the gate he turned, 'Smile Angelica,' he said, 'it was all bound to come out sometime…' as if I were in some way responsible for my predicament, then he waved and walked away.

I went indoors; I felt despondent, weighed down by Aileen's recent revelations, but also by an overwhelming sense that my life was spinning out of control and I could do nothing about it. I was caught in a maelstrom of my own making, and there was no going back. Aileen's secret would become common knowledge, probably first thing tomorrow when the morning papers came out. Tongues would be wagging, fit to tie themselves into knots. I wondered what I had started.

CHAPTER 8

Aileen wasn't home when I got there, so I sat on the step and played Solitaire on my mobile, until the battery ran out. She came down the street at last, carrying two string-bags full of groceries, and I rushed to open the gate. She looked much better than she had the last time I visited, she had some colour in her cheeks, and she was wearing bright red lipstick.

'It's great to see y', Angel, we'll have some lunch. Sure, it's a fine day.'

I was worried; she hadn't called me Angel since I was about eight years old. I took her bags and followed her into the house. It smelled of lavender wax polish, and everything gleamed. Three giant, cardboard boxes stood next to the door, along with several black plastic bags overflowing with clothes.

'What's all this, Mam?' I asked her, 'Is there anything left in the house?'

'I've been having a clear-out. I need to put the past behind me, wipe the slate clean. I'm going to replace it all, start again. I might move.' She took my hand, 'You've made me realise that my life has been nothing but a fantasy; I've avoided the truth for far too long.'

I should have been reassured, happy that she was

facing reality, but the change was too sudden, too unexpected.

'How will you shift it all?' I asked. It seemed too trite a question in the circumstances, but I asked it anyway.

She smiled, 'Ah, the lads from the Presbytery will be round to fetch it, I spoke to them earlier. You're not to worry.'

She started to fix lunch, so I tiptoed away to take a look in the bags and boxes. I'd have been happy to dispose of almost all of it; ornaments, and dusty books, and toys that I'd been telling her to throw out for ten years or more, but I knew that she loved them because they reminded her of happier times. My teddy-bear lay buried under a heap of old blankets, so I pulled him out and hid him in my bag. Another box was crammed with bed linen; most of it almost new, and presumably the contents of her 'bottom drawer'. Why did women of her age, and older, keep piles of bedding that would never be used? Were they preparing to open an emergency hospital, or a refugee camp, at a moment's notice? I went upstairs, almost expecting the rooms to be empty, the beds bare and unwelcoming, but my room looked fine, though rather stark without the pictures and cluttered shelves. Aileen's room had changed, the wardrobe doors were open, and I could see that most of the contents had gone, soon to be claimed by the church for their poor parishioners.

It reminded me of the pictures I'd seen of convent cells,

devoid of anything that might connect the inhabitants to their past lives; even the photographs of Patrick had gone. The downstairs rooms were the same; she'd kept just the minimum, a lesson in de-cluttering and minimalism for us all; except this wasn't my mother, not Aileen, who treasured all the bits and pieces that I would quite happily have tossed straight into the bin.

And now I had to tell her that her face would probably be on the front page of all the newspapers, possibly tomorrow morning, with the words, 'Abductor', and 'Child Stealer', emblazoned beneath, along with lurid details of her infertility, and her dubious motives. How would she cope? I had a dreadful suspicion that it might push her over the edge.

'Why aren't you eating your ham roll?' she asked, 'It's got your favourite pickle; I especially went out to buy it, because I knew you'd be round. Have y' no work today, darlin'?'

I shook my head, 'I've no work today...' it was true enough. I nibbled at the ham roll, just to please her. 'Mam...' I said at last, 'I need to tell you something. I have to warn you.'

She looked up, startled and fearful at the same time, and I noticed her lipstick had smudged down into the lines at the corners of her mouth. It was as if her mask was slipping, all her bravado melting away, revealing the fragile woman beneath. I forced myself to go on, but it was hard to know where to start; at the beginning

I supposed.

'After what you told me, I decided to trace my biological family,' the words seemed strangely clinical, 'and I found Finbar's mother, and his brother, Don.' I tried not to watch her face but instead looked down at the crisply ironed, and starched, white tablecloth, 'he told me the whole story.'

'Is that all?' she asked, 'It's exactly what I told you. And did you find Finbar?'

'No, nor Iris, but the thing is, that's not all…' I paused to gather strength, 'because someone overheard, and now the newspapers are on to it! It could be in the papers, maybe tomorrow morning.' There it was out, I'd said it. I stared at her, the colour had gone from her cheeks; she was as white as her freshly-laundered tablecloth. I waited for her reaction with dread.

'I'm sorry, Mam…' I added softly.

She nodded slowly, 'No, you're alright, Angela, it's time the truth came out, and you're not to worry about me, not anymore. I can take it, and I wouldn't have done anything different, even if I had my time again.' She seemed suddenly smaller, more diminished, 'Do y' think they'll lock me away, Angela?'

'No, Mam, definitely not, you'll probably just get counselling, a psychological assessment,' I really hoped they wouldn't lock her away, 'or community service; visiting the aged, maybe.'

'Will y' still come and sees me, Angela?'

'Of course, I will, Mam; you know how much I care for you. I'm so sorry for all of this.'

'It's not your fault, you mustn't think it is. Go now, I need to prepare myself for the…. for the shame…' She stood up, 'Tomorrow y' say? So, everyone will know who I really am, tomorrow.'

My eyes were starting to fill with tears, so I blew my nose; she was so calm and accepting of her fate that I didn't want to spoil things. 'I'll come around, shall I? A united front; whatever happens we'll brave it out, together.' I was trying my best to sound cheerful.

'Yes, Angela, please do. I'll wrap your roll in foil; you can have it for your tea. Thank you for being such a wonderful daughter, you've made it all worthwhile, my life would have been nothing without you,' then she kissed me gently and we parted.

I'd reached the end of the road before I realised that I'd left without my ham roll, with the 'favourite pickle' she'd bought especially for me, just because I liked it. It shouldn't have mattered that much, but it did, and it felt like yet another act of treachery. I wondered briefly if I should go back, but I couldn't face her, I'd make it up to her tomorrow.

CHAPTER 9

The cats had moved in with me now that Carolyn had deserted them to join Jono in the attic bedroom. I found them comforting, and I felt more relaxed having them there. Maybe it was just the company of living things around me, but I slept better with Baggy sprawled across the end of the bed, and Fluffy next to me, practically sharing my pillow. Sometimes she would reach out with her paw to stroke my face, as if to make sure that I was still there, or still alive. It was her gentle touch that woke me from a deep sleep to the grim reality that my life had become. It was seven o'clock, half an hour before the paper shop on the corner was due to open, heralding my true identity to the people of Dublin. My persona, crafted so carefully by Aileen and Patrick Sullivan, was none other than Angelica Malone, stolen daughter of Iris Malone and Fin Delaney.

The cats stalked around, rubbing themselves against my legs, and staring resentfully at me, obviously wondering why no food was forthcoming. I filled the kettle and switched it on, and gazed back at them, and at the toaster, as if it were an object entirely alien to me, rather than something I'd used almost daily for the past twenty, or so, years of my life. I gave up on the idea of breakfast almost straight away; I wasn't in the least hungry in any case, and someone else would have to feed the cats, for a change. I pulled on my jeans, threw my jacket over my nightie, and went out into the street. It was cold and overcast, and still not quite light. I blew on my freezing fingers and wished I'd remembered my gloves. It was only seven fifteen, but with any luck they'd already be open; some people liked to pick up their newspapers to read on their way to work. Then I saw her, a girl with untidy hair and a puzzled expression, staring back at me from the newspaper stand.

'Smile, Angelica,' Marty's words rang in my head. Someone, an accomplice, must have been waiting for me to open the door, and how obliging of me to wait politely on the step; well, I hadn't smiled, which was good because it would have been even worse. I rushed in and bought two copies, I wasn't sure why I wanted two, one was bad enough; was I subconsciously enjoying the notoriety? After all, I'd never been in the newspapers before; then I remembered that I had, twenty-five years ago, to be precise! I scurried home, switched the kettle back on, fed the neglected cats, and sat down at the table to read my story.

"**IS THIS ANGELICA?**" asked the headline, followed by an emotional piece of mawkish prose, along the lines of "the poor little child was snatched from her loving parents", and no mention of the fact that Finbar Delaney was a violent brute of a man, who beat poor little Iris senseless whenever he had the opportunity. It went on to say that, "The Gardai is still waiting to question Aileen Sullivan, whose husband is only recently deceased... They confirmed that an investigation is underway."

So, there it was, in black and white, for all to see, and I was certain there would be worse to come in the next few days. As Don said, if I was lucky, I'd have just a week of it, and that would be that, but the fate of Aileen was still to be decided, and I was afraid for her.

Jono and Carolyn got up eventually. I was beginning to wonder how it was that Carolyn still had a job, but I suppose if he sacked her too there'd soon be no one left to run Mr O'Donnell's failing business, other than Padraig, on the rare occasions that he managed to turn up. I showed them the newspaper.

'You'll be needing to see your mam,' said Carolyn, 'you don't know how she's going to take it. The police will be round there first thing, and probably the Press looking for her side of the story. We should go with her, Jono?'

Dublin was manic, solid with rush hour traffic, and a light fog had descended, slowing everything to a crawl, so it was almost ten by the time we arrived. My heart stopped when I saw the ambulance blocking the road. A police car with a flashing, blue light was parked just behind it, and there was a crowd of onlookers. They separated to form a path when two paramedics, carrying a stretcher, came out of my mother's house.

'You go, Jono,' whispered Carolyn, 'find somewhere to leave the car. Come on, Angela.'

I heard her as if from a distance, as I stumbled out of the car on legs that were holding me upright and propelling me slowly forward, even though my brain seemed to have become disengaged from the rest of my body. We pushed our way through the crowd, or rather Carolyn did; I had no strength, and I owed the fact that I was standing at all to Carolyn, who'd wrapped her arm tightly around my waist to support me. They were just closing the doors to the ambulance when we got there.

'It's my mother,' I managed to gasp, 'she'll want me to go with her…'

'You'll have to follow in a police car,' said the paramedic, and he slammed the door shut. He beckoned to one of the officers, 'explain to him…' he added gently.

I heard muted conversation as Carolyn explained the situation, then she hugged me, and murmured, 'Try not to fret, Angie. I'll wait for Jono to come back, then we'll come and find you.'

We took off, back through the city in a volley of screaming sirens, and along strangely, empty roads, as cars and buses parted to let us through. I noticed a few elderly people touched their collars as we passed; it was a mark of respect, or fear, and it filled me with dread.

Carolyn and Jono had already arrived by the time I was allowed to see her. She was in an intensive-care ward and I was shocked by the tubes attached to her body, and by the number of patients in the room, at least eight, who all appeared to be hovering between life and death. She looked younger, her face was serene and unlined, and she seemed to be sleeping peacefully, as if her troubles were forgotten. She didn't appear to be in pain.

'Can she hear me?' I asked the nurse.

He thought for a moment or two as if considering whether I was strong enough to cope with his reply. 'I don't think she can,' he said at last, 'I'm afraid it doesn't look good. Was she depressed about anything?'

'You mean she did this to herself, on purpose?' My words were ragged and choked with tears.

'I'm sorry, I thought you knew…'

I shook my head.

'An over-the-counter painkiller; she's taken too many. We'll do our best, but her major organs could fail at any moment. If she doesn't respond we'll take her to a private room so that you can be with her. We should know before too long.'

They moved her to a small room soon after, and I

was told that I could sit with her for as long as I wanted. Carolyn stayed with me all day, but she had to sit in the waiting room; it was just as well because I didn't feel up to talking, and I was, irrationally, obsessed with the fact that I hadn't gone back for my ham roll, with my 'favourite pickle'.

Kitty turned up around two in the afternoon, she was crying, but she was angry too. I wondered why Roisin wasn't there, or her husband, and why hadn't one of the boys come with her to offer some support? But she told me she'd insisted on coming in alone, and that my Uncle Jack was waiting in the car. 'It wasn't fair to involve the children,' she said.

She still worried about her children, even though all four of them were now upwards of twenty-five, and three of them had children of their own to worry about. She held me close as soon as she saw me, and apologised profusely for Aileen's misdemeanours or, as she put it, Aileen's sins, which made me think it was most likely her children's spiritual welfare that was making her determined to keep them at bay, rather than the notion that it might be too upsetting for them.

Then she turned her attention to Aileen. 'What made you do it?' she wailed, 'May the Lord-in-all-his-mercy forgive you...' She continued in this vein for about half an hour, until it became just too much for her and she ran out of the room yelling into her mobile, 'that she needed to be picked up, right away!'. It was quiet after she went; the expression on my mother's face hadn't changed, and I was pleased because it seemed to indicate that she hadn't heard any of Kitty's accusations, she'd suffered enough already.

Roisin telephoned me not long after, to say how sorry she was for all of it. They were shocked and upset, but why hadn't I been around to see her new babby, William, who was the cutest, and sure to cheer me up; like it would be that easy!

Aileen died that evening. I'd had the chance to tell her that I was sorry, and that I loved her, though I doubt she'd been able to hear me. They'd done their best, but her system had failed, and if they had been able to revive her, she would have remained in a vegetative state. She'd taken far too many pills for it to be just 'a cry for help', though they were careful to explain to me that only a few could cause irreparable damage; maybe they were afraid that I'd do the same. No one had asked me about the newspaper article, perhaps they hadn't connected it to us, or maybe they were just too busy to read it. One thing was certain; it wouldn't have been overlooked by the police, suicide never was, even though it was no longer a criminal offence, and Aileen's suicide would be of particular interest to them.

I was an orphan, probably an orphan twice over, and that had to be a record; unless Iris and Fin turned up to reclaim their missing child, but I wasn't hopeful.

My new family took me home and fussed around me, Carolyn and Jono that is, not Don Delaney who had precipitated the situation that I found myself in. Or did he? Because I was the one who insisted on looking for him; or you could say that it was Aileen and Patrick who had brought it all about in the first place, by stealing me from a field in Kilkenny.

'We're going to find Iris,' declared Carolyn, 'she is still out there; I just know she is, and when she sees the newspapers, she'll turn up to claim you.'

Claim me…! Like I was a lost umbrella, forgotten, and left on a bus. I wasn't sure I wanted to be claimed, I wasn't even certain that I wanted parents anymore. They were nothing but a heavy weight, draining your energy, while you struggle to please them, and conform, and make them proud.

I was free, at last; perhaps there were advantages to being an orphan, after all.

A week later I still hadn't been claimed, and I was sure that if 'they' were out there, they would have been in touch by now.

I'd spent many hours down at the police station, going through my personal details over and over; and they'd questioned me relentlessly about my abduction, which seemed rather odd since I was only three months old when it happened. Eventually, they concluded that I was indeed Angelica Malone, and they promised to contact the various bureaucratic and administrative institutions so that I could be granted my 'real name' and obtain all the relevant papers. No one could be prosecuted as the offending parties were both dead. They also said, they would try to trace the whereabouts of Iris and Fin, but as they hadn't heard from them in more than twenty years, they weren't hopeful, and I already knew that Fin's family had searched for him without success. None of it helped my mental state and I'd swing from euphoria, at having solved the mystery of my existence, and joy at the prospect of actually having a passport and a birth certificate, to black-hole depths at the loss of two people who'd spent twenty five years of their lives raising me, and whom I still loved, in spite of it all.

CHAPTER 10
KILKENNY
1993
Aileen Sullivan

Aileen, married for fifteen years, and with nothing to show for it; apart from a few cheap sticks of furniture, and a rented cottage, marooned in the middle of nowhere. Her sister, Kitty, had given birth three times, and in the first five years of marriage. Three little boys, one following another, with barely enough time to draw breath in between; and now she was pregnant again with her fourth and hoping for a girl.

Aileen was certain she would have truly valued a little one, whatever it was. How could it possibly matter, she wondered, they were all babies, weren't they? And now she didn't even have them around, not since they'd decided that life would be better in Canada. 'More opportunities for the children,' said Kitty, 'a new life, in a country where there's more space; and the weather's better.' Then the photographs began to arrive, in the post to begin with, and then, almost daily, on screen; three little brothers celebrating a birthday, or kicking a ball, or running across a snowy landscape.

She was pleased they were so happy, so fulfilled, but nevertheless, it was a constant bombardment that only served to remind her of what she had missed. It looked idyllic, she had to admit, though rather flat, and not nearly as beautiful as Ireland.

It was unfair; why was it so easy for some and yet impossible for others? Those women who popped out babies, year after year, like farm animals, seemingly unable, or unwilling, to prevent it; and those who couldn't care for them, or didn't want yet another child, producing half a dozen, and sometimes more. She was a failure, unable to accomplish the very thing she'd been put on earth to do.

Angela had been their salvation, such a pretty and sweet-natured child, who truly befitted her name, for she was as beautiful as an angel in every way; and the fact that she had arrived in such an unconventional way made her all the more special.

It was a golden, autumn afternoon when Aileen took the path across the farm. She was gathering sloes from the blackthorn in the hedgerows, and was just a stone's throw from a small, dilapidated cottage when she found the baby lying in a hollow beneath a gooseberry bush; well, not exactly a gooseberry bush, but something very similar. She was wrapped tightly, in a pink shawl, and when Aileen gathered her into her arms, she just gazed up at her with large, grey eyes, and smiled as if she knew, somehow, that this was her new mother. Aileen glanced around, there was no one in sight, and it was perfectly still; not so much as a whisper of breeze ruffled the leaves, even the birds had stopped their constant chirping. It was almost as if, for a moment, the world had stopped, so she dropped her basket and, clutching the baby tightly in her arms, ran back the way she had come, in the warm, October sun.

Patrick came home soon after; he'd been gone since five and he looked worn out, but he was whistling when he came in.

'What have you got there, Aileen?' he asked her cheerfully, but his face fell when she told him how she'd found the baby, who was snuffling frantically into her woolly cardigan, trying to find milk that would never be there.

'But that's someone else's child,' he said gruffly, 'his mother will be frantic wondering where he is. We should take him to the Garda.'

'She, she's a she, Patrick, and her name is Angelica, look, it's embroidered on her shawl; but I'm going to call her Angela, after St. Angela Merici. No one wanted this baby, or they wouldn't have left her in a field, a fox could have taken her, and the nights are cold. She would have died; she's ours now.'

'They might come back for her, Aileen, did y' think of that?'

'Well, and why would I let her go back to a mother who'd leave her to die in a field? She's the answer to our prayers, Pat, she's been sent to us, we can't turn her away; we can give her a good life.'

Patrick shook his head, she looked happier than she'd been for years; if they'd only had children of their own, she would have been content.

'Just till morning then,' he said wearily, 'and then we'll take her back.'

'Maybe,' murmured Aileen, and she rocked the baby in her lap and sang to her quietly.

CHAPTER 11
DUBLIN
2018

I hadn't seen, or heard, from Don since Aileen died. I think he felt guilty about how his desperate search for his brother had led to her suicide.
This time Jono didn't drive me, I took the bus, I had plenty of time to spare; now I was no longer working.
Kitty had forgiven her sister and was planning a grand funeral, so I didn't have to concern myself with that. I got the impression that she thought it was her duty because they'd been blood relatives, which I wasn't. Nothing was said to that effect, just intimated, and I should have felt excluded, but I didn't, I just felt relieved.
It was raining when I got off the bus which added to the drabness of the street. The children's play area was deserted and full of muddy puddles where the grass had worn away. Don was expecting me, and the front door was half open; we'd barely spoken when I called him, he said he was just on his way out, but I wasn't sure I believed him. He agreed that I should visit my

grandmother; he said she'd been asking for me but, unsurprisingly, he seemed reluctant to see me again.

She sat in her chair, bundled up to the neck in blankets as before, and her eyes were half closed, as if she couldn't decide whether to be awake or asleep.

'She's having a doze,' whispered Don, she spends most of the day like that now. It's a recent thing, only a few months back she'd be talking the hind-leg off a donkey, given half a chance; she always liked company. She's hanging on to see if Fin comes back, you raised her hopes.' He paused and looked abashed, 'I'm sorry about what happened to your mam, Angela, I feel…'

'That it was your fault?' I glared at him, but he avoided my gaze. 'No, it's fine, Don; and it wasn't your fault,' I added reluctantly, 'actually, it was mine.'

He looked up then, 'No, it was hers, her fault, Angela, all hers. I'm just sorry that it's ended like this. You mustn't blame y'self, darlin', she should never have taken you.'

The old woman stirred, 'Is that my Angelica? Have y' found my boy yet? Have y' found little Fin?'

I knelt next to her and took her hand, 'Not yet, Gran, I'm still trying though, and when I do, I'll bring him to you, I promise.'

It wasn't much, but it seemed to placate her because she smiled to herself and dozed off again into half sleep.

'Come into the kitchen, I'll make coffee,' said Don, 'I'm

guessing you won't want to be going for a drink?'

'What with your mate Mick? What do you think? Did you find out who took your phone? Was that even true?'

'Sure, it was, Angie, but maybe I wasn't as put out as I might have been.'

I knew then that I'd been set up. 'Did they pay you for the story?' I asked, but he shook his head. 'How could y' think such a thing of your own uncle? All I want is to find my little brother for the old woman, before she goes on her final journey.'

I didn't stay long, just had my coffee and went. Grandmother was sleeping when I left; her breathing was ragged, and irregular, and I decided to visit again soon. She wouldn't be around for very much longer, though she'd still have managed nearly thirty years more than Aileen, hanging on till the bitter end, unable to live and unable to die, trapped between the two; it wasn't an inviting prospect, and it didn't help my depression at all. I decided to go round to see Roisin and little William, named for his paternal grandfather, maybe the new babby would cheer me up! It was worth a try.

Roisin didn't come to the door straight away, and when she did it wasn't the Roisin I knew. This one looked bedraggled and sleep deprived. Chloe was pulling at the bottom of her shirt, and grizzling, and her nose needed wiping, and I could hear the unmistakeable mewl of a new baby crying from a room upstairs.

'Oh, it's you, Angie,' she said, 'I've just put William in his cot; he won't leave me, every time I put him down, he yells like he'll never see me again. I've been up all night, and this one is too coldy for nursery, they don't want them if they're under the weather, though she probably caught it there to start with. Make me a cuppa, Angie, I need reviving, I'm a mess!'

The kitchen was a mess too. I struggled to find a couple of clean mugs, and a beaker and juice for Chloe; then while the water came to a boil, I wiped all the work surfaces and put the dishwasher on. It took me all of five minutes.

'You're an angel, sure y' are,' she said when I gave her the tea and a sandwich.

''Chocolate spread, it's all I could find,' I explained when she wrinkled her nose, 'it's delicious... I might have to buy some.'

'Mam was coming, but she had to visit the undertaker, and Father Paul, and a florist about the tributes. It's going to be grand, a royal send-off, and they're allowed to be buried in consecrated ground now! I'm sorry she died, Angela, I liked your mam; she was a nice woman, even if she wasn't really your mam. And I'm sorry not to have been around to pay my respects, but I'm just too exhausted to do anything...' and she burst into tears. God! If it wasn't one thing it was another, and to think I'd come to cheer myself up! Instead, I'd walked into a mad house. Why didn't anyone lead a normal life, but what constituted a normal life? I wasn't sure I knew; one that was angst free, I supposed, where everyone was happy, and life ran smoothly with no hiccoughs or surprises, but how would that be normal? It was an illusion, just a façade, and it suddenly occurred to me just how adept we all are at hiding our true circumstances.

I sat Roisin in a chair and picked up the little one. She clutched me tightly around the neck with her sticky, chubby little fingers, 'Would you like something to eat, Chloe?' I asked her, but she didn't reply, she just sucked her thumb and nodded. We went into the kitchen and I gave her a biscuit while I buttered bread and cut up a banana, Chloe looked as if she might have had too many biscuits; then I switched on the television and settled her down to watch cartoons. Roisin was still crying, but it was quieter than before. 'What's the problem, Roisin?' I asked, 'I'll help as much as I can. I'd better fetch the babby for starters,' but even then, she didn't react.

William's face was bright red, and his cries had turned to faint splutters, as if he'd given up on any hope of attention. I lifted him out and hugged him, wrapping a shawl around him, as his legs felt icy cold, then I headed back along the landing to the stairs.

'Is that you, Roisin?' called a voice. It was Sean; why hadn't Roisin mentioned that Sean was home? I stopped outside their room, Roisin and Sean's room, the master-suite. What did that mean? Why not the mistress-suite, or did that have too many unwelcome connotations?

'No, it's me… Angela,' I called back, but there was no reply, so I tapped lightly on the door; then opened it just a crack, and peeped in. The room was in darkness as the blinds were drawn, and there was an overpowering smell of sweat.

'Are you ill, Sean?' I whispered, 'Can I get you anything?'

'Go away, Angie, and take the babby with y', I don't want to see him! Just tell Roisin to come.'

The babby started to wail again so I patted his back and rocked him, and he settled down and nuzzled into my shoulder. 'You won't find anything there,' I murmured, 'let's go and find your mammy.'

Roisin had stopped crying, though she still looked miserable. I changed William's soaking nappy and gave him to her, and she clamped him to her breast, 'Are you feeling better,' I asked, and she nodded, 'Thanks, Angie, you're a star, sure you are.'

I wanted to enquire why Sean was upstairs in bed, instead of at work; or at least, why he wasn't helping with his children, but I decided to wait until the baby was fed. They looked so content sitting there, no one would guess there was anything wrong.

After several minutes I couldn't wait any longer, 'Roisin, what's wrong with Sean? Is he sick?' I asked her, then I waited again, while she decided whether she should tell me.

'He's depressed, would you believe?' she said quietly, 'Or he says he is. He won't get up, or wash; he just lies there, all day. I can't even get in to change the sheets. I've been sleeping with the children this past week.' She gave a bitter laugh, 'What's he got to be depressed about? He hasn't gone through nine months of pregnancy, looking like a whale, while trying to keep the house nice, and holding down a job, and caring for a toddler, and now a baby as well.' She paused for breath before continuing, 'The doctor came to see him this morning; him, can you believe? He told him to get up, but he refused! I don't know how I'm going to manage; he won't go to work; he won't even let me open the curtains! What am I going to do, Angie?'

I didn't know what to say, or where to begin. 'It's a medical condition, Roisin,' I said at last, 'he can't help it, I'm sure he'd get stuck in if he could. He's not a bad man; you've always told me how reasonable he is. Surely the doctor can give him a certificate, and then at least you won't be worrying about paying the bills.'

'It's not just him, Angie...' she eyed me resentfully, 'it's Mam. She's gone to pieces since she lost her sister. Now all she thinks about is giving Aileen a good send off, so she's no use to me either. And I know she was your mam, but no one is helping me, Angie, no one, and I can't cope anymore, it's all too much!'

Suddenly everything had changed. I'd been relieved that Kitty was organising the funeral, and I'd just gone with it, not realising that Roisin desperately needed her too, but I didn't know what to do. I couldn't tell Sean to get up and face his responsibilities, he'd tell me where to go, in no uncertain terms, and why not, it wasn't my business. Equally, I knew that nothing would persuade Kitty to relinquish control of Aileen's funeral; all I could offer was the help that Roisin needed, till everything returned to some sort of normality. Suddenly, I had a job, albeit unpaid. 'Don't worry, Roisin,' I said, 'I'll help you, it will be a pleasure, and I've nothing else to do for the moment. I'll stay until I've put Chloe to bed and cooked the dinner; then we'll decide what to do next. Now, where do you keep the vacuum cleaner and the mop? I can start by giving the place a bit of a clean.'

CHAPTER 12

I stayed for nearly two weeks, until two days before the funeral when Kitty turned up. 'You can go now, Angie...' she told me, 'Thank you for helping Roisin and the children; you know how busy I've been with my sister's service and burial, but everything's arranged now. It's going to be wonderful!'
I noticed she said, 'my sister' rather than 'your mother', but perhaps I was being oversensitive, and how could a funeral ever be 'wonderful'? She turned to Roisin next. 'Get your things, Roisin; I'm taking you and the children home with me until that lazy heap of a husband decides to rise from his bed.'
Roisin didn't argue, and neither did Sean, in fact he seemed glad to be rid of us. Kitty dropped me at the end of my road, and although I was sad to see them drive off, I felt happy to be free of the responsibility. It surprised me that I'd considered Roisin to be so fortunate for I knew now that her life was far from perfect. Still, at least Sean was being treated for his depression, with counselling, and various medications, so hopefully, their life and marriage would soon be back on track. He'd resented my presence in the house, but I had no choice but to ignore him, he'd always been

so friendly in the past and I just had to keep reminding myself that he was ill.

On the third day of my stay I'd opened the door to the postman. 'Parcel for Roisin, from Canada,' he chirruped, 'and how are you this morning, Angela, are they treating y' well?'

I took it inside and gave it to Roisin, 'You've got a very cheery postman,' I said, 'look, he brought you a present.'

It was a baby blanket, hand-knitted in a pretty powder-blue, and almost identical to mine. Along one side, where the plain stitches met the purl, 'William John', was woven in bright blue, silk thread. I held it to my cheek, and it felt, somehow, familiar. Was this Iris's way of letting me know where she was? No, that was ridiculous and no more than wishful thinking; how could it be anything else?

'Who sent you this shawl, Roisin?' I asked her, 'It's exactly like mine, the one I came in.'

That sounded ridiculous too, as if I'd come in a package from some distant destination.

'Mam still has friends in Canada, Christy and Paul; we never see them, but they like to keep in touch. Perhaps they bought it in a local craft shop, it looks hand knitted. Oh, Angela, surely you can't be thinking that Iris made it?'

Canada, was it possible that Iris was in Canada? If she was, it was no wonder she hadn't read the Irish newspapers. Had she fled to Canada to get away from Fin? Or was she trying to forget me? Did she want to start over in some place completely different, where she could put the past behind her?

Carolyn and Jono were at work when I got home. The cats were pleased to see me; they sat next to me on the arms of my slumping chair, like sphinxes guarding some ancient, Egyptian tomb. Very little had changed in my absence; the notoriety, that Carolyn had predicted, was reserved for Aileen rather than me, and then it was only brief. No one had contacted me from my 'real' family, but then Iris might be on the other side of the world, and maybe Fin was dead, or just didn't care. What if they were both dead? Two fathers and two mothers gone to the grave, and me only twenty-five!

Still, at least I was now in possession of various documents that proved I existed, and I'd already applied for a passport in a name I didn't recognise as my own. My birth certificate said I was Angelica Mary Malone, and stated that my father was Finbar Delaney, and my mother, Iris Kathleen Malone, both residing in Dublin at the time of my birth. Who was she? And who was I? I wasn't sure I knew anymore. And who was I left with now, apart from my adoptive cousins? An ancient grandmother on the brink of dementia, and the treacherous Don Delaney; they didn't feel like an acceptable exchange for Patrick and Aileen, and I yearned for a time when I was naively happy being Angela Sullivan.

I switched on the television and I was still sitting there, flanked by cats, when Carolyn returned just after two; I was more than happy to see her.

'Mr. O'Donnell has given us the afternoon off.' she explained, 'He's worried about the business, reckons there's too much competition. Between you and me, I think he'd already been drinking when he came in. So how are you, Angie? Are you bearing up? At least it took your mind off things, looking after Roisin, and the children and all.'

I laughed; I supposed the 'all', she was referring to, was Sean.

'I'm in need of a rest, but thanks for asking! You will come to the funeral with me, Carolyn, won't you?'

'Of course, I'm coming, and Jono too. I've organised flowers, I hope that's okay. They're white lilies in the shape of a cross, but if you've already ordered some, then fine, we can take them from us.'

Flowers…! Carolyn had ordered the flowers! Whatever was the matter with me? How in the world had I forgotten something so important, so vital, to the proceedings?

'Don't worry it's fine,' she added, 'I never mentioned it before because you had so much to think about already. I hope you don't mind. Don't forget to call the florist with your message for the card.'

I hugged her, 'Thank you so much, Carolyn, I'll refund you the money. I don't know why I didn't think of it, it's unforgivable!'

'How are you doing, Angela?' asked Jono when he came in, 'Are you still after finding Iris? Has no one been in touch at all?'

'No, not so far, Jono,' I replied, 'but there's time, perhaps they will.'

He nodded, 'Yes, someone might see the story and tell her, sometimes it takes a while for the word to get around.'

'There's the blanket, though,' I said quietly, and then wished I hadn't. He would think I'd taken leave of my senses.

Carolyn came and sat down next to me, 'Well, don't stop there, what's all this about a blanket? Have you got a lead?'

'Someone sent Roisin a baby blanket, that's all...' I hesitated, 'it's identical to mine.'

She put her arm around me, 'Aw, come on, Angie, they could have used the same knitting pattern, it's easy to knit a baby shawl. Did you ask who sent it?'

'Roisin said it was from people they knew when they lived in Canada, and it's not just any shawl, it's got William's name sewn along the edge. It's identical to mine, except it's blue, instead of pink.'

I felt like crying, but I wasn't sure why. Surely, I wasn't pinning all my hopes on such a tenuous connection.

'Well, I suppose it could be a clue,' murmured Carolyn, but I could tell by her expression that she thought I was clutching at straws.

'Your mother might well have run off to Canada,' said Jono, 'she may have relatives there, the Irish are everywhere,' he grinned, 'you might have relatives there as well, Angie. Iris could have knitted the blanket, or her mother; what did you say her name was? Kathleen…?'

I nodded, was he humouring me?

'Well, maybe they're still knitting blankets for babies. Kathleen's probably not very old; she'd be in her seventies, sixties even. Have you asked Roisin where it came from?'

'Don't get your hopes up, Angie,' murmured Carolyn, 'it's a bit of a long shot.'

It was, I knew. I saw her glance at Jono.

'Roisin said she would find out where it came from. You never know…' I paused, 'I suppose I'll just have to wait until she gets a reply from whoever sent it. I'm going to write to Fin's sister, Maura, she might have some idea where they went. I just have to get through this week first.'

Yes, I would find Iris, but first I had to bury my other mother.

CHAPTER 13
Roisin

There was always something different about her. Angela, I mean; she just didn't fit in; those huge grey eyes, and the straw-coloured hair, and with us all so dark and fair skinned, but then she was adopted so there'd be no reason why she should resemble any of us. Still, there was a strangeness about her; like she knew on some instinctive level that something wasn't quite right.

Aileen and Patrick smothered her. I suppose that's what happens when you only have the one child to worry about; they were over-protective; I wouldn't have been able to stand it. She wanted to come travelling with me, but Patrick put his foot down; he said she had to find a job, not go gallivanting off around the globe. I always suspected there was more to it; it was probably Aileen who said she couldn't leave, but then she couldn't have left anyway, because she didn't have a passport, and no hope of getting one either without dropping them in hot water, because they'd stolen her.

They seemed so normal, Mr and Mrs Average, and

Aileen was dull as chastity; she always behaved like she had a secret, but Patrick was full of life. He loved a drink and a craic of a Saturday night! Poor Angela, they even encouraged her to move in with Conor just to keep her here. I knew what he was like the instant I set eyes on him, and I was proved right; the state of her when he'd finished, poor girl!

I couldn't believe it when she told me they found her in a field. It would have been grand if they'd saved her and handed her in, but instead they kept her and let that poor woman go on, year after year, not knowing if her child was alive or dead. How could anyone do such a thing?

I know it was sad for them, Aileen wanted a child and there was Angela, lying under a bush, just like in a fairy tale. It would have been hard to resist picking her up, and maybe she thought it was the right thing to do, but now they're gone, Patrick too, and both no age at all.

It's been hard on Mam; Aileen was the only sister she had, and she hasn't stopped crying since she passed, but Angela has been my salvation; she's helped me to get back on my feet when everything became too much. She finished up staying till Mam came and took us back home; not Sean, just me, and Chloe and William. Sean was still in bed when we left; he said he was depressed, but to me it felt like he just didn't care anymore.

The funeral was a grim affair; the sky opened, and the rain fell in torrents soaking everyone. Irish rain, cold and unrelenting, and heavy enough to wash away all the sins we're so obsessed with. The church was full; there are so many of us, second and third generations, and friends and neighbours of Aileen, and old Mrs. Gaffney who lived next door.

The Irish certainly know how to do a funeral, the congregation smartly dressed in black, even a few veils on the old women. It's funny how they turn out for death, often people you don't see in years, yet there they are at the wake, knocking back the Guinness, and the rum-punch, and all that free food. God, forgive me; say twenty 'Hail Marys', Roisin, and you'll be pure again, cleansed, innocent, all ready for the next wicked thought or misdemeanour.

Jono and Carolyn were there, either side of Angela as if to prop her up, but she didn't really need it. She's moved on, already... so maybe my problems have helped her to see how lucky she is; free of all the expectations, and the responsibilities that go with them.

CHAPTER 14

It was over. Aileen was gone, buried next to Patrick in the soft earth. Their house had been rented, rather than owned, so there was very little left that I wanted, or needed. Most of it had been disposed of anyway, in her massive clear out, as if she had foreseen her death. Maybe, subconsciously, she'd already wanted her life to be over and done with, now that the lies were exposed, and all the things she valued most were gone. What was it she said to me? That day when we sat opposite each other at the kitchen table, when she admitted how she'd come by me, and her justifications for keeping me. 'Time goes by without us noticing and it's not until we've nearly run out that we realise how little we have...' Those words would stay with me always; and suddenly, finding Iris seemed even more imperative. Not Fin, I didn't care whether or not I found Fin.

Reporters stalked the churchyard like crows seeking carrion. Their dark coats flapped winglike in the driving rain as they tried in vain to protect and conceal their cameras. They flocked around me when I tried to leave, each promising to pay me for any interesting information relating to my abduction, as if I had some fascinating, and preferably sordid, tale to tell. But there was nothing in my upbringing that would attract the attention of their readers; I was worth no more than a brief paragraph, or three. My childhood had been ordinary, and Patrick and Aileen faultless in their regard for my wellbeing. I didn't need anyone to pay me for a story that didn't exist. I was stolen, cared for, went to school, grew up. End of! Nothing interesting of note, only my beginning; and I had no memory of that.

It occurred to me afterwards that maybe I should have contrived some tale; something to keep me in the public eye, and on the front pages, but it wasn't in me to lie, or to exaggerate trivialities.

Afterwards, Carolyn scolded me for my lack of foresight. 'You made a mistake there,' she said, 'I despair of you! There's no such thing as bad publicity. Iris might have seen the story, or someone who knew her. Go back and say you'll take the money, make something up, anything...'

Maybe I would, one day, but for the moment I felt as if I'd done enough damage, me and Don between us. There had to be another way; I'd write to Maura, Fin's sister. Perhaps she'd been in touch with Iris, maybe she'd even known from the start where Iris had gone. Don said it was she who always made the effort to keep in touch.

Dear Maura (I wrote),
Have you heard from Don?

No, that wouldn't do! I screwed the paper into a ball and threw it into the bin; then I sat there for at least ten minutes wondering how to begin.

I imagined Maura opening the envelope, how would she react at receiving a letter from a niece who had disappeared, without trace, nearly a quarter of a century ago? With shock, definitely... and joy, perhaps... or disbelief. What if she had a weak heart? I'd caused enough trouble already.

I still hadn't got her address from Don, I'd put off calling him after the funeral, and now it seemed too long a time, and I felt embarrassed because I hadn't been back to see my grandmother. Why hadn't I asked more about his sister when I had the chance? What sort of person was she? Did he have any photographs? I tried again...

Dear Maura,
I hope this won't be too much of a shock for you after so many years...

Yes, it was better, so long as she didn't think I was preparing her for bad news; after all it was good, wasn't it? I was alive, I was back, Angelica had returned from oblivion.

I continued...

My name is Angela Sullivan, or it has been for most of my life. You knew me briefly as Angelica Malone, daughter of Iris Malone and your brother, Fin Delaney.

My parents, the ones who cared for and raised me, have recently passed away; Patrick first, of a heart attack, and then my mother, Aileen, soon after. It was only after Patrick died that Aileen told me the truth and, now I know my real identity, I would very much like to find my biological parents so I can reassure them that I am well, and healthy, and none the worse for my beginnings. It must have been very hard for them when I went missing, and I'm sure they will have wondered ever since what became of me.

    I hope you don't mind me contacting you. I know it's many years since you left Ireland, and Don tells me that there is very little contact between remaining members of the family. I've been to visit your mother, my grandmother, on two occasions, and she is well enough for such as old woman though she's becoming sleepier by the day.

Is there any chance that you have kept in touch with Iris? Or Fin? Don mentioned that he went missing soon after my disappearance; maybe you know something of his whereabouts?

I hope we can meet up sometime soon,
With very best wishes, your niece,
Angelica Malone

    Then I re-wrote it, minus all my crossings out, and put it in an envelope; I'd have to get the address from Don, and I wasn't looking forward to seeing him. I could telephone, but far better to go around to the house. Anyway, now that I'd found my grandmother, I felt compelled to visit her, for all I knew she might soon be departing as well; in fact, half of her seemed to have left already. I set off straightaway, before I had the chance to change my mind. It wasn't as if I was doing much else. I called him to say I was on my way and, this time, he seemed pleased to hear from me.

There was a note on the door when I got there; it said, 'Angel, just gone to the post, make y'self at home. Back soon, Don.'

Angel? Only Aileen had ever called me that. I pushed open the door and walked into the gloomy room, and there she was, dozing in her old armchair. A cat was sleeping on her lap, its head resting across her substantial belly; they both looked warm and comfortable. It hadn't been there on my previous visits, so I took out my phone and snapped a picture to post to Maura with my letter. She'd probably like a photo of her mother, and maybe she would come for a visit if she realised how ancient she'd become; although Grandmother had never once mentioned Maura, only Fin. It was Fin she wanted to see, before she left for good.

'Pension day...' explained Don when he returned, 'I pick it up every week from the post office. How are y' Angie?'

'Not too bad, thanks, Don, all things considered.'

I took out the letter I'd written to Maura, 'Will you give me Maura's address, please? I've explained everything to her; I hope she doesn't get too much of a shock.'

'I'll get it for y',' he said, 'it should be in one of the drawers. We haven't been in touch for a while. Ah yes, here we are.'

'Don't suppose you've got any photos in there, have you, Don?' I asked him.

'Maybe in the other drawer; there could be one or two…' he opened a second drawer and rifled through it. 'Yes, here we are,' he said at last, 'but they're old, taken more than twenty years ago in the town, it must have been the last time she was here. We've aged a bit, I reckon.' He screwed up his eyes and held it as far away as he could, 'My arms aren't long enough these days! Will y' look at that! It's me…' he shook his head, 'and Mam, and Da, this is Declan, and Maura; she had long, black hair, back then.'

'Can I keep one of these, please, Don. Maybe I'll visit her one day. I was going to send her this.' I held up the photo I'd taken on my mobile, and he gave up squinting and fished around in his pocket for his glasses.

'Well, will y' look at that, it's a grand photo, Angela! And is it your cat, there on her knee?'

I laughed at that, 'I came on the bus, Don, and I wouldn't be bringing my cats on the bus, now would I? I thought it was your cat! It was asleep on her lap when

I got here, it's keeping her company. Do you think I should wake her to say hello?'

He sighed, 'No, we'll leave her; she's not too good these days. I don't know how much longer I can keep her at home; best you tell Maura she's going downhill fast, just in case she wants to see her.'

'No, Don, you tell her. She's your sister, she should take some responsibility, and so should your brothers. It's not fair leaving you to cope with everything.'

The old woman murmured in her sleep when I stood up to leave, and the cat leapt off her lap. I went over and kissed her cheek, but she didn't wake.

'I'll be off, Don,' I whispered, 'see you again.'

The cat and I exited at the same time, the cat to the left, no doubt in search of another soft lap to sit on, and me to the right. I wondered for a moment if I should pay Sean a quick visit to see if he'd improved at all, but I decided against it. Things were depressing enough without inviting more misery into my life; instead, I headed straight home; I'd post my letter tomorrow.

CHAPTER 15

I was bored, I'd happily given up work but, now that all the chaos was over and done with, I had nothing to do.

Carolyn and Jono were working, and friends and family were occupied with jobs, or babies, or both. I wasn't just bored; I was lonely too. My project had stalled. I'd found Don, and I'd written to Maura, and now all I could do was wait for her to get back to me. I doubted she would know where Iris was, in any case, but maybe she'd invite me to England, and it occurred to me that I should have written my email address on the letter. She could have sent me an instant reply; instead here I was, awaiting snail-mail. What if she'd moved? She might not have bothered to tell Don; it wasn't as if they were close.

My other non-lead was William's blanket, and it was plain that everyone thought I was mad to even give it consideration. Plus, I doubted that Roisin had written her thank-you notes, so I wouldn't be finding out any time soon, but how amazing it would be if it turned out that Iris was in Canada. I could visit her there; though did I really need an excuse to go to Canada? With my new passport, and cash, I could go anywhere I pleased, but not yet, first I had to find Iris! I wrote a quick note to Maura, just to tell her that she could contact me by email and went straight out to post it.

I had become a watcher, observing other peoples' lives; watching as they went to work each day, or took their kids to school. My life had shrunk, and I merely existed, wandering parent-less, and job-less, from day to day. I checked the post over and over, hoping for word from Maura, and pestered Roisin whenever I saw her, 'Will you be writing to your friends in Canada anytime soon? Be sure to ask them where they found William's blanket', and, 'Have you heard back from your friends in Canada, Roisin?' and she'd look back at me with an expression that conveyed a mixture of sadness and sympathy, and, more than a smidgen of irritation. 'No, Angela, not yet, I'll tell y' as soon as I do, be patient just a little bit longer...' and she'd add, 'I don't want you to be disappointed, Angie, but I very much doubt they'll have any connection to Iris.'

Her children looked forward to my visits, although Auntie Kitty was less keen. 'So, you've not got a job yet, Angela?' It was spoken as a question, but she meant it as an indisputable fact; one that condemned me. She might just as well have said, 'You're a waste of space, sure y' are, doing nothing useful with your life, and living off your inheritance', as if I were the daughter of some property magnate, or a spoilt princess with a trust fund. Nothing could have been further from the truth; the way things were going; my legacy would be gone in no time.

Roisin never mentioned going back home to Sean. 'Sure, he's doing well, he's much improved...' she would tell me when I asked, but it quickly became apparent that she didn't particularly care either way. Her life had improved immeasurably; she'd given up her job at the supermarket and informed them that she wouldn't be returning; and her mother, Kitty, was an on-site nanny for the children. There was also a willing playmate for the little ones who called in two or three times a week, she being 'yours truly'.

I was deep in a rut of my own making, and I worried that Carolyn and Jono would grow tired of me moping around.

Carolyn and Jono were in the kitchen when I got home from visiting Roisin, they were laughing and Jono was cooking something complicated with noodles, spring onions, and a slab of tofu. He stopped chopping and put down the knife.

'Ah...' he said, 'Angela, at last; we were just talking about you!'

'All good,' added Carolyn, and she grinned as if to reassure me.

'Are you still thinking of going back to university?' asked Jono, 'We were just saying, you could apply for next year, if you hurry, and you'd still have several months to get used to the idea. It's so easy to get into the habit of drifting along without making any decisions.'

He was right, it was exactly what I was doing.
'I'm happy to help,' he added, 'if I can. Is there anything that particularly interests you? You're very good with the cats, have you considered becoming a vet nurse? I could pull some strings; maybe you could even train as you study.'
Carolyn laughed, 'And we all know you're useless in an office.'
It was indisputable; I was hopeless at anything that required me to sit down for any length of time. I liked his idea. 'Thanks Jono, you're right,' I replied, 'I am good with animals, well, cats, anyway. See what you can do, I'd really appreciate it!'
'In the meantime, we're off to London...!' shrieked Carolyn, 'Jono wants me to meet everyone, the English side of the family, and his friends from uni.'
He grabbed her playfully around the waist and kissed her on the forehead, 'Yes, the whole mob of them, and it's time we took a trip to Wicklow; we should have gone before, but I was worried they'd frighten you away, they're a fearsome mob.'
'Oh really, well, wait till you meet the Kavanaghs; I bet yours are chicken feed compared to mine!'

I listened to their cheerful banter and wondered, would my life have been like that if it hadn't been for

Aileen, and Patrick, and Fin? Was Fin the reason I'd been abandoned, alone and vulnerable in a field, waiting for Aileen to come along and pick me up? But the rest of them were just as guilty, Iris and Mary, and Kathleen; they should never have left me, and maybe, if Aileen had waited a bit longer before downing a bottle of pills, the courts would have realised it and exonerated her. Perhaps I had brothers, and sisters, somewhere in the world, maybe in Canada.

Carolyn was rattling on non-stop about Buckingham Palace, and Trafalgar Square, and how they'd be staying with Jono's aunt who, lived in West London, which was 'nice and central', according to Carolyn, who had already planned their itinerary; departure by plane on Friday, a market on Saturday morning, and sightseeing on the Sunday.

I foresaw a lonely weekend ahead of me. Maybe I'd ask Roisin again if she'd heard anything from Canada.

I waved them off on the Friday. Carolyn was already fretting about the flight and being so far from home. I watched as the taxi drove around the corner, she was still waving, and a feeling of envy suddenly overwhelmed me; I hoped it didn't show in my face. I walked slowly back indoors; the place felt empty without her infectious chatter.

I was pathetic. The whole world was out there, just waiting for me to take that first step, but I couldn't do it! I was stuck in limbo. I went back to bed for two hours and only got up because it occurred to me that I might become like Sean if I didn't, and the idea terrified me; and I was hungry, so two good reasons not to give in to lethargy.

The whole weekend stretched before me, empty days when I would be alone. I weighed up my options, I could visit Roisin and the children, they always made me welcome, even when Kitty didn't; and the boys, Roisin's brothers, might be there, it was a while since I'd seen them.

I tried to imagine how my situation would look to an outsider, without all the feelings that engulfed me, the shock, the grief, and the confusion. From the outside it was fairly simple, two people, who weren't really my parents, had died; that was all. They had, very kindly, left me enough money to laze about, as I was doing now, or, to find something worthwhile that I really wanted to do. I had time to spare, a chance to decide on the direction I wanted my life to follow. How many people were given that opportunity? The quest, for the woman who left me alone in a field, was merely a diversion. If I found her, it would be great, in fact, it would be amazing, but I couldn't let it take over my life; for a start, I might never find her. My upbeat meanderings suddenly took a dive. I was fooling myself because, first and foremost, I really did want to find her, I needed to find her. I'd been doing so well, and almost convinced myself that it wasn't that important in the scheme of things, but it was.

I got dressed and went out, unsure of where I was heading. I turned left and walked briskly towards the city centre, quickening my pace as I passed O'Donnell and Henry's Travel; God forbid that anyone should want to talk to me. A quick glance confirmed that customer numbers had diminished to nil. I could see Mr O'Donnell perusing some papers at the desk that used to be mine. Padraig was there too, hanging lametta along the edges of the shelves and straightening brochures. He looked up and waved a feeble salute, as if unsure whether it was me. I turned away quickly; things must have been bad for Mr O'Donnell to insist that Padraig come in. I walked on, unaware to begin with that I was following the route I'd taken on the day of Aileen's 'confession'. At least this time it wasn't raining; now the trees were bare, and the blue winter sky bathed everything in an eye-watering brightness. The streets were bustling, and the shop windows already embellished with tinsel and fairy lights, even though it was still November. I turned away from the main streets and cut through the back road, where I'd sat on the wall in the pouring rain; it seemed a lifetime ago.

Eventually, I found myself in front of the house that I'd shared with Aileen and Patrick. I stood back so that the woman who was sweeping the step didn't see me, and for a moment I really wished it was Aileen, but it wasn't, it couldn't be, because she was in the cemetery, next to dear old Patrick. Tears ran down my face, I was crying for Patrick and Aileen, but also for me. I shook myself, dried my tears, and moved closer. I wanted to see how much had changed. This woman was younger than my mother; she looked to be in her forties, and she was wearing jeans with kitten heels, and a full face of make-up. She looked across at me and smiled as I walked past, and I smiled back. I noticed that the curtains were floral, and brightly coloured, and the windows were no longer covered in shrouds of off-white lace. I was tempted to stop, to ask her if she was happy in her new home; I'd have liked to see inside, to find out if she had brought life to the place, to perhaps ask her if she had a family, but I didn't. I just walked on, and that was that, everything that linked me to my life there was gone.

I went home after that, slowly, heading north to Grafton Street, where I stopped at McDonalds and queued for fifteen minutes for a burger and fries; then, clutching my rapidly cooling paper bag, I strolled across the Green to Iveagh Gardens, where I found an empty bench and a flock of hungry gulls, every one of them intent on sharing my lunch.

CHAPTER 16

On Saturday I called Roisin and she drove round straight away to pick me up. 'And, before you ask...' she said, 'no, there's nothing yet from Canada, but I've written, so it's down to them now.'
The back seat was empty. 'Where are the little ones?' I asked, 'didn't they want to come for a ride?'
She grinned, 'William was asleep in his pram, and Grandpa and Chloe are making a swing at the top of the garden. It's fantastic, Angela, I have my life back; shall we take a trip to the shopping centre, or find some lunch? The shops are pretty crowded.'
'Pub lunch then,' I said, 'let's head out of town.'

It was after three when we arrived at Kitty's house on the outskirts of the city. Their home was big and draughty, and no one seemed too bothered about putting anything away. Their old dog was sleeping in his basket near the kitchen range; he looked up briefly to acknowledge my presence but obviously decided I wasn't worth the effort of rising from his bed. The air reeked with the smell of boiling broccoli, so I went across and turned the flame down. 'Mam always overcooks the greens,' explained Roisin, 'we're having roast beef for dinner.'

I finished up staying the night; it was lucky I'd thought to put out extra food for the cats. We shared the double bed in Roisin's old room; Chloe was on a camp bed in the corner, and William in his cot. I'd only ever had to share a bed when I stayed with school friends for sleepovers, and, of course, during my time with Conor. It seemed odd, as if we'd retreated to some primitive, tribe mentality; I almost expected Kitty and Jack to wander in and join us. Little Chloe was snoring softly; light breaths, punctuated by occasional yelps, she reminded me of the cats. I really hoped they hadn't eaten all their food in one go. William was wriggling in his cot, maybe he was having a bad dream; did babies have bad dreams, I wondered.

'I won't go back to Sean,' said Roisin suddenly, 'it was a mistake. I didn't allow myself time to mature, to see the world, and experience life as an independent woman.'

What was she talking about? I felt irritated, she had more than I could ever hope for, and yet here she was complaining, when it was Sean coping with depression, and losing his family, and probably his home.

'You've been halfway around the world;' I said, 'you've seen far more of it than me! At least you could do that; and you've got your babies, you wouldn't be without them, would you? And what about Sean, will you share custody, and the mortgage? It's not that easy, Roisin, he can't help the way he is.'

'I'm aware of that; I know it's not his fault. I already knew he was like that when we were at university. He was always depressed; I thought I could make him better.' She turned away from me, 'I've got to sleep now, Angie; William will be up in the night.'

He was, twice, the first time at around two, when Roisin switched on the lamp and staggered round the bed to lift him from his cot, and the second time at five, when she seemed oblivious to his wails. I picked him up and walked the floor, rocking and patting him; if he woke Chloe, then we'd all have to get up.

Someone was tapping gently on the door, it was Kitty. 'Give him to me,' she whispered, 'I'll make him a bottle. Roisin needs her sleep.'

I handed him over and went back to bed; no wonder Roisin didn't want to go home!

On Sunday, Roisin's eldest brother, Tim, turned up with his wife, Kate, and their three boys, twins of nine and a seven-year-old. They raced around the house, screaming like lunatics and trampling Chloe when she didn't move out of the way fast enough. I was relieved when they went, and so was the dog. As soon as the front door closed behind them, he was out of his basket and cocking his leg up the nearest fencepost, he'd been too frightened to venture outside before. Roisin spent most of the day chatting at length to Kate, mainly about how difficult motherhood had turned out to be. I knew she'd be fine now though, because her mother had taken over her role almost completely, as proved to be the case that evening when she gave them their tea and got them ready for bed.

'I'll take you home now,' said Roisin, 'Mam has everything under control.'

I nodded, 'Yes, please, Roisin, that would be grand.'

The house was in darkness when we drew up outside, it was empty, just waiting for me to occupy it, to turn on the lights, and the television, and feed the cats. Yesterday, I minded that it was empty, but now I was glad. 'Thanks for everything, Roisin,' I murmured, 'I've had a great weekend.'

She waited until I'd unlocked the door before driving off, and I turned and waved. The cats miaowed and nuzzled my legs. 'Come on, guys,' I said, 'let's find you some food, and then we'll put the kettle on.'

CHAPTER 17

Carolyn and Jono came home on Monday afternoon, I was pleased to see them. They'd been due to arrive earlier, but the flight was late so Jono said 'hi' and bye' and dashed off to the surgery to make sure all was well.

Carolyn had promised Mr O'Donnell that she'd be in for the afternoon, it was the only reason he let her have the Friday off, but she decided he would have to do without her, as she was worn out from the journey and her hectic weekend in London. I wondered if Padraig had turned up to help, but I somehow doubted it, not if he was expecting Carolyn; and anyway, the brochures had already been tidied and straightened, and Padraig wasn't much good at anything else. Maybe Mr O'Donnell should have kept me on, I was far more reliable, and he would probably take me back if I asked; I shuddered at the thought. I'd spent a couple of hours online, assessing whether I had the right qualifications for vet nursing, and the idea appealed to me. Maybe I could start by volunteering at the cats' home.

Carolyn didn't stop talking from the moment she got in the door. I was treated to every little detail of her trip, how they'd travelled around the West End in an open-topped bus, even though it was freezing, and how the Christmas lights in Regents Street were totally amazing. I tried my best to sound and look enthusiastic, but she went on, and on, until I was searching for an excuse to escape.

'And,' she continued, hardly drawing breath, 'I met Jono's friends from university, you should have been there! There was this gorgeous man, just right for you, his name is David and his wife has left him. It's really sad, she sounds like a right cow, sure she does.'

'Thanks for thinking of me, Carolyn. It's just what I need, a depressed man who's going through a divorce,' like poor Sean, I thought, though I didn't say so, 'and why would he be interested in someone who lives in another country?'

'Wales,' said Carolyn, 'he lives in Wales.'

'Oh, good, that's alright then,' I laughed, 'but Wales is still another country, even if it is a bit nearer.'

'I got you some chocolates; I knew you wouldn't want a tiny model of Buckingham Palace, or a plastic snow globe. Oh, and I've kept this English newspaper, I thought you might be interested in one of the articles.'

'Thanks, Carolyn,' I replied, 'lovely chocolates, we'll eat them later. Maybe you can get me the globe next time.'

I put the chocolates down on the table and opened the newspaper "WHERE DO I COME FROM?" asked the header, then, "Recent DNA advances mean that it is now possible to trace your roots back through several generations", and further down the page, "discover relatives you never knew existed. They might live in your street; they might even live next door…"

'What do y' think, Angie?' she smiled encouragingly, 'They analyse saliva from a mouth swab and, just from that, they can give you an accurate account of your place of origin, and any relatives that share your DNA. You might be able to find Iris! Or Fin, and any children they've had since; maybe you've got brothers and sisters, and cousins…'

I didn't know what to say, why hadn't someone mentioned before that this test existed?

She went on, 'of course, it does depend whether they've done it too, but it's worth a go, isn't it?'

It was, definitely worth a go!

Maura's email dropped into my 'in box' the following morning.

'Angelica…!' It began, and I could tell she was pleased, and surprised, because it was followed by a line of alternatively startled and happy emojis.

'I can't tell you how happy I am that we've found you, after all this time!

I telephoned Don as soon as I received your email, just to check we hadn't fallen victim to some heartless hoax, or scam, but he assured me that you really are Angelica, my baby niece, who disappeared all those years ago!

I left Ireland when I was young, so I met you just once when I went back to visit the family, and then only by accident. We bumped into Iris, in the street; she was pushing your pram and you were snuggled inside, staring out at the world around you, even though you were just a few months old. You already resembled Iris; she was always a pretty girl. Sadly, my brother, Fin, was never nice to her, and I shouldn't say it, but I doubt they'd have been together at all if you hadn't arrived on the scene. I was in England when my mother wrote to tell me you'd been abducted. We were distraught but, secretly, I hoped Iris had somehow taken you out of harm's way, because she disappeared soon after. Then Fin vanished too. My father and brothers searched for years without success, but anything could have happened to him, he had so many enemies; I was always surprised that he got to the age he did. Don said that Mam never got over it, her precious boy going missing like that, but it must be a great boon in her old age, to have you suddenly appear out of nowhere.'

I scanned the lengthy email impatiently, searching for the answer to my question and found it in a small paragraph near the end, it said;

'I'm very sorry, Angelica, but I have no idea where you might find Iris, or even where you could start your search. As I said, I didn't really know her at all, and I avoided Fin as much as I could.

Thank you for visiting Mam, and for sending news of her. Don is a good, kind man, but not a great communicator.
You're welcome to visit us, please come when you have time. We have three grown up children - your cousins - all with children of their own. It must be strange for you, suddenly to find that that you have a whole, new family.
Welcome back, Angelica! Much love, Maura.'

So, she didn't know where Iris was, or Fin, though it turned out I had cousins and nieces, and nephews. I also had an aunt, and four uncles, or five if I included Maura's husband, though I'd only met Don, and my ancient grandmother. I emailed back by return, to thank her for her reply, and added that I'd love to visit as soon as I was able; then I attached the photograph of Grandma with the random cat, that I'd never got around to printing, or posting, and promised to send more ASAP.
I wasn't sure when it would be though because every time I thought of her, huddled in her chair in that airless room, my heart sank into my boots. As for Don, his life seemed to consist of aimless drifting between the post office, and the pub.

I felt disappointed with them all; they were ordinary, and not dissimilar to Patrick and Aileen, in fact, if anything they were worse! Why was I even bothering?

CHAPTER 18

My de-oxyribonucleic acid test, to give it its full name, arrived two weeks later. It wasn't what I'd expected at all, consisting of a small plastic tube and a sealed envelope in which to return the sample. Carolyn was horrified when she saw it and I explained the process, which involved filling the plastic tube with saliva.

'Well, just let me know when the result comes,' she said, 'I have no wish to see you spitting into that bottle!' I couldn't say I relished the idea either, but I went off to the bathroom where I completed the test, filled in the forms, and sealed the envelope for posting. Then we both went off to work.

I'd responded reluctantly to Mr O'Donnell's pleas for help, but only part-time, I told him, and just for a few weeks, until he managed to find someone to replace me. He was very grateful, apparently my input had been far greater than Carolyn's and Padraig's combined, and Padraig managed to create more chaos than he solved, almost every time he crossed the threshold of O'Donnell and Henry.

I felt happier than I had for weeks; extra money was always useful, and it gave a framework to my day. In addition, I still had my afternoons free, just in case I decided to offer my assistance at the home for unwanted felines. I felt rested and at ease, everything would work out and, if I wanted, said Mr O'Donnell, I could continue to work part-time. It made a difference having every afternoon to do as I pleased; Christmas wasn't far away, and it was fun to wander the fairy-lit streets as the sky darkened. I hadn't been back to see Don and his mother, I knew they were family, yet I felt no rapport, no instinctive connection. I made up my mind to go when my two weeks of work was up, I'd buy a present for Grandma, and take a selfie with Don to email to Maura.

Roisin listened patiently while I told her about Don and my Grandmother, and Maura, and then invited me to spend Christmas with them. 'Those people are not your family,' she'd replied, 'how can they be? You don't know them; not like you know us! And anyway, it sounds to me like they don't care for anyone, not even their own mother.'

'Don does,' I said, 'he cares for her all the time. It's his job, I expect he gets a carer's allowance.' I hadn't thought of it before, but it was probably true.

'Yes, he sounds like a good man, but the others are useless. I thought you said that Fin had four brothers; so how come you've only met the one? No, Angela, we're your family, me and Mam, and Da and all. You must come to us for Christmas!'

She seemed to have forgotten Sean completely. She never mentioned him unless I asked, and it made me realise how women can be just as cruel as men, though in a different way, not that I ever really doubted it. I mentioned him now.

'So, Roisin,' I said, 'and will Sean be seeing the little ones over Christmas?'

She blushed, and her expression hardened.

'He's off to see his brother, Angie, and, to be honest, he's in no fit state to care for two small children!'

I left it at that. 'Can I come for the day, Roisin?' I asked her, 'I'd love to see Chloe playing with her toys. I won't stay though; your mam will have enough to do with all of you, as it is.'

Yes, Christmas day would be grand, just enough to keep the blues away. She nodded and smiled, 'Yes, Angie, I know it all gets a bit much, especially if you're not used to the racket!'

I wondered briefly if I should offer to house the dog over the festivities, but decided against it, after all, the cats would never approve of the competition for food and attention.

CHAPTER 19
DUBLIN
1993

Iris was beautiful from the moment she was born, one precious little sister in a country where huge families were the norm. Mary could still remember that day clearly, though she had only been five herself, but already rotund and rosy, and quite cherubic. She soldiered through life, while ethereal Iris wafted, appearing more vulnerable than she actually was, for there a hard streak that kept her going, in spite of everything.

The Delaneys were well known in the part of Dublin where they grew up, one girl, and five boys, Fin, at twenty-six, being the last but the most attractive, and spoilt by everyone, not least by his mother.
Mary watched him from a distance. She knew well enough that he wouldn't be interested in her, not when there were so many others to choose from. She guessed he'd be there that summer evening when the heat sucked the humidity from the earth and formed ghost-like drifts over the grass. The band was playing 'Raglan

Road' in the corner of the bar, and its haunting refrain drifted out into the darkness, 'When the angel woos the clay…' Mary knew the words by heart, it should have been a warning, and if she'd heeded it, everything might have been different.

She was certain that Fin wouldn't want her, but she would capture him anyway, because Iris would snare him if she couldn't, and, just to be certain, she picked Rosemary, and sweet-scented herbs, and burned them together, murmuring incantations as the smoke rose, curling and intertwining, in the damp air. The love potion worked, she could tell it had, the minute they looked into each other's eyes.

Later she regretted it, and wished the spell could be reversed, but it was too late; the past could never be changed, the damage was done. Most of all, she regretted dabbling in what their mother described as witchcraft, though neither of them would ever tell Iris, because they knew she wouldn't forgive them if she found out.

Kathleen insisted that Mary wasn't to blame; it was Iris who was destined to attract unwanted attention from the wrong sort; that, and fate, never to be changed by mortal man, or woman, but only by God. In any case, Fin was just too attractive for his own good, or anyone else's, for that matter, and they were foolish not to have realised.

It ought to have made Mary more content, being

told that it was nothing to do with her after all, but guilt weighed heavy on her heart, and she could never shake the notion that it was her meddling that had led to their present predicament.

Most of all, she blamed herself for the loss of Angelica. She could never work out how Fin had traced them to the tiny, farm cottage where they were hiding, but she decided in the end that they must have been followed, either by Fin himself, or by one of his brothers.

Many years had passed, but she was still tormented by her own stupidity, convinced that she had made everything much worse. It kept her awake into the small hours, pursuing her relentlessly, and condemning her to relive everything that had happened, over, and over again, never fading, but instead, becoming clearer with each passing year. She knew it was in the past and that nothing could be changed, that was an indisputable fact, yet it made no difference.

They'd felt safe at last, and the bruises on Iris's face had faded to a dirty yellow, when Fin burst in. She remembered how the plaster cracked into a spider-web of fine lines when the door slammed back against the wall, and the white flecks of paint falling, slowly, to the floor, like snowflakes. It was an irrelevancy, yet nevertheless, as crystal clear in her mind as if it were yesterday.

'You can't have her!' screamed Iris, when she saw him, and she seized his arm in a futile attempt to hold him back, but he threw her to the floor. Angelica was asleep on Kathleen's lap in the back porch, but she was stirring and looked about to cry, 'Quick, give her to me,' whispered Mary, and Kathleen thrust the baby into Mary's arms and she ran out of the house into the lane, and then across the fields, until she could no longer hear Fin's ranting, or Iris's anguished cries.

It was a beautiful afternoon in autumn, and an overwhelming feeling of peace descended on her. She was determined that Fin wouldn't take the baby, so she decided to hide her until he was gone; then she'd console Iris, and put witch-hazel on her bruises and, when it was safe, she would find Angelica and they'd move on. Mary put her down in a soft, grassy nest in the shade of the hedgerows, under the hawthorn and shiny rosehips, and powdery, autumn sloes. She looked at home there, wrapped in the little, pink shawl that Kathleen had knitted, with her name embroidered along the edge where it changed from plain to purl; and she didn't even murmur when Mary kissed her gently on the cheek and crept away.

Kathleen hid, covering her ears to shut out the sound of his voice, hardly daring to breathe, dreading his footfall on the stairs, and the strong arms that would seize her ankles and drag her out from under the bed. She heard him leave eventually and watched from the attic window as his van disappeared into the distance, and then she ran back downstairs. Mary was there too, hiding in the trees, until she was sure that he'd really gone and, when she was certain, she went in. She was afraid of what she might find, but Iris was still alive; Fin knew just how far he could go, he also knew that Iris wouldn't involve the law if she could avoid it. There was always the danger that Angelica might be taken away, or worse, that he might be given part custody of the child, and she wouldn't want to risk that.

'Where's Angelica...?' asked Iris as soon as she saw her; her face was swollen, and her left eye was almost shut. 'Where is she, Mary?' she repeated, 'please tell me he hasn't taken her...'

Mary tried to smile, 'She's safe, Iris, I've hidden her and when we're sure he won't be back I'll fetch her, and we'll leave. We can go across the fields; we'll find somewhere else to stay, somewhere safe.'

'She won't be walking anywhere,' said Kathleen, 'look at the state of her. It was as much as I could do to drag her to a chair. It's time to get the Garda; he'll kill her if he comes back. Stay with her Mary, I'll run down to the village and then we'll fetch Angelica.'

'No...' wailed Iris, 'I'll be fine; don't tell them, please. They'll take her away. Mary, go and get her, how could you leave her alone, she'll be afraid, and hungry. I want her back now!'

Mary hugged her gently, but Iris winced and pulled away.

'Leave her a little longer, Iris,' she murmured, 'just a little longer, try to be patient, she's safe and warm, she won't come to any harm; she's strong, and the fresh air will do her good.'

Mary was waiting outside when Kathleen returned. She'd begun to worry about Angelica, and was wondering whether she'd done the right thing by leaving her; equally, she didn't dare desert Iris, what if Fin came back? She felt racked by indecision; maybe she should have stayed with Angelica; what if Iris was right and she was hungry, or cold? She saw Kathleen coming along the road when she was still some distance away and took off immediately, back across the fields, retracing her steps along the hedgerows until she came to the hollow in the grass where she'd left Angelica, but the baby was gone! Mary couldn't believe her eyes, was it the right place? It looked the same, the grass was flattened, just very slightly, though not enough for anyone to notice, only someone who had negligently abandoned a baby, and then, with a heavy heart, she began to search for blood, or any sign that Angelica had been taken by a fox.

It was then that a terrible thought occurred to her, had Fin been watching? Had he looked out of the window, just long enough to see her fleeing across the field with the tiny bundle, and then come searching? Perhaps he'd parked somewhere nearby and walked back and carried her away; she might just as well have given her to him. How would she tell Iris that she had failed? That she had, stupidly, allowed Fin to take Angelica from them, unhindered by feeble, shrieking women? What could she possibly say that would ease the pain that Iris would feel when she found out that her baby had gone? It wasn't as if he really cared for her; he was too selfish to tend to the needs of such a young child. He only wanted to hurt Iris in any way that he could, and he wouldn't be content until he had destroyed her completely.

She walked back to the cottage slowly, rehearsing the words she would say to Iris, reassuring words, insisting that he wouldn't harm Angelica, that his mother had raised six children, and the police would get her back in no time, but she knew she'd be wasting her breath, because nothing would help when Iris found out that Angelica had gone. Worst of all she would blame Mary; she'd accuse her of stupidity, and jealousy, because she lacked a child of her own, and with no hope of having one either, because no man would ever look at her.

Kathleen was waiting on the front step, 'Where is she?' she asked, 'Where's Angelica?'
'She wasn't there! Oh, God, I think he's taken her... Fin... there's no other explanation... where else could she have gone?'
Kathleen buried her face in her hands and when she looked up her face was wet with tears, 'Oh Jesus, Mary

and Joseph, how will we tell Iris? Listen to her; it will be the death of her; more than she can bear. Quick, think of something. How could you have been so stupid?'

Mary suddenly felt angry, with herself, but also with Iris.

'Why must I always take the blame?' she snapped, 'And why do you always defend Iris? Anyway, it was you who gave her to me to hide, it's not my fault. I thought she would be safe; I love her too. I want her back.'

'Yes, Mary, I know you do, and we're both to blame.' Kathleen sighed and crossed herself, 'God help us... Well then, you'd better go up and tell her.'

CHAPTER 20

In the dark days, following Angelica's inexplicable, vanishing trick, Fin kept his distance, knowing that the Garda were watching him. They'd questioned him for some time about the injuries that Iris had suffered, though she'd refused to make a formal complaint against him in case he had stolen Angelica, and she didn't want him to take it out on the child. Neither she, nor Mary, nor Kathleen, could think of any other explanation for her disappearance. The whole area had been searched by young and old, pacing the fields with their sticks, poking into rabbit burrows, and fox holes, and frightening every living creature for miles around; and they'd appealed for information, but not a single witness had come forward.

Iris was a mess, veering between manic hysteria and anger, and worst of all, a kind of disengagement with the world and everyone in it. Hardly a day went by without hours of ragged weeping, when she'd refuse to get out of bed; then fits of rage would overtake her and she'd storm around the house, hurling plates, and slamming doors, and screeching at anyone within earshot. She wouldn't wash, or eat, but just cried constantly for her missing daughter.

It soon became clear to Mary that they would have to take flight once more, because as soon as the police called off their search for Angelica, Fin would be around to finish what he started. It was then that she told Hanna Jenkins about their dilemma.

She'd arrived early, before Hanna opened her bookshop, leaving Kathleen and Iris holed up in the house, too afraid to open the front door, or even the blinds, in case Fin was watching the house. The day before, Kathleen had spotted his brother, Declan, parked just across the road so she knew Fin wouldn't be too far away. Beside Declan, there were three more brothers, James, Don and Tommy, as well as a sister who had run off as soon as she was old enough, but Declan was closest to Fin, in age and temperament, and his reputation for violence was renowned.

Hanna Jenkins was a plump, little Welsh woman in her early sixties, and, in many ways, Mary was like a daughter to her, in place of the children she'd never had. She looked out of the window when she heard the bell and, when she saw it was Mary, she dragged a pink, plastic curler from her hair, and threw on her candlewick dressing-gown, and bustled to the door; then they sat in the small kitchen behind the shop and ate eggs and bacon, while Mary updated her on everything that had happened. Naturally, Hanna already knew that Angelica had disappeared. It had been in all the papers, and on the television, but she'd been unaware of Fin's violent rages, though, now Mary mentioned it, she'd wondered why Iris had looked in such a terrible state in the photographs, with her bent fingers and bruised eyes.

Mary was already starting to worry because she'd been gone for over an hour, but she needed to get away, if only for a short while. The constant wailing from Iris and her mother, was enough to drive anyone insane! Hanna was gazing out of the window deep in thought. In her mind's eye she pictured herself, sitting on a swing in a green garden; a tiny girl with dark eyes and a grubby face, surrounded by a completely different landscape, a grey and forbidding place, where the cool mist would descend in moments, hiding the hills and peaks, and muting the sound of the sheep.

'You must go to Wales,' she said at last, 'no one will find you there. My sister lives in a small village; her house is large, and she was widowed last year. She asked me to go back, but my life is here now, with my books. She will find you work I'm sure; the garden is too much for her, and no one knows more about plants and trees than you, Mary. She has no family, so you'll be company for her; we're a childless bunch these days, except for the likes of the Delaneys. Her name is Megan, Megan Rhys; I'll call her this afternoon, I'm sure she'll help you.'

Mary could hear Iris as soon as she turned the corner. Declan was still sitting in his car across the road; he was flicking the ash from his cigarette into the gutter, but he got out when he saw Mary approaching. 'What have you done with her? What have you done with Angelica, you old witch? Did you bury her? Haven't you told her yet,' he nodded towards the house, 'that crazy sister of yours? And tell her to stop the screeching, Mary, or they'll cart her away to the mad house, sure they will.' He moved closer until their noses were almost touching, and she recoiled at his reek of alcohol and stale cigarette smoke.

'You'll never be free of us; you do know that, don't you? The child is better off wherever she is, than with you old bitches.'

'Make up your mind, Declan, is it witch, or bitch?' She stared straight into his eyes, defying him to look away, determined to ignore the foul smoke on his breath.

'Whores... whores, and witches...' he whispered menacingly, and he spat on the pavement next to her.

Mary waited until he'd slammed the car door. She could see him sitting at the wheel and he glared back at her, scowling, and white with rage. He seemed to be having trouble getting the key into the ignition but he managed eventually and she watched as he drove away and then ran to the front door and let herself in, turning the key twice when she got inside, just to make sure it was locked. It was lucky that Kathleen hadn't put the chain across, or she wouldn't have been able to get in at all.

'Where have you been, Mary?' asked Kathleen, 'We've been afraid; they're always out there, Fin, and Declan; they take it in turns to terrorise us.'

She raised her voice to counter the wails, 'Go and pack, Ma, we're leaving. I've found us somewhere safe to stay where they can't torment us anymore.'

Iris was clinging to the banisters at the top of the stairs and she stopped wailing when she caught the words, 'pack and 'leaving'.

'Leaving…? But where are you taking us, Mary? And if no one will find us, how will I know if they've found Angelica?' and she started bawling all over again.

'Don't worry, I'll keep in touch with Hanna Jenkins,' replied Mary, in what she hoped was a soothing voice, 'I'm doing my best, Iris, so try to stop crying, please.'

'I wouldn't be crying at all if it weren't for you, Mary!' screamed Iris, and she marched upstairs and slammed the door.

Mary held back the tears, there was too much to do. Now wasn't the time to be going to pieces, even if everyone else was. She had to keep a clear head. Why had Declan called her a witch? That bothered her nearly as much as the threats of violence. It was lucky they weren't alive a few hundred years earlier or they might all have been burned for witchcraft. On the other hand, he had called them whores, and there was no truth in that, and there never would be!

CHAPTER 21
WALES
1993
Megan Rhys

It was good to hear from my sister, Hanna. We speak rarely these days, but I know she's always there, if I need her, and I'm here if she needs me. We lead a solitary life here in the Welsh Hills, it doesn't have to be, not anymore; communication is far easier than it once was. It's now a matter of choice, but it's still a good place to hide away and, according to Hanna, these women need sanctuary. My life has been lonely since Gar passed away, and I'd let time go by, accepting my isolation more, and more, with each passing day. It's good that Hanna is forcing me to engage in life again, making me confront it, instead of being swept along towards the inevitable end, with few diversions, aside from the chapel choir.

It was a beautiful day in May when they arrived, the roses were out in the garden, and the hedgerows were bursting with sweet-smelling grasses and wildflowers smothered the lanes and paths.

I went to the bus stop to meet them; they'd been travelling since dawn and they looked exhausted, making me feel ashamed that I hadn't thought to take the car down. My house is no more than a quarter of a mile from the bus stop, but it's up a steep slope and I wasn't sure if they'd make it, especially the thin girl who looked as if she might collapse if it weren't for the larger one holding her up. I guessed she was Mary, the woman who knew everything there was to know about plants, Hanna mentioned her to me when she telephoned.

So, the thin girl was Iris, the one whose baby had been stolen. I noticed that her hair needed a good wash, and she was so emaciated that her clothes were hanging from her bony, coat-hanger shoulders like rags, devoid of form or content. Her expression held such sadness, it showed in the empty gaze of her eyes. The older woman, Kathleen, was rake-thin too; she was pulling a large holdall on wheels. It rattled on the path, announcing their arrival to the whole village, not that anyone missed much anyway. It was the only luggage they had, apart from Mary's battered, tapestry bag and an old briefcase.

Iris and Kathleen didn't smile, they were silent, hostile even, and I guessed straightaway that they didn't want to be there. They each spoke to me just the once, to tell me who they were, but it was hard to miss the resentment whenever Iris looked at Mary; later I discovered why. I gave them soup, and a cob loaf, and told them where they were to sleep, and that was that. I left them to it and went to sit in the study with Dylan, my shaggy, old mongrel. He looked at me sideways, as if to say, 'what have you done now, you silly old woman?' It was almost as if he'd taken over the task of reproaching me for my foolishness, but it was easier to take from a dog than a man. Hanna told me that the reason Iris needed to leave Dublin was because a man was threatening her. Gar had never threatened me, not physically, at least, but there were many times when I'd have happily throttled him. Still, it was good to have other people in the house, lately I'd been nervous about intruders; although it was unlikely that anyone would venture all the way out here to intrude on me.

Mary and Kathleen looked brighter after a night's rest, but my sleep was disturbed by Iris, who wailed incessantly until three when she suddenly fell silent. I got up at one point and stood in the doorway to her bedroom, afraid that something might have happened to stop her wailing, but she was sleeping quietly, so quietly that I held my breath and listened, to ascertain whether or not she was still alive. Why Mary and Kathleen were able to sleep through it, I'll never understand; I can only assume they'd grown used to it.
Iris stayed in her room for most of the following day. Kathleen sat with her for a lot of the time, and I sent up snacks that came back untouched. Iris didn't speak to

me if she could avoid it and acted as if she were merely tolerating me to appease her sister.

Mary told me what had happened; how Fin had threatened to kill Iris, and that he'd accused them of hiding Angelica. I couldn't help worrying that their sudden disappearance would only reinforce that view, and I hoped he wouldn't find out that Hanna had been instrumental in helping them to escape.

Mary insisted they had no idea where the baby had gone; she seemed to think Fin had taken her, but it was obvious to me that she blamed herself for everything.

I showed her around Morgans Croft; Gar's beautiful house that had been in his family for generations. Then we went out into the garden; my acre of lawn, and flowerbeds, and a copse of small trees and shrubs. The Wisteria was in bloom, and bees hummed around the bluebells and the early honeysuckle. I could see she was impressed, and she looked at home in the garden, it accommodated her shape, curved and organic, like a sculpture by Henry Moore. It suited her personality too, she seemed to be grounded, down-to-earth; how odd that both expressions refer to the land; and she seemed to be aware of the magic in all growing things, a rare quality. I explained to her that her task would be the upkeep of the garden, and if she could grow some vegetables it would be a bonus. Kathleen, and in time, Iris, could help to clean and run the house, and keep me company. In return, I would give them a somewhere to live and a small salary. I felt happy, I hoped it would work, and maybe, one day, Iris would find her baby again.

CHAPTER 22
WALES

The flower beds were full of weeds. Bindweed wound about the clematis, and choked the roses, and ground-elder forced its way up through the paths, but Mary set to work, determined to tame it. She was hoping to repay Megan in some small way for her kindness, and, maybe, she would be able to tell Hanna that everything was working out for the best. She planted potatoes, and sowed rows of carrots in the vegetable patch, and lettuce and tomatoes in the greenhouse, and amongst the tomatoes, she planted some of her special seeds. They would look very similar to tomatoes once they had grown, but, in any case, who would suspect otherwise. She chose a sunny, sheltered spot for the rest of her herbs, mint and marigold, and blue borage, it always looked so pretty, floating in a glass of gin. She still referred to her book of spells from time to time, but only for medicinal purposes as she no longer had any desire to concoct potions that might influence the lives of others.

Megan was enthusiastic about her gardening skills and often wandered out into the garden to watch, and to bring her cups of tea, or cold lemonade. She was a tiny woman, less than five feet tall, and she wore a raffia hat a size too large for her, and daisy-sprigged, cotton dresses that brushed the grass as she walked. It was a warm day in May when Megan appeared at the door of the greenhouse, where Mary was pinching back the tomato seedlings.

'You're doing a great job with the garden, Mary,' she paused and blushed slightly, 'you've made it look beautiful. You've put in so much time; Gar would be so pleased…' she paused again, and Mary's heart sank, because she'd guessed what Megan was about to say.

'It's Iris, isn't it? I'm so sorry Megan; I'm hoping she'll improve as time goes by. I understand completely if you want us to leave.'

'No, I'm sorry, Mary; it's just that her crying keeps me awake at night, she never seems to get any better. It's awful of me to complain, I do feel sorry for her… And your mother is so depressed, and occupied with Iris, that nothing gets done…'

'We'll go, Megan, it's been good of you to have us for so long. Thank you for tolerating the disruption we've caused.'

'But I need you to do the garden,' she said, adding, 'I don't want you to go, Mary!'

'They can't manage on their own;' replied Mary, 'they'd likely be dead within a week!'

'Let me finish what I have to say,' said Megan. 'I have a

suggestion. I own a small house just outside the village. It's very run-down, and in need of renovation, but you could do it up. You'd still be able to come and do my garden, and you can stay from time to time, if you need to get away, and maybe, one day, Kathleen will feel up to helping around the house; perhaps Iris will too, she can't go on like this.'

Mary was unable to speak, for a moment she just stared, open-mouthed, at the small, grey-haired figure in the giant, straw hat, and then she threw her arms around her and kissed her on the top of her head.

'Stop, you're squashing me,' laughed Megan, 'let me go!'

Mary was overcome with gratitude; she wiped away the tears that were streaming down her cheeks. 'I don't know how to thank you,' she murmured.

'That's settled then,' said Megan, 'we'll take your things down there now. We'll need sheets and blankets, and mops, and buckets… you and I will go first to make sure it's fit for habitation. Leave Iris and Kathleen here, we'll fetch them later.'

The cottage was small, just two bedrooms, and a tiny attic accessed by a narrow, wooden ladder. Iris would have to sleep up there, the rungs would never take Mary's weight, and Kathleen might fall down it and break her neck. Anyway, Iris would at least be out of the way, thought Mary, even if her cries still reached them. The roof was covered in creepers and Mary could hear wasps buzzing so there was probably a nest among the tiles, but she knew that mint, wormwood, and thyme would see them off. Inside there was an ancient sofa, a table with four chairs, and a rudimentary kitchen. Layers of dust had turned the curtains a dirty grey; it clung to every surface and coated the threadbare rugs, but Mary was sure they would be happy there.

'My Grandmother's house;' explained Megan apologetically, 'after she died, a couple rented for a while, but that was some time back. I'll need to get the electricity reconnected so you'll be in the dark for a few days, but I've got some lamps and some candles you can have, and the evenings are getting lighter. We'll give it a good spring-clean then we'll go and fetch Iris and Kathleen.'

They set to work, washing the floors, and polishing the furniture, then they threw the rugs over the washing line and beat them with a broom, until the grass underneath was shrouded in dust. The grimy curtains were dunked in a tub to soak, but after an hour or two they were no cleaner and Megan decided to discard them. 'I've lots of curtains,' she said, 'you can have some of mine.'

CHAPTER 23

Almost a year had passed since Angelica's strange disappearance. Mary wrote to Hanna a couple of times, to thank her for her help, and to enquire if there had been any news, but Hanna said there was none, and the search was called off some time back. There was no local gossip of any note, and no 'remains' had been found, so she hoped that Angelica was somewhere alive and well. She thought long and hard before writing the word 'remains', but decided it was still a better option than 'body', or any of the other alternatives.

Megan's little cottage was now cosy and quite presentable. Mary worked tirelessly, inside, and out, whitewashing the walls, chasing away the spiders and cleaning the windows. She'd mowed the lawn, and filled the borders with geraniums and fuchsias, though they were fading fast and wouldn't survive the frost when it came. More importantly, she'd managed to persuade Kathleen to start sewing again, and she'd altered the curtains and made brightly coloured bedspreads and covers for the ancient sofa.

In July, Mary baked a simple sponge cake to mark Angelica's birthday. She iced it and put a single candle on the top, but then decided it looked lonely and took it off before anyone noticed. Kathleen and Iris refused to eat the cake, even though Mary insisted that she was quite sure that Angelica was somewhere and, maybe, celebrating her birthday. She might be walking by now, thought Mary, but she didn't dare elaborate for fear of making Iris feel worse than she already did. It was so tiring, attempting to keep everyone happy, and perhaps she was being unrealistic for even trying.

Sadly, Iris was still in a state of despair. She ate just enough to keep herself alive, even though she told them frequently that she would prefer to be dead, and the only reason to keep going at all was to find Angelica, and if, in the meantime, she had the opportunity to kill Fin, well, that would be another good reason for staying alive. However, gradually, at a rate that was barely noticeable, her mood seemed to be lifting. Every morning she would climb high into the hills, often disappearing for several hours, and when she returned her face was glowing, as if the solitude had helped her to leave some of her despair behind.

Mary spent as much time as she could tending Megan's garden at Morgans Croft, and the two women had become firm friends. She was very similar to her sister Hanna, so for Mary, at least, the place was beginning to feel like home, and she would happily have moved in, as the quiet and isolation suited her, but she still couldn't contemplate leaving Iris and

Kathleen to their own devices.

'It might be the best thing you could do,' insisted Megan, 'they need to stand on their own feet. What about you? Are you going to go on supporting them until you drop dead from exhaustion?'

Yes, I probably will, thought Mary, but she kept that to herself.

It was less than a week later when they heard frantic knocking at the door.

'Mother of God, who's there at this hour of the night?' cried Kathleen.

'Angelica,' murmured Iris, 'what if they've found her?'

Mary raised her eyebrows, 'Well, I doubt she'd be hammering on the door, Iris, but there's only one way to find out!' and she got to her feet and went to open it.

Megan was on the doorstep. She was wearing an old, candlewick dressing gown and for one brief moment Mary thought it was Hanna. It was evident that she'd run down the hill because she was shivering and out of breath, and her legs were splattered with mud. Mary helped her to the sofa. 'Make some tea, Kathleen,' she cried, 'hot and sweet; and Iris, put some logs on the fire, and get some blankets; she's cold. What's happened, Megan? Has someone frightened you?'

Megan tried to answer but the words wouldn't come, she just sat perfectly still and gazed at the television screen with unseeing eyes.

'Don't worry, tell me when you can,' whispered Mary, and she went into the kitchen to see if the kettle had boiled. She was making an effort to remain calm but fearing the words she might hear when Megan was able to explain, for she'd already guessed that something had happened to Hanna. Why else would she have run down the dark, muddy lane at this hour, unless she'd been assaulted by an intruder, though that seemed unlikely?

She went back into the room and turned off the television, unsure of why she hadn't thought to do it before, and then she sat down next to Megan and waited for her to speak.

'Hanna's dead, Mary. I'll never see her again,' she murmured, in a barely audible whisper, and Iris began to cry.

Kathleen got up to put another log on the fire and it spluttered into life, filling the room with the smell of scorched wool as tiny, glowing embers landed on the hearthrug and flared briefly before turning to charcoal. No one seemed to notice.

Mary wrapped another blanket around Megan's shoulders, but she shook it off.

'She died in a fire,' she murmured after a long pause, 'they said her books were like kindling, old and dry, she was in the shop, between the shelves. She must have been trying to stem the flames, why else would she stay?'

Then Mary started to cry and, no matter how hard she tried, she couldn't stop, and soon Megan was attempting to comfort her, patting her on the back and urging her to drink the cold, oversweet tea. Mary still couldn't stop crying, it was as if all the events of the past had suddenly descended upon her in that one moment, like a dam that had, quite unexpectedly, burst. She'd always managed to keep the tears at bay for the sake of those around her, those who were weaker; who couldn't cope with anything that life threw at them, and Iris and Kathleen couldn't have been more surprised if she'd dropped dead in front of them. It spurred Iris into action, and she dashed off into the kitchen to make fresh tea, while Kathleen scurried up the stairs to find more blankets.

Megan slept in Kathleen's bed, while Kathleen slept on the sofa in front of the fire. She lay awake, long after everyone else had given in to exhaustion and fallen asleep, listening to the sounds of the mice in the walls, and the barn owls swooping around the house like winged ghosts. Her thoughts kept her awake; they darted from one disaster to the next, the wretched series of events that had brought her to where she was now. Could her life have been different, or easier, she wondered. Maybe she'd taken a wrong turn somewhere along the way, or was it all pre-arranged, by some higher authority, this path she was destined to follow? She slept at last, but her dreams were full of ghosts. Her mother was there, and her father. They faded gradually into the mists of sleep, but then Liam arrived, looking emaciated and weary, and holding the stick that he'd always relied upon after his fall from the roof; then there was Hanna, the dead woman, whom she'd never met when she was alive, before the fire took her. After that, she searched in vain for Angelica, but she wasn't there. She slept more soundly then; somehow it was comforting to know that Angelica wasn't in the realm of the dead.

They awoke to a calm, windless day, the rain had stopped and the last of the leaves had fallen, leaving the branches of the trees stark against the sky. Only the large beech, at the end of the garden, clung onto its leaves, but they were brown and withered. The inhabitants of the cottage were enmeshed in a pall of lethargy, drifting from chair to kitchen, and back again, lost in their own thoughts. Mary felt as if a heavy burden had been lifted from her shoulders. Her outburst had been cathartic, but nagging doubts remained because she was convinced that Fin had been somehow responsible for Hanna's death. She didn't voice her suspicions, far better that everyone believed the fire to have been an unfortunate accident. Unwittingly, she was already attempting to alleviate everyone's pain by refusing to confide in those around her. Would it do any good if she made them feel worse than they already did? No, she would keep it to herself; she would manage, and later she could take Megan home and she would sneak off to the greenhouse. Her plants were doing well, though she might need a sunlamp soon. Cannabis sativa needed light; she smiled to herself then glanced around to see if anyone had noticed, now wasn't the time for brevity.

CHAPTER 24
Mary

Mary's fascination with plants began when she was quite small. If asked, Iris would tell you how she could still picture Mary, mashing rose petals into a jam-jar of water that gradually turned into a dirty, yellow liquid. They always expected it to smell of roses but, in fact, it carried little scent at all, other than a faint whiff of fresh leaves, squashed into mush. Nevertheless, they sprinkled it with abandon, dabbing it behind their ears, and inside their wrists, just as they'd seen their mother, Kathleen, dabbing her scented cologne. And they made lavender bags, sewn together with darning needles and thread, with giant stitches that allowed the tiny, lavender seeds to escape into their beds when they put them under their pillows.

That was when their father was alive. Liam Malone was considerably older than Kathleen and in ill health for the last twenty years of his life. He'd part-owned a roofing business but had been forced to sell his share after an accident when he'd fallen from the top of a two-storey house. It was lucky it wasn't three-storey, or he wouldn't have survived; as it was, his life was never the same. He was awarded compensation from the insurance, although, some said, he was drunk when he fell, and though Liam denied it and always insisted he'd been pushed, it was never proven either way. Luckily, when he eventually died, Kathleen was left with enough in the bank to see her comfortably to the end of her life.

Things hadn't been easy until her marriage, but her mother, father and their eight children, had always managed to scratch by; even so, her mother was delighted when Liam told them that he was in love with Kathleen and wanted to marry her. She was beautiful, and the image of her mother, and her grandmother, with large grey eyes and lustrous hair. They'd wanted eight children to carry on the family tradition, coincidentally, Liam had also come from a large family of eight, though at least three of them had died from old age by the time Mary was born. By then, Kathleen had suffered several miscarriages, and two still births, and was ready to give up, so when Iris followed five years after Mary, she considered her a bonus.

The two girls loved one another but couldn't have been more different, in looks and in temperament. Mary resembled her father, who was heavily built, and strong, until his accident. There was something profoundly reassuring about them both; they were stolid, and reliable, at least on the surface. Iris, on the other hand, was like a sprite; mercurial, and spirited, and slender as a reed; or an Iris. She skipped school to run across the fields and wade in the streams, forever looking for some new way to worry Kathleen; unlike studious Mary, who was always anxious to please and would plod around, trying to organise anyone who would listen. When she wasn't at school, she would haunt the local bookshop, until old Miss Jenkins would enquire if she ever intended to buy anything, telling her 'this isn't a library, you know!' and, 'You're supposed to buy the books! Who will want them when your sticky fingerprints are all over the pages?', as if Mary would ever contemplate having dirty fingers.

However, as Mary got older, she and Miss Jenkins became firm friends, which was to prove fortunate later. It was during one of her rummages among the shelves that ten-year-old Mary discovered 'the book', which not only offered remedies for various ailments, but also provided a chapter on spells that could be made at home in a saucepan, rather than a cauldron, and guaranteed success, provided the correct words, or incantations, were recited. One single leaf of Rue would see off a headache, and a bagful, hanging above the door, could ward off 'the evil eye'; while Calendula, or common marigold, was suited to all ailments, including athlete's foot, as well as a salve for sunburn. It could also strip a witch of her powers, and one never knew when that might be useful. She was very careful not to tell anyone about her new-found interest as a great deal of suspicion surrounded anyone who had strayed from the Holy Roman Church, regardless of the fact that it too relied on fear and superstition for its very survival.

Her knowledge of Cannabis Sativa and its uses, and rather dubious benefits, came much later.

CHAPTER 25

Mary was certain it was Fin who'd started the fire, or, maybe, his brother, Declan, with his habit of dropping smouldering cigarettes anywhere he pleased; though she was sure it wasn't an accident. They would have visited Hanna with the sole intention of forcing her to tell them where Iris had gone. Declan knew that Mary had visited Hanna shortly before they disappeared, and they were well aware that Hanna and she had been good friends for many years, and would want to keep in touch; and even if she'd refused to tell them, there would have been letters from Megan, and probably Mary too, lying around for anyone to see. If Fin came, it would be her fault; yet again. She wondered if they should leave, but where would they go? No, far better to cling to the faint hope that it was an accident, down to faulty wiring and old books, a fire just waiting to happen, and nothing sinister at all.

She didn't have long to wait. It was only three weeks later when she looked out of her bedroom window and saw Fin in the lane. He was alone, as far as she could tell, and standing stock still, as if waiting for someone to notice, and come out to greet him. Mary sat down heavily on her bed and it juddered under her

weight. She wondered briefly if she should call the police, but what good would that do? He wasn't committing any offence, and there was no evidence to suggest otherwise since Iris had always refused to bring charges against him. Mary tried to stand, but her legs had turned to jelly, so she craned her neck to see out, but it was impossible. Eventually the frantic beating of her heart slowed, and she managed to get to her feet and, holding onto the sill for support, peeped around the curtains, but Fin wasn't there.
'Iris...' she gasped, 'I must warn her...' and she ran down the stairs in a state of panic, almost falling in her haste.

Fin was blocking the kitchen doorway, and Iris was trying to open the door to the garden. She was making small, yelping noises, like a frightened animal, and clawing at a handle that obstinately refused to turn.
'Give up, Iris,' he spoke quietly, but his voice was full of menace, 'you'll not get away, not this time, not until you've told me where my daughter is, and I don't want your lies...' He swung round when he heard Mary approaching, 'Well, it's our Mary,' he laughed, 'and looking as lovely as ever.'
Mary stared at him defiantly, 'She doesn't know where her daughter is, so just go away and leave us in peace!'
'Well, Mary, d' you think I've come all the way from Ireland only to leave empty handed? Where have you hidden her? I'm a reasonable man, but I like to get my

own way, and you know what happens when I don't.'

'Will you burn us to death like poor old Hanna Jenkins? That was you, wasn't it Fin? You might as well admit it.'

He laughed again, 'It was an accident, Mary. I didn't mean for your friend to die, she had only to co-operate; it wasn't too much to ask, now was it?'

'You're a murderer, Finbar Delaney, sure you are. I'm fetching the police; I should have done it the minute I saw you.' She backed away, but he grabbed her wrist and threw her into the kitchen.

'I saw you, Mary,' he sneered, 'twitching the curtains like the old woman that you are. Why don't you mind your own business, leave us to sort out our quarrels, we don't want, or need, your interference! She's coming back to Dublin, with me…'

He seemed to stagger towards them then, his fists raised, and a startled expression on his face. Mary scrabbled to her feet ready to protect Iris as best she could; instead, there was a crash that seemed to shake the house. Kathleen stood in the doorway holding a bloodied claw-hammer, and Fin was lying sprawled across the floor.

CHAPTER 26

Fin was a big man, but tall and muscular rather than fat, and he seemed to take up most of the kitchen floor. Blood poured from the hole in the back of his head where the hammer had cracked his skull almost in two; who would ever have dreamt that Kathleen could wield a hammer with such force? Now, she stood in silence in the doorway, her right arm hanging limply by her side, still clutching the hammer as if ready to hit him again, should he have the audacity to recover and attempt to stand. It wasn't likely, the sound of splintering bone had filled the tiny kitchen, followed immediately by the crash as Fin slammed onto the floor, banging his head on the stove on his way down. No one screamed, they just stood in silence for what seemed an age. Eventually, Mary crept forward to look at the gaping wound in Fin's head,
'You've killed him…' she whispered… 'Oh, God, what have you done?'
Kathleen raised the hammer again, 'He might not be dead; what if he's pretending? Shall I hit him again?'
Mary inched around the body carefully to avoid the blood. 'Give me the hammer, Ma. He's definitely dead.'
Kathleen stared at her, as if trying to make up her

mind; was he dead, or not? Then, placated, she dropped the hammer onto the floor where it landed with a metallic thud.

'We should call the doctor, Mary. You never know for sure...' and she buried her face in her hands and began to moan softly, 'they'll hang me if they find out I did it...'

'Hush,' murmured Mary, 'they don't hang anyone, not anymore. There's nothing we can do; he's gone, and we'll have to deal with it. Don't worry, I'll sort it out, I always do, don't I? Anyway, it was self-defence; he would have killed Iris if he'd had the chance!'

'So, how is creeping up behind a man, and striking him with a hammer, self-defence?' enquired Iris. 'They'll say we lured him here, so that she could kill him! Anyway, she's right; maybe he's not quite dead.' She prodded him hard in the chest with her foot to see if he moved, 'No, he's dead, I reckon, but we might as well bury him, just to be on the safe side.'

They watched, shocked into silence, as the pool of blood grew and started to run across the uneven floor.

'I'm going to be sick...' yelled Iris, and she ran over to the sink and threw up.

'Mother of God,' cried Kathleen, 'she's run straight through it, it's all over her shoes. What if she'd slipped?'

'Pull yourselves together,' said Mary, 'help me get him outside. Open the door, we'll pull him.'

Kathleen edged around the kitchen to open the door, all the while staring transfixed at the blood that was already beginning to congeal.

Iris's eyes sparkled, 'Look how easily he slides. You've done it, Ma… you've set us free. We can go home.'

'Hush, Iris,' whispered Mary, 'no one must hear!' She wondered briefly if they'd both gone mad. Iris seemed to be relishing the way Fin's body slid across the bloody kitchen floor and bumped down the stone steps onto the damp grass; and here she was, trying to sort out the mess they'd created, yet again!

They were out of breath by the time they'd dragged Fin to the small patch of trees where their garden met the wood. Mary stood up and stretched, her body wasn't suited to dragging heavy weights around, 'Iris, make y' self useful, cover him with leaves! We'll come out and bury him later.'

They walked back up the garden and into the kitchen. The blood had turned a rusty red, though brighter in the middle where Fin's head met the floor, and the tiles were splattered and sticky underfoot, but they set to work with hot water and bleach and soon all traces of recent murder had been eradicated.

Then they went back to dig the hole where Finbar Delaney would spend the next twenty-four years.

CHAPTER 27
DUBLIN
1995
Mary

It was odd how everything seemed to improve after Fin's demise. It had drawn a line between their old life, and the new. Naturally, they still mourned the loss of Angelica, but at least they were now certain that Fin hadn't taken her. They were even more certain that Finbar Delaney was dead and buried, so made up their minds never to mention him again. Their only concern was that Declan might one day turn up on their doorstep. Fin and Declan had always been close; he'd be missing his brother and they knew that he wouldn't give up easily.

Mary was spending more time up at the 'big house', as they'd taken to calling it. Since the fire that did for the bookshop and Hanna with it, Megan had become depressed, she was anxious whenever the house so much as creaked, especially during the night, and she begged Mary to move in as her companion, but how could she even think of leaving Iris and Kathleen?

They'd go to pieces if she didn't manage them. She'd spent a whole week at Morgans Croft after the traumatic night when Megan arrived on their doorstep, cold and mud splattered. She hadn't intended to be away for so long, but she feared for Megan's safety if someone didn't care for her. She hadn't seen her sister for many years, but, if anything, that made the shock of her death even greater.

Mary spent the entire week running frantically between Megan and the cottage, where Iris and Kathleen were subsisting on a diet of tinned fruit and toast. The upside of this was that she was getting fitter and thinner by the day, especially as she was trying to fork over the newly weeded flowerbeds whenever she found a spare moment. Iris sulked over her neglect, and Kathleen scolded her for leaving them. 'So is Megan more important than us now?' she'd ask, and Mary would explain patiently, over and over, about the debt they owed Megan, and Hanna, for helping when they had nowhere else to go.

It wasn't their fault, she reasoned. They were just damaged by circumstances. There was always an explanation for the way people behaved.

Christmas came and Megan asked Mary to go with her to chapel to join in the carols, suggesting that, one day, she should join the choir. Kathleen was horrified when she told her. 'It's not a proper church, or a proper religion, Mary! Why ever do you go there? And why do you have to spend so much time running after that woman?'

Mary was finally beginning to lose patience. Iris spent far too long sitting around brooding, and weren't Iris and Kathleen supposed to be helping Megan with the cleaning in the big house? That was the agreement, and it was time they were made to accept their responsibilities; they owed Megan that, and Mary too.

It was three months later when Megan asked Mary if she would accompany her to Dublin. Both she and Mary were named in Hanna's will, a copy of which was in the hands of Mr. Percy, her solicitor. Luckily the bookshop had been adequately insured against fire so the legacy was substantial, and they were the sole benefactors. Megan couldn't possibly make the journey on her own, and since Mary stood to gain it was obvious that she should go with her.

Mary could think of several reasons for not returning to Dublin. For a start, how could she leave Iris and Kathleen? They hadn't coped well the last time she left them, if she was in Dublin, she wouldn't even be able to pop back and forth to help and reassure, but Megan insisted. 'We owe it to Hanna,' she said, 'we didn't even get to the funeral, and she's remembered you in her will. I can't go without you, Mary. I know why you don't want to go, but we'll avoid all those familiar places where you could bump into Fin, or his family and that will be up to you. I'm not used to cities, and I don't know Dublin at all.'

Well, we won't be running into Fin, thought Mary, and she smiled, safe in the knowledge that they would always know where Fin was.

It was settled and, just over a year after Mary left Dublin, she was back again. Nothing had changed, and why would it, just because she had?

The hotel was in the centre near the Green; she'd often walked past it, but never for a moment dreamed that she would, one day, be staying there. Her room was next to Megan's, a 'charming room with an ensuite bath and shower'; that was the way it was described in the brochure, but Mary thought it clinical, and too far off the ground; she'd never been fond of heights. Still it would be grand to have someone else cooking the meals, and making the bed for a few days, and she was glad to be back in Ireland. It hadn't been easy to just pack up and leave at a moment's notice. Her life should have been here, with the people she loved, they smiled at her when they passed in the street, and she smiled back. Perhaps she was being over sentimental; they didn't all smile, not anymore. Still, she liked the noise of the traffic and the bustling crowds, and the quaint architecture.

She telephoned Kathleen every morning before breakfast and Kathleen responded with a litany of woes. 'Mary, there's a dead rat on the path!' or 'Mary we've no bread, and the baker has shut early!' or, 'Iris went out yesterday and it was nearly dark when she came home. I was beside myself with worry, sure I was! I thought she'd had an accident! Won't you come home, Mary?'

There was a chill March wind blowing in from the bay when Mary set off. She was alone, as Megan wanted to rest, and she walked slowly, relishing the breeze and the sun on her face, and breathing in the fresh scent of the daffodils in St Stephen's Green. She was home and suddenly she wanted to stay. This was where she belonged, the place where she'd arrived in the world, and where she'd grown up, and if not for Iris, she would still be here. Kathleen's house, and Mary's home for nearly a quarter of a century, was empty and neglected; would anyone have noticed, apart from Fin and Declan? Of course, they would, their neighbours must have wondered where they'd gone. They'd have gossiped amongst themselves, each putting forward their own theories as to why a middle-aged woman and her two daughters would, to all intents and purposes, have disappeared off the face of the earth. And what about Fin and Declan, had they pursued them, pestering them for answers, and making accusations of collusion? She decided straightaway, to go and see; after all, no one would be watching for her, not after all this time, and she turned and walked briskly in the direction of home.

There it was; a pretty Georgian terrace, with a short flight of steps up to a burgundy-coloured front door and a patch of grass where she'd played for hours as a child, threading daisies, or reading, always reading; and waiting for Iris to return from whatever mischief she'd managed to find. She watched from across the road, wondering if the key would still be under the flower pot, there would be post for sure, it would be piled up on the door mat, all the ridiculous supermarket offers, and free newspapers, and probably some unpaid bills too. She made up her mind, she would take a look.

She crossed the road, glancing around to make sure no one was watching. The gate squeaked when she opened it and a curtain twitched in the window of the house next door, but she ran up the steps anyway and lifted the stone pot that sat next to the boot-scraper. The key was still there so she inserted it in the lock and went in, quickly closing the door behind her. Heaps of paper lifted in the draught from the door; it almost filled the hallway, ankle deep. Mary went straight to the kitchen for a rubbish sack, thinking how lucky it was that, with all that kindling, the house hadn't gone the same way as Hanna's. A quick glance confirmed that most of it was only fit for the bin; including several notes from Fin, each more threatening than the last, and one, slightly nearer the top of the pile, full of apologies and pleading for Iris to contact him. Apart from the dust, the house looked unchanged; it was interesting that no one had taken the trouble to come in and check that they weren't dead in their beds. Someone must have been removing the free papers from the letter box, unless they'd finally realised the house was empty. It took some time to gather it all into piles so that it fitted into the black plastic sack, and she was exhausted by the time she'd finished.

Now she was here and seated on the sofa staring out at the overgrown garden, Mary had changed her mind; it was nice to be back, but it didn't feel the same. She thought of Megan and Morgans Croft, and the peaceful Welsh countryside and, to her absolute amazement, she realised that she missed it. She had moved on, it was time to sell and it would make a considerable amount of money. In the past few days, she'd learned that Hanna had left her fifty percent of her worldly goods, and a hundred or so books. Fortunately, the books hadn't survived the blaze, because taking them to Wales would have been almost impossible, and she would never have been able to part with them. It seemed as if everyone was intent on throwing money her way, and yet she didn't feel that she needed it. Megan had already indicated that she would 'remember her' when she died; as it was, she paid her well for her efforts in the garden, and they had the cottage to live in, and Kathleen wasn't poor. It made Mary smile; it was good never to have to worry where the next meal was coming from. There was also the possibility of creating a little business of her own from her labours in the greenhouse. She could always find a market for herbs, and organic vegetables, and for her illegal 'produce' too, though she'd never sell that, well, not too blatantly, only to those she could rely on to be discrete. The last thing they wanted was the law poking around in their affairs, not with Fin rotting in the copse at the end of the garden.

She stood up and left, placing the key back under the pot, and glancing around warily before she went down the steps.

'Can I help y' with that, Mary?' enquired a voice. Mary looked up, the neighbour five doors along was looking down at her from his front door. I put your rubbish out just after you left, but the bin has been empty for some time now. Here, let me take that off you, if you leave it out it'll be all over the street in no time!

She'd been caught in the act, breaking, and entering, but it was her own property; so why did she feel guilty? 'Dan, it's good to see you,' she smiled. He was always attractive, even as a lad, and one of Iris's many admirers who'd often follow her home from school. She'd been more than happy to let him carry her bags.

'Where have you been, Mary? We've missed you, and how is Iris?'

Mary handed him the plastic sack, 'It doesn't weigh much, it's only paper, but I'd be grateful if you could dispose of it...' she paused, reluctant to give away anything that might be used against them. 'We had a spot of bother,' she said quietly, 'after Angelica was lost... Iris's husband blamed us, and we had to move away.'

'Yes, Fin Delaney,' his eyes narrowed, 'he was here, many times, and that brother of his, Declan; my wife found them intimidating, and she wasn't the only one. We told the Garda in the end; then it stopped. Karine saw him once in the town, a while ago that was, nothing since, though his brother was back snooping around. None of them can be trusted. I feel for Iris, losing the babby and not knowing where she'd gone. Why did she do it, Mary? Why did she take up with Fin? She could have had anyone!'

'Yes, Dan, I know, anyone, but she settled for Fin and look where it's led us. I'm sorry they made your life difficult, and Karine's, really, I am. I'd better go, you never can tell, they might be back.' She refused to be drawn into saying more than was necessary. Even if Fin couldn't return, Declan might.

'Bye, Mary, be sure to tell Iris I was asking after her, and Kathleen. Oh, and will y' tell her I saw Ronan a while back, and he was asking what became of her. I'll keep an eye out for the house until you return.'

Mary tried not to show her displeasure; how many more times would she have to hear how wonderful Iris was? She was never without admirers, following her home, and hanging around outside the house hoping she might appear at the window, and she only had to smile sweetly for them to consider the wait worthwhile. Ronan and Iris had been friends since they were tiny children, but even when they were older, she seemed content to remain just his friend, though he obviously worshipped her.

She forced a smile, 'Thanks, Dan!' She waved goodbye and set off up the road while he stood on the step and watched until she turned the corner.

'I won't be back,' she murmured to herself, 'and neither will Iris!' No, Iris could just kick her heels in the middle of nowhere and be grateful that it was Fin and not her, that was lying in a shallow grave.

They sailed out of the bay on a sea that was as smooth as polished, grey marble; it lapped gently against the sides of the ship with a soft slapping sound, and the still air magnified the sound of the engines. A light rain began to fall as they approached Holyhead, but it wasn't until they reached Nefyn that it started to snow in a flutter of light feathery flakes, wetting their cheeks, and powdering the trees and the fields in a glaze of crystalline whiteness. The sky was sepia-yellow, and overcast, when they reached the village where the driver dropped Mary first, having been assured by Megan that she would be fine, and that she'd welcome having the place to herself after the chaos of Dublin.

He gazed heavenwards, 'There's more to come, yes, plenty more up there. We could be snowed in by tomorrow.'

The cottage was in darkness. Mary opened the door and stepped over the threshold; the room felt colder than outside in the lane because the glass in the windows was thin, and the curtains were open, and the fire had been allowed to go out. 'Iris...' she called, 'Mother, where are you?' Kathleen crept from the shadows of the kitchen. 'I seen him, Mary! Fin, he's out there, in the garden.'

'Ma, whoever is out there it can't be Fin; he went away if you recall? To a better place; or perhaps a worse one...' she added, under her breath.'

'Say what you like, Mary, I'd know him anywhere. He's come back and he's taken Iris with him.'

Mary felt a shiver run down her spine. 'Where is Iris, Ma?' she asked.

Kathleen gazed out of the window into the darkness, 'She's been gone all day, out there, up into the hills, like she always does, but she's usually home by now, and it's snowing. You shouldn't have left us Mary; you'll have to go and find her.'

'Why do I have to find her? I'm tired, I've been travelling all day; and how do I know where she's gone?'

'She's your sister Mary, you've only the one. She could

die out there in the hills.'

'Let me make up the fire, Ma, and then we'll talk about it. And turn on the lights, or she won't fathom where she is.'

Another hour passed and Kathleen became more agitated with every minute, murmuring prayers, and fingering the beads on her Rosary.

'She's here! Thanks be to God!' she cried at last when Iris came running up the path and flung open the door. Her eyes were shining, and she was laughing, 'I've had such a day, we've had to rescue the new lambs, they were trapped in the snow almost up to their necks, the poor little things... Oh, Mary, you're back!'

Mary breathed a sigh of relief, Iris was home, so she excused herself and went to her bedroom where she opened the window a tiny crack to let in the night air, and soon the room was filled with the sweet scent of a special type of weed, lovingly tended in Megan Rhys' outhouse because the greenhouse had become too cold for its particular needs.

Anyone looking up would have seen the silhouette of an obese young woman, leaning against the sill, obscured by a stream of fragrant smoke that wafted through the open window into the lane, where it seemed to float like a grey cloud before vanishing entirely in the cold air.

CHAPTER 28

DUBLIN

2019

Angelica

The results of my test arrived by email in the first week of January. They came in the form of a circle, comprised of coloured segments, that showed I was fifty-one percent Irish, so no surprises there, it was just as I expected. More interesting, were the other regions mentioned, Sweden and Norway, and Germanic Europe, and two percent of me that hailed from the Caucasus, wherever that was. I'd have to resort to a map to find out. It also offered information on the stories and events that my DNA suggested I was a part of. It was all fascinating, but where were the details? Was I hoping for a list of names, my father's, or better still, my mother's, and their likely whereabouts? I showed Carolyn and Jono, and they agreed it hadn't helped, but a few days later the emails began to arrive, proclaiming, 'New discoveries for Angelica Malone'! It seemed I had relatives all over the place; third, fourth, fifth, and even more distant cousins, some from as far away as Australia, and a third-cousin in Canada, a Ruth Randall; my heart pounded uncomfortably, did she know my mother? 'Send message' said the box next to it, but I hesitated. Perhaps I'd check with Don first to ask if he'd heard of her, or any of the others for that matter. He would think I was completely mad for even asking.

I'd intended to visit my grandmother before Christmas, I still had her present tucked away at the back of my wardrobe, a pink, woolly cardigan that I'd wrapped in tissue and silver paper; I doubted she would ever wear it. To be honest, I felt nothing for her; there was no natural affinity, but then it was hard to recognise any spark of life that might indicate who she was, or who she had been. I felt sorry for her, and for her situation, she hardly left her chair, but sympathy wasn't the same as love. Don said a woman from the social services came once a week to bath her, he'd never been able to manage it, 'she was his mam', he said, 'and she'd never have wanted it.'

Mr O'Donnell had found a new assistant, so my days were free again. I wondered how long it would last; the wages and conditions didn't exactly encourage people to hang around. It suited Carolyn because she was happy to take full advantage of his good nature, and he'd have let her get away with murder for a quiet life!

I took the Artane bus from the centre and walked

the remaining mile or so, it gave me time to think. The door was wide open when I arrived, and the room was cold. Don was smoking on the doorstep, 'I'm after airing the room,' he explained, 'she's warm enough with her shawls, and the cat.'

I walked across and knelt beside her. 'How are y' Grandma?' I asked, but she just stared at me, and I realised she'd forgotten who I was. I put the present into her cold hands and the cat jumped off her lap and ran through the open front door. 'It's Angelica,' I said, 'look I've brought you a Christmas present. I'd have come before, but I've had so much to do.'

It was a feeble excuse, but she didn't acknowledge it, or my presence.

'He's gone!' she moaned, 'he's run off!'

'She means the cat,' said Don, 'she's taken with it, and it helps keep her warm.'

'Maybe, you should get her a cat of her own,' I suggested; it seemed like the obvious solution.

'Oh, and who would look after it after she passes?' he asked, 'I'd be saddled with the cat then; as it is, my life isn't my own.'

I felt selfish for even suggesting it.

'Can I buy you a drink, Don?' I asked him, 'I need to pick your brains.'

He nodded, 'Sure y' can, darlin'... though there's not much for you to pick. I'll leave the door open; the cat might come back!'

'Will she be alright on her own with the door open?' I queried, 'Someone might come in...'

'No one is after stealing her, and if they did, they'd soon be bringing her back. Anyway, Mrs Shaunessy will be here soon, to give her the weekly bath.'

I glanced over my shoulder as we walked up the road and saw the cat creeping back in. I was pleased, she didn't know me, and Don was indifferent, but the cat seemed to really like her.

Mick was still behind the bar, he looked younger than ever. I waved at him politely and went to sit in my 'usual' spot in the corner.

'To what do I owe this pleasure?' asked Don when he came back with a pint of Guinness and a vodka and tonic. It was a bit early in the day for vodka, but, given the circumstances, I welcomed it. I took out the list of names I'd copied down from my email, 'I just wondered if you knew anything about a Ruth Randall, she lives in Canada, apparently she's our third-cousin. Have you heard of her?'

Don sipped his drink, 'No, can't say I have. It's hard enough keeping up with everyone here; and in Canada, you say?' he scratched his unshaved chin, 'No I've not heard of her.'

I thrust the paper under his nose, 'Look, Don, can you tell me if you recognise any of these names?'

He squinted at the list and I realised he was having trouble seeing it. 'Here give it to me,' I said, 'I'll read them out, one at a time. Stop me if any of them sound familiar.'

I read the list slowly, so that he had plenty of time to mull them over, but he rejected them all. 'Fin's not there...' he replied, 'nor Iris.'

I put it back in my bag and stood up to go.

'Ask Maura,' he added, 'she might know, it matters to her, it doesn't matter to me, not anymore, I've caused enough heartache as it is.' He didn't stand, or give any indication that he was leaving, and I assumed he was there for the day, 'Thanks for the drink, Don,' I said, 'I'll be in touch if I come up with anything important.'

The door was still open when I passed the house, so I popped my head around. A large woman, with a tight, grey perm, was helping Grandmother to her feet, Mrs Shaunessy, I assumed. There was no sign of the cat. I withdrew and hurried off; she didn't need me; I could have been anybody.

As soon as I got home, I emailed Maura to ask her if she knew a Ruth Randall. I don't know the name, she replied, but why don't you write to her? What harm would it do?

She was right, it wouldn't do any harm; so why was I so reluctant to get in touch?

'It's because you're afraid,' explained Carolyn, 'you're terrified that it will lead nowhere. You've been following clues that, so far, have only led you on a wild-goose-chase, and now you're pinning all your hopes on some distant cousin in Canada who, until now, didn't even know you existed. There's only one way to find out, write to her and ask if she's heard of Fin Delaney or Iris Malone. Did you send the whole list to Maura?'

'Hardly,' I replied, 'there's far too many, and not a single Delaney, or a Malone.'

'Pick the first dozen or so and ask her,' she said, 'she won't feel inundated if you just send a few.'

Maura answered by return, 'I'm sorry, Angela, there's no one I recognise. Come and see us; you can show me the website; maybe someone familiar will turn up, you never know. And we'd love to meet you.'

It would be nice to meet Maura and her family, I decided, at least they seemed fairly normal.

I still hadn't written to the mysterious Ruth, but I'd realised why I was so reluctant. It was true, nothing I'd done so far had produced the result I wanted, namely, to find Iris. Worst of all, my meddling had led to the death of Aileen. She wasn't my biological mother, or even my adoptive mother, but she was the only mother I'd known, and now I didn't even have her. Still, there was a slight possibility that Iris had gone to Canada, after all, that was where William's blanket came from, and it was exactly the same as the one I'd arrived in. I sent a quick message to Ruth, to ask her if she knew Iris or Fin, and explaining that I was a relative who had lost

contact with them. She came back straightaway to say that the only Malone she'd heard of was Molly, who lived 'in Dublin's fair city'. No doubt, she thought she was being amusing.
I decided to visit Maura.

CHAPTER 29

Carolyn was in the kitchen when I got up the next morning; she was sitting at the table eating toast and jam, like she had all the time in the world, and it was already gone eight thirty. 'No work today?' I enquired. She grinned up at me, 'We're never busy before mid-morning, and I've got something to tell you that couldn't wait!' She fidgeted impatiently while I switched the kettle back on and opened the pantry to take out the cat food. 'For the love of God, Angela, will y' just sit down, it's important; the cats can wait!'

I pulled out a chair and sat, 'Well, what's so important that we have to starve the poor cats?' I asked, and they clearly agreed, because they were peering dolefully between me and their empty bowls.

'We're getting married, Angie… me and Jono. I wanted you to be the first to know!'

I was astounded, though why I'm not sure. It was obvious they were ideally suited, and they'd been friends for nearly four years, before their relationship turned from 'platonic' to 'romantic'. They knew each other's infuriating habits and moods already, it was tried and tested, no dodgy pub pick-ups for them. 'Amazing…!' I gasped, and I hugged her, 'I'm so happy for you, Carolyn, he's fabulous!'

'I hope his family like me, Angie; do you think they will?'

I'm certain they'll love you,' I said.

'We're off to see Mam and Da, and all, on Friday evening. We'll stay over the weekend; that'll be an eye-opener for him, he'll probably call it off.'

'Your family are great,' I added, 'so why wouldn't he like them?'

'I'll tell Michael when I get to work.'

'Michael?' I queried, 'So would that be Mr O'Donnell?'

'Yes, he really opened up to me the other day; said he was worried about Padraig.'

I nodded sagely, 'Well I can understand that, I'd be worried about Padraig too, if I was paying him.'

'Padraig's his sister's boy, he couldn't socialise, was bullied at school, the usual stuff; his mother thinks he might be autistic. It's not serious, just enough to make his life difficult.'

I gave her a fresh cup of tea and loaded the toaster with a couple of slices for me.

'Thanks, Angie,' she said, 'it's been grand having you around. I hope you meet someone soon. We haven't fixed the date yet… for the wedding…' she added, when I seemed baffled, though maybe 'preoccupied', would have been a more charitable description, given my circumstances, 'so you won't have to worry about finding somewhere to live, not for ages…'

I hadn't thought of that. Carolyn and Jono would probably get a house of their own, and I'd be looking for another place to hang my hat. I'd miss them, life used to be so predictable, but now it was full of uncertainties.

'Can Michael get me a good deal on a flight to Bristol,' I asked her, 'I'm going to visit Maura. I just have to check on a date that will suit her.'

'Of course, I can, but are you sure it's what you want?'

'It's my only option,' I said, 'so far, she's the only close relative I've found that's even vaguely normal.'

She went to work soon after and I went upstairs to get my laptop.

'Dear Maura, I wrote,

Will it be alright for me to visit on the weekend of the third March? I'd love to meet you all! Angela x'

I couldn't think of anything else to say so I pressed send. Only then did it occur to me that I could have given her an update on the old woman, her ancient mother.

Roisin called soon after to complain that 'her mother had taken over her life, and her children.'

'Does that mean you're going back to Sean?' I asked.

'No, it means I'm looking for a job, something challenging. I might try teaching; it's just a short course on top of my degree.'

We chatted for some time, mainly about how difficult

her life had become, while I made reassuring noises along the lines of, 'I'm sure Chloe loves you more than your mother,' and 'no, you're nowhere near too old to change your life'. I could hardly fit a word in; when had she become so self-obsessed? At last I did, 'Have you heard from your friends in Canada, Roisin? You know… the ones who sent William the blanket.'

'They're not my friends, Angie,' she replied, 'they're my mother's friends, and no, I've heard nothing yet. I'll be sure to tell you when I do.'

The email device on my mobile pinged and I breathed a sigh of relief, it was the perfect excuse to make my escape from my latest role, as Roisin's psychologist and life coach. 'Got to go, Roisin,' I said, 'email, it might be important.'

I opened it, 'New discoveries for Angelica Malone,' read the heading, and just below that, 'view this DNA match'. My hands were shaking as I pressed the link. 'Close family match,' it declared, 'possibly half-sister or first cousin', and next to that was a tiny picture of a young woman who looked about the same age as me. It said her name was Neve. I read it again, just to make sure; well, either was possible, I could easily have a half-sister, Iris and Fin would almost definitely have gone on to have more children; and then there were Fin's four brothers. I knew that Don had never married, but he might still have produced children, even if he'd never been aware of the fact, and what about Tommy,

Declan, and James; and didn't the article in the newspaper refer to Iris having a sister? Maybe, Neve was one of Maura's grown up children; the possibilities were endless, I could have numerous first cousins, and half-sisters, and brothers. I should have been happy, but the idea shocked me. I was still sitting there trying to come to terms with it all when it pinged again, informing me that I had a message, and that I should, 'press link to view.'

It was Neve and all it said was, 'Who are you?'

I'd wanted to ask her the same question, and to be honest, I think I might have put it more politely. Maybe she hadn't meant to sound curt, unless it was because she was wondering why she'd never heard of me, until now. I chewed my lip for a moment or two, wondering what to write, after all, if she was the daughter of Fin, or Iris, they might have kept my existence, and my unusual departure, a secret; one of those family traumas that are shut away and never permitted to see the light of day, unless someone like me suddenly turns up out of nowhere to ruffle the status-quo. I wrote a quick message, 'Thanks for contacting me, Neve! I'm hoping for news of my parents, Iris Malone, and Fin Delaney, we've lost contact. Can you help with any info?' and pressed send; then I wrote another asking if I could have her email address so that we could contact each other without using the site, and I sent that too.

I expected her to reply by return but she didn't, and

in the end, I decided to clean the place, just to occupy myself while I was waiting. I'd washed the kitchen floor, and started on the dusting, when her message came and I went through the whole tiresome business of linking to the site, and finding the relevant page, yet again, but I was shaking like a leaf and my brain just wasn't connecting with my fingers. I was a nervous wreck by the time I'd found it, it said, 'I haven't heard of Fin or Iris, but if you want to contact me, send me your email address. I need to know more before we proceed.'

'Before we proceed', I didn't feel encouraged by her attitude, but I sent it anyway and then went back to the dusting.

She finally contacted me around midday, by which time there wasn't a speck of dust to be seen, and the whole place reeked of furniture polish. She wasn't the chattiest person I'd ever met, but she'd written a brief 'hello' and told me she lived in Cork with her father and sister. I started to type a reply, but it was hard to explain my situation. 'Hi Neve,' I wrote, 'it's good of you to get back to me, and I assure you I'm not some kind of scam. I was adopted at three months and I'm hoping to trace my birth parents. I've managed to find my grandmother, and an aunt and uncle, but it would be nice to find my father as he was the youngest son, and his mother is hoping to see him again before she passes.'

Her reply came straight away, and her tone had changed completely. She said how sorry she was to hear about my grandmother and that she would do all she could to help, but she wasn't aware of any Delaneys or Malone's, which was odd as she'd been working on a family tree, and, 'how was that possible if we were so closely related?'

I was starting to think the same thing, but I wasn't keen to point out the remaining possibility, that somewhere along the line there was 'a mix up', or in simple terms, someone's father hadn't really been their father. I was about to reply, but then she wrote again asking if I'd be prepared to meet. We'd be able to discuss it further, and she might be able to 'fill a few gaps on her family tree,' and, 'how did I feel about getting the train to Cork the following weekend?'

CHAPTER 30
CORK

I accepted her invitation, I had nothing much else to do, and the daffodils would be coming out; not that I needed any excuse because, above all, I was curious; how was it possible that we were cousins, or, even more amazing, half-sisters?

I recognised her from the photograph as soon as I got off the train. We weren't at all alike; she had sandy coloured hair and freckles, and she was taller than me, and fine boned. We greeted each other with a shy 'hello' and a brief hug, and then, for a moment or two, neither of us seemed to know what to say. I followed her out of the station to her car, a nearly new Mercedes, 'It's not mine,' she said, 'it's Dad's; I've been driving since I was seventeen, but I've never had a car of my own.'

We drove about five kilometres into the soft green of the countryside. It was somehow easier to talk in the car; it was less confronting if we didn't have to look at each other. I told her how I came to be separated from my parents, and that I'd been brought up by Aileen and Patrick, the couple who had taken me; and that they'd recently passed away, but not before Aileen had explained how she'd found me in the field. It felt strange telling her, as if I almost didn't believe it myself.

'I was suspicious,' she said, 'I couldn't understand how we could be related at all, especially when you told me about Iris and Fin. I've been compiling a family tree for some time, it's quite extensive and goes back many years, but their names have never cropped up, and I've never heard of anyone called Angelica. It's an unusual name, isn't it?'

'Yes,' I agreed, 'it is unusual. Aileen called me Angela; it's hard to think of myself as anything else.'

After that we drove for a while in silence. There was so much I wanted to ask her, but I didn't know where to start; like, if she had been so suspicious when I first popped up on the website, why had she changed her mind, and to the extent that she'd wanted to meet me, and invite me to her home?

I didn't have to ask, 'I'm sorry if I seemed unfriendly at first,' she said suddenly, 'it was just strange finding out that I was so closely related to someone I'd never heard of. All sorts of thoughts run through your mind. At first, I thought it might be a mistake; then I started wondering if maybe my mother had given birth to an illegitimate child, before she had me. I expect you're wondering why I didn't just ask her.' She turned her head briefly, away from the road ahead, to glance at me, and I nodded. 'She left my father some time ago; she joined a religious cult, the Palmarians; I doubt you've heard of them, they encouraged her to break all ties with us. She went soon after the birth of my sister, Rose.'

I was horrified; her life was almost as complicated as mine; almost, but not quite. 'That's dreadful!' I murmured, though it didn't seem sufficient a response. She continued, 'My dad thought it might have been due to postnatal depression, but she never came back. It was a long time ago; anyway, that's why I couldn't ask her.'

'But her name isn't Iris,' I said, 'so there's no reason to think that.'

'No, none at all, or I'd have tried harder to contact her. It's not what changed my mind though.'

I waited for her to elaborate, but she didn't, and I didn't like to ask.

We stopped soon after, outside a large detached house with iron gates, it was a world away from the small terrace where I'd spent my childhood.

'We're here,' she announced, 'and I ought to tell you before we go in that it was my father who changed my mind. He said he knew Iris, and Fin, when he was a young lad in Dublin. He spoke fondly of Iris and said he wanted to meet you.'

CHAPTER 31

Ronan Kelly opened the door and came out to greet us. He was tall and slender, with a receding hairline, and a smile that reached all the way to his eyes and back again.

'Angelica Malone…' he murmured, 'you're just as I remember Iris, the very image; come in, come in… Meet my youngest daughter, Rose.'

I felt awkward, all over again. Was I supposed to hug these people, would that be over-familiar, or should I simply shake hands? I didn't have to worry; Rose, who was a slighter shorter clone of her sister, stepped forward and hugged me; then Ronan put his arm around my shoulders and led me into a vast kitchen where the table was set for a meal.

The conversation over lunch was convivial, there were no awkward questions; I had a feeling they would come later. Neve told me that she'd just returned from a year in Paris as part of her degree course; she said she was fluent in French, and Rose said that she was hoping to follow in a year or two. I might well have felt intimidated by their obvious wealth and sophistication, but they were so friendly, and hospitable, that I couldn't feel anything but welcome. Ronan explained that he had left Dublin when he was young, to join a building firm in County Cork; it had been a good move, if the house was anything to go by. He told me, again and again, that I looked exactly like Iris, and how much he'd missed her when she took up with Fin. He said that he remembered when her baby went missing, but always assumed that Iris had spirited me away.

'Fin was the sort of man you'd walk a mile to avoid, so I couldn't fault her if she did,' he said, 'but we won't dwell on that now. Can I get y' more wine, Angelica? That's a grand name y' have!'

'I'm not used to it,' I explained, 'so Angela will do just fine!'

At the end of the meal I got up to help with the clearing, but Ronan beckoned me to follow him. 'Come with me, let the girls do it; I want to speak to you.' I looked back at Neve and she smiled, 'Yes, go on, we're fine. I'll top up your glass and bring it in.'

The room was beautiful, with long, antique sofas gracing either end of an intricately woven Persian rug, and soft chairs placed cosily around a deep fireplace. At the far end I could see elegant French windows, draped in a heavy tapestry of gold and yellow, and beyond them, a garden full of trees that stretched away into the distance. I wondered again why I was here, and he seemed to read my thoughts.

'I think I may owe you some sort of explanation,' he said softly, 'Have a seat, Angelica, I've something important to say, and it might be best if we're both sitting down. Neve tells me that you and she have a close DNA match?'

I nodded, wondering what was coming next; and yet already half knowing.

'Iris and I were close, anyone will tell you that, but we were always friends, nothing more…'

I took a deep breath. I wasn't sure if I was relieved or disappointed.

He paused, 'Here's our drinks, thank you, Neve.' She went out again and closed the door. I took a large gulp of Pinot Noir, there was obviously more to come.

'…but I wasn't really content with that. She was obsessed with Fin to begin with, and he was a good-looking man, whereas, I was young for my age, and not particularly attractive, by comparison.' He grinned, 'She wasn't interested in me, but one night, after Fin had given her a black eye, and bruised ribs, she arrived on our doorstep. At the time we lived just at the far end of the same street, I was in the house alone…'

I nodded, and he continued, 'yes, you can guess what happened next; it was only the once. I never saw her after that; she spent most of her time with Fin, even though he treated her like…' he shook his head, 'Why are women so easily fooled by good looks, and flattery?'

I felt quite indignant, 'Not all women,' I murmured.

I took another large gulp of wine and nearly choked.

This couldn't be happening; was he saying that I was his daughter?

'I'm sorry, I shouldn't have said that! It's because I still feel angry every time I think of Iris with Fin! Maybe you've already guessed where this is going? I suppose the question is whether the DNA test has matched you with anyone in the Delaney family?'

'I've met Don, his brother,' I replied, 'and my grandmother, and I've contacted Fin's sister in England, but I didn't find them as a result of the test. I showed Don the list they sent me, he said he didn't recognise any of the names, but then they're all fairly distant, just third and fourth cousins; none that are close.'

'Have you got it with you?' he asked.

I opened my bag, 'I've got it here, but I've only copied out the first twelve, the others were irrelevant. After all, if he didn't recognise the first twelve there'd be little chance of him knowing the rest.'

I handed it to him, and he nodded as he read it, 'Yes, there's Neve, of course, and one or two others that I recall from years back.'

I couldn't reply; I was stunned into silence. It seemed I was sitting opposite my father, and he appeared to have reached the same conclusion. My search for Fin and his family had been pointless. Fin had nothing to do with my existence on the earth; and everything that had happened to me, since the moment of my birth, had been avoidable.

He took my hands in his and looked into my eyes, 'Welcome, Angelica, I'm so pleased you found us at last.' Then he put his arms around me and hugged me tight. 'Neve, Rose,' he called, 'come and meet your new sister!'

I caught the last train back to Dublin on the Sunday evening. It had been a strange day. I could see my reflection in the windows of the carriage, an unfamiliar face, with black shadows where normally there were none, and eyes that were flat and dead. She looked back at me, and for a moment I felt that I was outside looking in; it was an odd sensation, quickly dispelled by the artificial lights of a train speeding back to Cork, when my mirror image turned into clattering strobe flashes of light and darkness, before receding into the gloom of the countryside.

I'd awoken that morning to the sound of a man crying, it was Ronan, no doubt weeping for Iris, and for all those wasted years; and perhaps for my anguish too. Surely, it should have been me, crying for the loss of my mother, or perhaps bemoaning her stupidity, but I couldn't blame her, not really, not after Conor. If she was stupid, then so was I.

He'd recovered by the time I went down to breakfast and seemed happy enough; I don't think he realised that I'd heard. My mood was alternating between dizzy euphoria and melancholy, so maybe it was the same for him.

They'd begged me to stay, insisting that now I had so few links to the city it was the obvious thing to do; and that we had so much to learn about each other, and how it would 'give us all time to come to terms with the situation'. I was a situation; if anyone had told me a year ago that my life would take such a dramatic turn, I'd have laughed!

I explained how, although Aileen, and Patrick, were now departed, I still had my adoptive cousins, and their children. I even mentioned Kitty, though heaven knows why, because she'd probably not have noticed my absence anyway; and there was Carolyn, and Jono, and various other friends and acquaintances, they at least deserved some sort of explanation.

    I closed my eyes to shut out my doppelganger on the other side of the glass and thought instead about Iris. Hadn't she at least considered the possibility that I wasn't Fin's child? And what of Fin Delaney, was he so certain of her devotion that he never thought to question it? Now I was faced with the uncomfortable task of informing Don that I wasn't related to him at all; and that his mother wasn't my grandmother. I felt sad in a way as she'd been so happy to see me, but fortunately, if dementia could ever be termed as fortunate, she'd recently deteriorated to the extent that she barely knew who I was. Then there was Maura; I was supposed to be visiting her in a week or two for a joyful reunion; how would I break the news to them all, that I was a fraud, a cuckoo in the nest? And what about the old woman, would she ever understand that I was no longer the missing link to her beloved youngest child? No, far better to let her hope.

I made the decision, there and then, to hold back; I wouldn't tell Don, not until I'd spoken to Maura; then it might be better if she could let him know.
I didn't want to go back in any case; the cluttered house depressed me, and the pub wasn't much better; it reminded me of Don's treachery, and Aileen's short spell of notoriety that led to her death. It had all been avoidable, and the idea that I had been partly responsible cut into my heart like a knife.
I'd chosen to believe him when he told me that someone else had informed the press, because I still felt obliged to keep in touch; convinced that they were my only blood relatives. And I'd hoped that my continued liaison with the Delaneys might eventually lead me to Iris, but it was only a faint hope, and now I was pleased that the link had been completely severed.

Carolyn ran to greet me as soon as got off the train. I'd sent her a text just after breakfast to tell her the momentous news, and she in turn, had told me hers. Her family had taken to Jono as soon as he'd walked in the door.
'That's wonderful, Carolyn,' I said, 'you see, I told you

everything would be fine.'

She took my bag and hurried me out of the station to where Jono was parked. People were always giving me lifts; I made up my mind to learn to drive.

CHAPTER 32

WALES

2018

David

David watched the women walk away. Iris and Mary; they'd lived next door for as long as he could remember, but they'd always kept themselves to themselves. They were very different; a chalk and cheese couple who professed to be sisters, although some questioned this assertion.
'They're definitely lesbians', said one of the newer neighbours, 'it's obvious! I know the type...' He appeared to relish the notion, but David thought it unlikely. His parents knew their mother, Kathleen; they were never friends, but she was always pleasant enough, and not as guarded as her daughters. Unfortunately, she hadn't lived beyond seventy, so she was no longer around to confirm anything either way.

The remains of the man hung from the tree, like medieval bones on a gibbet, and observed by a crowd who seemed transfixed by the macabre scene; until the police shooed everyone away and began to take him down, folding him into a body bag, bony arms spilling out, sullenly resisting his brief loss of freedom after all the years confined beneath the roots.

It was later, when he recalled the way Iris had reacted, that he acknowledged his much younger self; the serious face staring up at him, tugging at his jacket, as if urging him to remember something long buried in his sub-conscious, a memory that he was sure he ought to recall. Instead he brushed aside his feelings of disquiet and thought about Iris. She was lovely, there was no doubt about that, and her slender frame and ethereal quality made her appear far younger than her sister.

He'd returned to the village only recently. His marriage had fallen apart so he'd come home, back to Wales, though he couldn't quite believe that it was actually happening until he drove across the Severn Bridge when his heart had, quite unexpectedly, soared and he'd opened the windows and screamed, 'I'm home...' into the roaring wind and the noise of the traffic. It was then that he decided that, maybe, freedom was what he'd wanted all along.

His parents' house was pebble-dashed and painted a crisp white. Inside, the ceilings were high, and there were long, narrow, sash windows and pale, wooden floors, and it was roomy, now that his sister had moved to Newport. His mother would have been happier if she'd found a job in the shop down the lane, just to have her close by, but it was fortunate for David, because her room was big enough for an office, so he could work online and begin to get his life in order. His wife, Claudia, had accused him of taking the easy option, of running away 'back to his mother', but he didn't care. He'd become desensitised to her vitriol, though he had to admit that it was a shock to discover her packing her bags, along with the sudden announcement that she'd fallen for her boss and was off, 'pronto!' He could see now that the last five years had been a mistake; neither of them had been ready for the restrictions that marriage had placed upon them.

'Ups and downs', said his father, 'you're supposed to work through them, not give up at the slightest drawback!' His mother had been more sympathetic; she'd disliked Claudia from the start and had never seen the need for him to take off to England, especially now that Lara had gone too, leaving her with a permanently empty nest.

His thoughts turned back to Iris, and how anxious she'd been to run away from the wreck of the man in the tree. It was hardly surprising as she wasn't alone in her revulsion; after all, it was the last thing that anyone expected to see, first thing in the morning. She was very beautiful; maybe he could get to know her better? It might mean that he had to put up with the other one, but it would be worth it, wouldn't it?

It was late, and the sun was sinking behind the hills,

when he finally found enough courage to saunter up the path, bursting with a confidence that was really only skin deep. Mary saw him coming and opened the door, 'Oh, David, isn't it? So, you're back, we haven't seen you in these parts, not for a while!' She didn't invite him in and, when he attempted to peer past her into the room, she closed the door slightly to restrict his view.

'I just wanted to check that you're both okay,' he said, 'you know, after everything that happened this morning, but if it's not convenient?'

'Who is it?' came a voice from inside, and his heart jumped when he heard it.

'Only the boy from next door,' called Mary, 'you know, David.'

'Well, bring him in Mary, we need company.' She peered around the door and smiled up at him, 'Come in, David, and have some tea, I've made some biscuits. Everyone around here is so dull, so settled in their ways. I'm glad you've come back; you were such a lovely little child; I used to watch you playing with your sister in the garden.'

Mary frowned at her, 'I don't think we need to have a conversation on the doorstep, now do we? All of the neighbourhood will want to join in, sure they will.' She stood back and held the door open and David saw that Iris was wearing a dove-grey shirt that matched her eyes, with denim jeans, at least two sizes too big and baggy around the knees, and that her hair was the colour of ripe corn and piled up in an untidy topknot that spilled out over her cheeks.

It was curious, thought Mary, the sudden change that had come over Iris since Fin popped out of the ground, like a cork from a bottle, almost as if the earth had had quite enough of him.

They'd come in and cowered by the kitchen stove, while Iris sobbed hysterically; even though Mary told her, over and over, that no one would connect them with the heap of rattling bones that he had become. She'd almost doubted it herself to begin with, and her hands shook when she poured generous measures of whisky to calm them. She'd sipped it slowly while Iris wailed; listening to the ambulance siren when it finally sped off, lights flashing, as if there were some hope that he might be revived, if they only hurried.

'He's gone,' whispered Iris, and she downed another measure of whisky, 'really gone this time!' Then she went to her room and slept for four hours and when she reappeared it was as if Finbar Delaney had never existed.

Mary wished that she could forget him too, but guilt weighed heavily upon her. It would stay with her until they carried her out in a wooden box and planted her beneath the earth, next to Kathleen.

Now she was chatting non-stop to David, laughing, and assuring him that they were fine, and they were glad the bones had been taken off to the morgue. That she'd always felt there was a disturbing presence in the garden, and how it couldn't be good for anyone's peace of mind having a dead body in such proximity, even if one didn't know it was there! God forbid she gets too carried away, thought Mary, she'll be telling him next that we put it there. But there was no danger of that because Iris appeared to have created an alternative reality, one that had engulfed her completely during her long nap.

Eventually, David wandered back up the path and she waved him goodbye from the doorstep, 'Come back again, won't you. I'll make some scones…' and she blew him a kiss when he turned to close the gate.

'You mustn't lead him on, Iris, he's far too young for you!' scolded Mary. 'All these years you've been content enough to hide away while we've both got old. We've allowed the ghost of a man long dead to destroy our lives.'

'But he's really gone now, Mary,' she murmured, 'Fin has really gone, and I'm not old! I've got so much to catch up on; and I like David, he's enthusiastic about life, no one has threatened him, or made him a prisoner.'

'You don't know that, he's not a child. He was living with a girl in London, so, where is she?'

'I intend to find out and then I'll tell you, Mary, I promise, but I'm certain of one thing, she's not under a tree at the back of their garden!'

Iris spent the next three days wandering in and out of the garden. Her good mood continued, and she spent a considerable amount of time offering tea to everyone who came and went, watching, with a kind of morbid fascination, while they took soil samples, and photographed the hole from whence Fin had emerged. He certainly knew how to make an entrance, and an exit, she decided, in life and in death; and whereas the idea would have upset her just the week before, she now decided it was all rather amusing. Sometimes David would call by, along with other curious neighbours, and they would join her at the end of the garden to observe the proceedings, while Mary glowered at them through the kitchen window.

On the fourth day the police returned to remove the orange tape draped around the trees to protect the area from contamination; not that anyone would have gone anywhere near it, as the ground was unstable and likely to give way at any moment. Iris felt that the earth was anything but contaminated, it had been before, but now, with Fin gone, it was cleansed. She was disappointed when they packed up and went home, leaving only the giant, upturned tree, which, they said, would be a new ecosystem, and become home to an infinite variety of wildlife, as the earth was so rich.

The excitement was over, and David finally

returned to his study and switched on his screen, but it was hard to concentrate, and boring after the chaos. He was gazing out of the window when he noticed Iris looking up at him. She waved and smiled, and then turned and began to walk briskly up the lane away from the village to where a tiny track led into the hills. He banged on the glass, but she was already too far away to hear him, so he grabbed his jacket and ran after her.

'Why didn't you wait for me?' he gasped, 'Where are you going?'

She grinned. 'You're not very fit, David! Look how far you ran, such a little distance and you're out of breath already! I would have waited, but I thought you were working; don't you have to earn a living?'

'There's plenty of time for that,' he replied, 'I'd much rather come out with you. And I know these tracks; I've lived here all my life. Look, see that bank of cloud to the west? It could come down and swallow this path in moments. It's very dangerous; there are vertical drops further up, no one would find you if you fell.'

'How old do you think I am, David?' she asked teasingly, 'I'm not some ancient biddy who's forever tripping over her feet. No, I think you're just looking for an excuse to come with me! You don't have to make excuses, I'm happy to have your company.'

He nodded, 'Fair enough, but I meant what I said, it is dangerous when the cloud descends, and the ground is still wet underfoot from the storm.'

'I've lived here for almost as long as you've been alive,' she replied, 'and I probably know these hills better than you! I can find my way down, even in the mist, and I know ways that take me almost onto the roof of the farm at the top of the valley. There have been countless winters when I've helped the farmer and gone out to rescue lambs when they've ventured too far in late snow. Have you ever done that?'

He blushed and shook his head, and she regretted being so forthright, so she added, 'Don't worry, it's fine, I forgive you... just don't do it again.'

They walked on in silence for a while, until scrub covered the tracks and the trees became weathered and bent. 'I never really noticed you before,' he said at last, 'you were just one of the women who lived next door. Sometimes I'd see you in the front garden during the school holidays, but I suppose the rest of the time we were off early on the bus, and home late, we were the last stop;' he laughed, 'though you were always a bit of a mystery, Iris.'

'A mystery? You were just a schoolboy, and I was never mysterious, sad maybe. Anyway, it's complicated and I don't want to dwell on it, I come up here to leave all that behind. I'll tell you about it one day, David, when I'm ready. So, where did your clouds go? Look over there, it's clear as spring water, and there's the sea in the distance. It's so blue! I miss the sea... and I miss Ireland.'

'You should go home, Iris. Why have you never been home?'

'How do you know I've not been back? As it happens, no, I haven't, not for many years. One day I'll tell you why, I promise...' she paused then added, in a small voice, 'I need to tell someone.'

He hugged her then, but only because she looked so sad, and she put her head on his shoulder and enjoyed the closeness. Eventually, she pulled away from him, 'That was nice, no one ever hugs me!'

'You mean you don't give Mary a cuddle? Well, that will disappoint some of the neighbours.'

'I'm well aware of the gossip, David. God, people are impossible! Anyway, you can tell them now that Mary is definitely my sister, and she's not in the least cuddly, I can assure you of that.'

'No one hugs me either,' he murmured, 'not since Claudia left, though she wasn't very affectionate at the best of times.'

'Now you look sad, shall I give you a cuddle? I'm only joking…' she added quickly. 'Tell me about Claudia, what happened there? And why don't I remember you getting married?'

'It was very low-key, just a register office, in London, and the whole thing was doomed from the start. I'd just finished university, but I was already twenty-five. I'd become what you might call a permanent student, I went straight from school, finished my degree and began my PhD, then I suddenly got tired of it all and applied for a job in London. Shall we turn back now? I suppose I should get on with things.'

'Yes, I'm starting to feel cold. But go on, you haven't got to Claudia yet.'

'Oh, yes, Claudia; must we?' he sighed. 'I went for a position in an advertising firm in Paddington. And that's where we met.'

'What, at the station, like the bear?' She was teasing him, but he nodded.

'Yeah, at the station, just like the bear! She was sitting on the platform looking all forlorn because she'd lost her ticket.'

'So, you took her home with you; this is all starting to sound very familiar.'

He laughed, 'Only if you've seen the film.'

'Or read the book! Well, did you, did you take her home?'

'I was staying with a friend, Jono, he's Irish, actually. We studied together, but he had another year to do. He was in London working during the long holiday, so we stayed with him. Next thing I knew, I'd got the job and we'd moved in together, Claudia and me, that is, not Jono. Things went down-hill straight away. You probably don't know what I mean at all; it's just… sometimes you get so desperate for change that you make choices you'd never consider if you were in a rational state of mind. I'd pinned so many hopes on my relationship with Claudia, but she wasn't who I thought she was. That makes it sound like it was her fault, but it wasn't, it was mine. I'd just got this person in my head, the one that I wanted her to be, and she wasn't, she was someone quite different. In the end she reminded me of some of the silly, spoilt girls I went out with when I was younger. I don't suppose you know what I'm talking about, do you?'

'I do, David, I really do; maybe next time I'll tell you why; or maybe the time after that. We're back now; I hope I'll see you soon.'

She ran off down the lane, and suddenly he felt incredibly alone in an almost unnatural silence; until the breeze got up and danced through the trees, rustling the leaves, and disturbing the flock of starlings in the topmost branches. He looked around anxiously; were there more dead men, with grinning skulls and tattered trousers, waiting to rise to the surface of the earth? He trotted the short distance to his parent's home and flopped down on the stairs. Iris was right, he was unfit, and he'd have to do something about it.

Iris slammed the front door behind her and leaned against it for a moment, closing her eyes, and relishing a new sensation. She felt incredibly happy and she wasn't entirely sure why, though she was certain it had nothing to do with the whiff of marijuana that was drifting out of Mary's bedroom.

'I'm back,' she called, 'I'll make some lunch.'

CHAPTER 33

Some weeks had passed since Iris was up at Morgans Croft. Once upon a time she'd be there twice or three times a week, helping to keep the house clean and tidy, but she wasn't needed now that most of the rooms were unused, and the furniture in them permanently covered with dust sheets. Megan was in her mid-eighties and rather frail. She pottered between her small kitchen, a cosy living room, and a bedroom on the ground floor, dusting and polishing when she felt up to it. On good days, she would wander around the garden after Mary, carrying bags of bulbs, or a basket to collect bouquets of herbs for Mary to sell to the restaurants in town. The only time anyone ventured up the stairs to the floor above was when Mary stayed the night, which was usually because Megan felt unwell, or unable to cope with being on her own.

Iris waited at the gate, watching anxiously as Mary drove up the hill, she seemed to be in control of the car, and the road was always deserted, but Iris still wondered if, one day, she would end up in a ditch.
She didn't mind being alone in the cottage, not anymore. She still slept in the warm, attic bedroom, just as she had when they first arrived all those years ago;

she liked climbing the ladder, and the isolation when she reached the top. She had few mementos of her life in Ireland, but pride of place, next to her bed, was a photo of tiny Angelica, wrapped in the blanket that Kathleen had knitted. It was faded now, even though she'd placed it behind glass in a pretty frame and shielded from the sun streaming in through the skylight.

She saw no reason to move down to Kathleen's room, that would always be hers, only now it doubled as Iris's workshop, Kathleen would have approved of that.

Mary disappeared beyond the bend in the lane. There were no screeching brakes or loud crashes and Iris breathed a sigh of relief and went to clear away the dishes before making her way upstairs to her workshop. There was a pile of hand-knitted blankets on the bed, each ready to be embroidered with a new baby name. Kathleen gave her the pattern, and taught her how to make them, which always amused Mary as she had been able to knit since she was six. To begin with, they sold them in a small gift shop in the town that was owned by a friend of Megan's, but now Iris had a thriving business online; and, in any case, the gift shop was long-gone as Megan's friend had sold up and retired some time back. Iris picked one up one of the blankets, it was pale lemon, like an early primrose, and destined for a baby with a gender-neutral name. 'Caspa Eden…' murmured Iris, as she threaded her needle with green silk thread, 'So are you a boy, or are you a girl?' There was still a demand for pink, and blue, for a flurry of Charlottes, and an outbreak of Williams; 'William George', William Peter, 'Freddie William', and a 'William John', bound for Canada. Didn't they make baby blankets in Canada? Iris didn't care, so long as they paid the postage.

As she sewed, she thought about her new friend. It would be good to have someone to confide in, someone who might reassure her that her daughter was still out there, and maybe looking for her at this very moment, but how much could she tell him? She'd sworn to Mary that they would never admit to burying Fin, but it would be lovely to tell David about Angelica. Where would be the harm in that? He was young, but not as young as she had been when Mary left her baby in a field.

CHAPTER 34

Iris was awake until the early hours, she was thinking about David; she liked him, and it was so long since anyone had noticed her. She could hear Mary padding about in the kitchen, so she wasn't sleeping either. It was probably because of Fin; she behaved as if she wasn't bothered by his unexpected appearance, but Iris knew that she was. It would be difficult to ascertain whether Mary was bothered by anything unless you'd known her for most of her life. She always insisted that she didn't miss Ireland, but how could that be? Their life here was good, and maybe if they'd tried harder to fit in, things might have been better, but now Fin had vacated his earthy grave in the garden, they could make up for lost time. They could get to know people, and travel, they could even go back to Dublin, if it weren't for Declan.

She dozed off eventually and was woken by someone knocking on the front door and Mary yelling from the bottom of the stairs, 'Iris, are you up? Your little friend wants you to come out and play!' Iris picked up her clothes and climbed down the ladder to the bathroom. 'Be there in a minute, David,' she called, hoping that it was really David, and not just Mary's

idea of a joke. 'Thanks, Mary,' she added as she left, 'at least I've got a friend now!'
David was sitting on the garden wall. 'Sorry about Mary,' she murmured, 'she doesn't mean it, not really.'
He stood up and kissed her on the cheek. 'Don't worry, I'm used to it; she reminds me of Claudia. I hope you don't mind me turning up uninvited. I don't want to stop you getting on with…. whatever it is that you do.'
'I knit baby blankets,' she smiled at his puzzled expression, 'and I embroider their names along the edge; some of their names are extraordinary. My mother taught me how to make them. She thought I needed something to occupy me when we first came here, after…' She paused unsure whether to go on.
'After what…?' he asked.
'Let's walk, it's a beautiful day. I might tell you,' she added, 'though I'm not sure if I should; we've only just met.'
'Oh, so we're going to talk about the weather instead, I thought you were Irish, not English.'
She smiled, 'Everyone talks about the weather; it saves an awkward gap in the conversation.'
They walked for some distance until the path narrowed and began to climb. 'After what, Iris…' he asked, when his curiosity got the better of him.
'After I lost my daughter…!'
She said it in a rush, to get it over with, and he looked shocked and slightly uncomfortable, 'How did she…?'

'She didn't die, David, she was stolen!' She gazed off into the far distance where the hills turned into towering peaks against the sky. David took her hand and waited for her to say more, but she didn't, and he blamed himself for her silence. Perhaps if he'd concealed his surprise, she might have been more willing to confide in him, but her answer had been so unexpected. 'I'm sorry,' he said at last, 'and I understand if you don't want to talk about it; it must be heartbreaking for you, never to know where she is.'

'Or if she's dead;' she replied softly, 'so you may have been right the first time. It's just that I always tell myself she's alive, and happy somewhere.'

'Have you tried to find her, Iris? It's easier to find people now; most people are online. Have you heard of six degrees of separation? It's the idea that we're all fewer than seven acquaintances away from anyone in the world.'

'What a strange idea...' she hesitated while he waited impatiently for her to go on, 'but yes, I wish I could find her. There are other reasons why I've never tried...' she paused again, wondering how much she could tell him. What would Mary say if he became too curious?

'You'd better tell me the whole story, Iris. I can't help you if you don't, and I want to help you; and I'd like to know why you've shut yourself away in the middle of nowhere for all these years when your daughter might be out there somewhere. What if she's looking for you?'

'Angelica… my daughter's name is Angelica.'

'Angelica, it's a pretty name, and unusual, was her father French?'

'French…! No, David, he was an Irishman, a violent Irishman. We were staying in a remote cottage in Ireland, miles from anywhere, but he came after us. We were never sure how he found us; not like the second time…' she bit her tongue, wishing she'd been more careful, 'he didn't find us the second time.'

'Did he take Angelica?' he asked.

'He accused us of taking her from him! Mary hid her in the field until he'd gone, but when she went back for her…'

'She'd gone…?'

'Yes, she'd gone too. We thought at first, he'd taken her, but now I think someone else did. Her father didn't really want her; he just wanted to hurt me, as he always did. That's it, that's my story; my daughter was stolen from me because Mary was stupid enough to leave her alone in a field!'

'You haven't told me why you've hidden yourselves away here. Are you still afraid of him?'

'Yes, I suppose you could say that; and his brother, Declan. He'd be here in an instant if he knew where we were.'

'Declan, and what is this other guy called, Angelica's father?'

'I'd prefer not to tell you; I want to forget him.' She'd

said too much already. David must never know that Fin had already found them, or that he had set light to Hanna's bookshop to find out where they were.

She shuddered remembering the day they'd killed him, or rather, the day that Kathleen killed him.

But they'd all buried him, under the beech tree!

'How old would he be now?' asked David, 'He might have mellowed and become…' he wasn't sure how to continue, become what, nicer, more tolerant, or less violent?

'Fin would never mellow,' there she'd said it, his name, just a slip of the tongue. Still, no one would ever connect a single name with the man lying in the morgue.

'Ah, Fin, that must be short for something,' he murmured.

'Forget I said it… Please, David, I've told you why we're here, I'd be grateful if you'd let it rest. Let's just enjoy our time together; I need to forget the past. I'm used to her being gone, really, I am. She'd be twenty-five now,' she added wistfully, 'just the right age for you.'

Why did that make him feel disheartened, he wondered? Fair enough, maybe Iris was older, but if it had been the other way around nobody would even notice, and the ones that did would be congratulating him.

Mary was out when they got back. He hovered on

the doorstep, while Iris toyed with the idea of inviting him in for coffee, and some of the shortbread she'd baked the day before. Mary would be furious if she came home and found him there, so it was almost worth it just to annoy her, but she wouldn't know unless she came back early, and anyway, Iris wasn't sure if she wanted him to stay.

'I won't invite you in, David,' she said instead, 'Mary will likely be back soon, and we don't want the neighbours talking, do we?'

'I am your neighbour,' he replied, 'and I think its fine.' He suddenly remembered his mother's face when he said he'd been out with Iris; she wasn't pleased. 'Stay away,' she'd told him, 'don't be drawn into something you'll regret.'

His father agreed, 'Yes, she's a strange one! At least the other woman makes some effort to be civil; Megan would be lost without her, but Iris...' he shook his head, 'why would a good-looking girl like that, bury herself away in the middle of nowhere; unless she's got something to hide?'

'I'll see you tomorrow, David,' said Iris, 'I've loads of knitting to do.'

'Well, I've never heard anyone use that excuse before! Look, I'm here for you, Iris, remember that. I'll help as much as I can, you only have to ask.' He turned at the gate and blew her a kiss and she closed the door and went back upstairs; 'Caspa Eden' was still awaiting her attention.

She unthreaded the green silk, wondering if she should maybe use the blue, or the pink, or perhaps both entwined, but they didn't match the yellow, so she discarded them and went back to the green. After all, what did it really matter?

David closed the front door quietly, anxious to avoid unwanted questions from his mother. His computer screen was dark, but it came alive as soon as he touched it, displaying long rows of statistics; he sighed, there had to be more to life than this. He closed the site and instead wrote 'six degrees of separation', then deleted it straightaway and instead wrote, 'results relating to DNA tests', but he deleted that too, and he was just about to write 'Angelica, Ireland', when he stopped himself. There wouldn't be many women with the name Angelica in the Irish Republic, would there? And surely, anyone stealing a baby would change her name, they'd be stupid not to, given the circumstances, but it wasn't just that, it was because he'd suddenly remembered how afraid she was when she told him about Fin, and his brother Declan. What if he inadvertently revealed where she was hiding? And why would Iris still be afraid after so many years had passed? There was something she wasn't telling him; he cleared the screen and reloaded his spread sheets.
He would tell her about the new DNA tests; it would

be entirely up to her if she wanted to proceed. He stared at the columns of figures and tried hard to concentrate, but again he felt someone tug at his sleeve, and the phantom face with serious brown eyes stared up at him from somewhere near desk height. There was something important he ought to recall, he was sure of it, but the memory, for the moment, escaped him.

CHAPTER 35

Despite everyone's disapproval, Iris and David began to meet every morning to climb the paths into the hills. Their walks never lasted for more than a few hours, at the most, so even Mary couldn't complain that Iris was wasting her time. Her friendship with David lightened her mood and, when she got home, she would set to work with renewed energy, and her list of orders grew. Mary did her best to avoid him by hiding in the kitchen when he came to the door, and she avoided his parents too, which wasn't easy as they were retired, and out, and about, more than they once were. As usual, Iris was making everything difficult, and Mary, frequently, told her so. Naturally, Iris didn't agree and retaliated, accusing Mary of jealousy, because her 'only friend was an old lady, who couldn't even get up the stairs, let alone a mountain'.

It was on one of their early morning walks that David asked her to go to London with him, 'It's only for the weekend', he coaxed, 'you'll enjoy it. You can meet the gang, all my mates from uni. They'll love you, Iris, especially Jono, he's Irish, he has the same accent as you!'

'Oh, so you want them all to think that you're running

around with someone who's old enough to be your mother, now why would I do that?' she asked, 'And what would your own mother say? And Mary would have a fit!' Iris was suddenly tempted to go, just to annoy them.

'You're not old enough to be my mother, Iris! Anyway, we're not running around, as you put it,' and he added, 'we're good friends; and I'd like you to meet my other good friends.'

'Maybe I'll come one day, David, just not yet. I'm far too busy!' She walked briskly ahead so that he couldn't try to persuade her, 'Ask me again in a year or so, I might change my mind; one day…' She quickened her pace, but he lengthened his stride to catch up with her.

'Wait, Iris, slow down!' God, the woman was infuriating; he was starting to sympathise with Mary! 'I want to tell you something. I promise I won't try to persuade you to come to London with me.'

Iris stopped and turned to face him, 'Well, what have you to tell me, David?'

'I wasn't sure if I should mention it…'

She grinned at him, 'Yes, and now you have, so spit it out.'

'Did you know…' he hesitated, wondering if he should tell her, 'you can get DNA testing kits online? All you have to do is rub a cotton swab around the inside of your mouth, and from that they can match you with anyone else who shares even the smallest part of your

DNA; like your daughter, for instance, and lots of other people too.'

'I'll think about it…' said Iris, 'I'm not sure Mary would like that at all; she goes on endlessly about people knowing our business, and snooping into our affairs; though actually, it would serve her right!'

'Well, think on it, and let me know what you decide; there would probably be nothing, so don't get your hopes up.'

CHAPTER 36

His mind was in a turmoil, and he could feel the beginnings of a headache just over his left eye. How could he sleep when there was something nagging at him, something that frightened him every time he got too close?

He had a vague recollection of thick undergrowth, and tall trees closing in on him, confining him, gloomy in the rain that dripped through the branches and trickled down his neck, cold, and wet. He remembered the texture of rough bark pressing into his cheeks, and shrill voices, and the terrible dread that he might be discovered. But what had he seen, and why had it come back to haunt him since the storm when that heap of bones sprung out of the earth, entwined in the roots of the fallen beech? Something had awakened a long-suppressed memory, something so terrible that he'd refused to acknowledge it, pushing it far away, deep into his subconscious, so that it couldn't harm him.

They'd said the man was buried almost twenty-five years ago, a quarter of a century, thought David, almost my lifetime, but not quite. He'd have been just five, six years old at the most, so who would have been living in the cottage? Was it Iris, and Mary, and their mother,

Kathleen, who had always seemed old to him? And what was it, Iris said? 'Not like the second time he came after us.' She'd tried to take it back, but it was too late, he'd already noticed the fear in her eyes when she said it, and the way she clasped her hands together to stop them shaking.

He turned over, covering his face with his palms, trying to sooth the ache that had turned into a dull throb, and suddenly, in his mind's eye, he saw the man's head turn towards him, and dead, sightless eyes that seemed to gaze at him, seeking him out, and he saw the three women standing over the muddy hole in the ground, and the blood puddling on their thin, cotton dresses in the pouring rain. It was all coming back to him, snap, snap, snap, like rapidly moving stills in an art-house movie.

'Iris…!' he sat up abruptly and the pain in his head multiplied into bright, flashing stars. He would have to talk to her, first thing in the morning, but not in the hills with the wind blowing the way it was now, rattling the windows and doors, carrying their voices away into the valley and beyond. It would need to be somewhere quiet, where he could see her face, and observe her reactions, watching as her expression changed when she realised he'd seen her, that he knew! Did Iris murder Fin; the violent man who pursued them, demanding she return his daughter?

Sleep was no longer an option, so he got up and

switched on his computer. The complicated columns of statistics stared at him from a blue background, and he stared back.

Poor little kid, he thought, living with that all these years, and the small boy at his side looked up at him, and smiled.

CHAPTER 37

Iris was up earlier than usual. The overnight gale had made sleep impossible, blowing the remaining leaves from the trees and finding its way indoors to lift the curtains, making them billow like phantoms in the draught; and it howled down the chimney, covering the hearth with a black layer of soot and dirt.

She left Mary in bed and, closing the front door softly, she crept out into the lane to see if David was up and about. She usually got his attention by throwing a handful of earth at his window, though he'd said, just the other day, that his mother complained because it dirtied the windows, and if the earth became too hard it would probably sail straight through the glass. 'So, what do you suggest?' she'd asked when he told her, and 'Maybe you should just come and find me instead.' 'You could send me a text,' he'd replied, though he knew it wasn't likely because she always forgot to charge her phone.

His face, when he peered down at her was pale, as if he'd hardly slept either. She paced up and down while she waited for him to appear at the door, and when he did, he looked sullen and weary.

'Shall I go alone, David?' she asked, 'You don't look

well.' He smiled, but it wasn't his usual, open smile, it looked false, as if he were trying too hard.

'I didn't sleep, and I haven't had breakfast! Listen, Iris, I want to talk to you.' She made a face, 'Oh... that sounds ominous, what about?' 'I'll tell you later,' he said, 'and anyway, I've checked the weather forecast and I don't think we should walk far today. How do you feel about a drive into town for coffee, or lunch? It will have to be later though; I need to get some work done first.'

He closed the door and headed back to bed while Iris stood on the doorstep feeling bewildered. She was confused, had she upset him in some way? He seemed distracted when he was normally so pleased to see her. Still, she had plenty to do; a large department store had just requested an order.

They left around noon when Mary had already gone to see Megan. David's father was watching from the window when she got into the car, he made no effort to hide his disapproval.

'You're a better driver than Mary,' said Iris, after several minutes of silence. He didn't answer but she persisted, 'Well, what is it you want to talk about, David? Have you lost your tongue?'

'No, Iris, I haven't lost my tongue,' he turned briefly to smile, 'got to concentrate on the road, it's wild this morning.'

The sky was yellow when they parked on the road

outside a small café. It was deserted, apart from a couple of gossiping women huddled together at a corner table, but they ordered coffee and teacakes, and ate in silence. Iris was worried, why was David so sullen? He wouldn't even look at her or respond when she tried to lighten his mood. Was it something she'd done? She racked her brain, but nothing came to mind.
'I'm sorry, Iris, I'm just tired,' he said at last. He paused, wondering how to go on, 'and there's something I need to ask you, but I'm not sure how…' but Iris wasn't listening, she was looking up at the sky,
'It's snowing, David; look it's so gorgeous, such big feathery flakes.'
'Quick…' he yelled, 'get in the car, if we don't leave now, we'll never get back!'

Iris turned her eyes away from the road and stared at his pale, anxious face, and at his clenched knuckles gripping the wheel; they frightened her, they reminded her of Fin. Was he angry with her? Or was he just trying to keep control of the car? She said nothing, she didn't want to antagonise him, far better that she wait until he was ready to open up. It couldn't be that serious, she decided, maybe his mother had been having a go at him about the state of the windows. She would have to stop throwing earth at the glass. Honestly, some women were so fussy!

David wanted to talk; to say, 'I know what you did,

Iris,' but the words wouldn't come, and how could he ever retrieve them if, by some remote chance, he was wrong?

It was already getting dark; this wasn't the place to live if you were easily depressed by bad weather, and the snow was heavy, falling in large, soft flakes; they fluttered across the windscreen like exotic, white butterflies, obscuring the edges of the road.

'We should have come back earlier,' he growled, 'or better still, not have come at all.'

'Pull over; we can walk the rest of the way,' said Iris, 'it's only a few miles. Look, there's a space by the next farm gate, we can leave the car there. Come on, David, it will be fun, and we can't go any further in the car, can we?' She was laughing when she opened the passenger door and climbed out, 'Come on, I'll help you!'

He inched forward uncertainly, anxious to avoid the ditch. 'You're fine,' she cried, 'just a bit more to the right.' She was smiling at him, coaxing him forward; he swung the wheel down and brought the car to a standstill. 'Right, you're clear of the road,' she cried, 'not that anyone will be passing. Maybe you should leave the key in the ignition in case the farmer needs to move it.' Her face in the beam of the headlights looked happy, but more than that, exhilarated, and she was holding her palms out to catch the falling snow. He was confused, how could this small creature in a bobble-hat be capable of murder?

'I'm not sure I'm that trusting,' he muttered, 'if the snow melts overnight someone might steal it!' He followed her reluctantly, glancing back, once, or twice, at his keys dangling in the ignition. Was he really taking advice from someone who had, very likely, murdered her husband; and, it seemed, without the slightest regret or compunction?

'Best keep on the grass,' he added, 'it's not as slippery as the road. Here, Iris, take my hand.'

'But if I fall, we'll both go down.'

'I'm prepared to risk it!'

She grinned, 'You're just after holding my hand, come on, admit it.'

'I've got a better idea,' he murmured, and he wrapped his arm around her shoulders, 'see, we're both warmer this way!'

He could be wrong, he decided; maybe he'd had a nightmare, due to an overactive imagination, but he knew he was fooling himself because he remembered now, as clearly as if it were yesterday, the way that Fin's sightless eyes had turned to gaze at him when she kicked him. How could one person be capable of so much joy, and yet so much evil? Today should have been one of those memorable occasions, to be tucked away and looked back on with humour, and nostalgia, but instead it would be forever marred by the knowledge that Iris had probably killed her husband.

No, that wasn't fair; he'd yet to hear her side of the story; there were always two sides to consider. She was smiling at him now, and her cheeks were aglow amid the swirling flakes of snow.

It was almost dark when they reached the village. Iris had taken off her hat and stuffed it in her pocket, complaining that it made her feel too hot; he noticed the snowflakes melting in her hair and vowed he would remember her like that. The cottage was in darkness when she opened the door and switched on the downstairs light. 'The car isn't in the lane so Mary will be up at Morgans Croft,' she explained, but she shouted up the stairs anyway, just to be sure, in case she'd had to abandon it somewhere, as they had. 'Mary, are in your room? Would you like something to eat?' and then she went across to the fire and began to pile logs in the cold grate, 'It's freezing in here,' she murmured, 'I'll get the fire going, then I'll make the tea.'

'I'll do that,' he said, 'while you get the tea. There's no sign of Mary, she'd have appeared by now, I'm sure, especially if she thought you had a visitor. What is that smell?'

He sniffed the air, 'Wood smoke, but there's something else... whoa, that takes me back! It's Marijuana...! Iris, do you smoke weed?'

'Oh, you mean Mary's medicine; it's the only thing that keeps her sane. At least, that's what she says. I hope she's with Megan, I worry sometimes that she's not in a fit state to drive. Here, I've made hot chocolate, it's more warming than tea, and it won't keep you awake, you look as if you can do with a good night's sleep. Well, how romantic is this? Sitting in front of a roaring fire, mugs of hot chocolate; perhaps we should be drinking Irish coffee in tall glasses. It's a good thing I'm saving you for my daughter when she turns up, or you wouldn't be safe!'

Black shadows danced around the walls in the firelight, and the flames reflected in her eyes as she stared into its depths, 'Maybe you will meet her one day.'

'Iris, I have to tell you, I remember something…' he hesitated, unsure of how to go on.

'Remember what?' she asked, 'What have you remembered, David?'

'I don't know how to tell you; it's difficult for me, especially feeling the way I do…' he paused, 'the way I've felt about you since the morning of the storm when...'

'Hush don't go on,' she put her finger to his lips to silence him,' it was horrible. I don't want to think about it.'

'The thing is…' he paused again, 'the thing is… that man; I know who he is.'

'Who was he, David?' she asked, and he noticed she was trembling.

'It was Fin, the one you told me about, Angelica's

father. Did you kill him, Iris?'

'How can you even ask me that? You've ruined everything, how could you? I was having such a lovely time and now...' she didn't cry, she just went on staring into the flames. 'He deserved it,' she murmured softly, 'he deserved everything that happened to him. He was evil, and just for the record, I didn't kill him, I only helped to bury him.' She stopped suddenly, 'How do you know?'

'I saw you, Iris.'

'You saw me? What do you mean, you saw me? Don't be ridiculous; how is that even possible? You were no more than a baby when it happened.'

'I was five, or maybe six, I'm not sure exactly. It depends how long he's been dead, but I was there, Iris, in the wood, when you buried him.'

'But why have you waited till now to mention it?' She looked at him accusingly, 'What's stopped you from telling the police?'

'I've only just remembered.'

'So you've told no one?'

'No one; I didn't tell anyone at the time. I must have been in denial, refusing to acknowledge what I'd seen. I was only small! I probably thought I'd get into trouble for straying. I remembered last night, everything, I'm not sure why.'

'Well then, shouldn't you be afraid? No one knows you're here; what if I decide to hit you over the head and plant you in the garden? Not that I could if I wanted to,' she smiled wryly, adding, 'the ground is too hard, and buried under a shroud of snow.'

A shroud, he shuddered, did she have to be so dramatic? 'I thought you said you didn't do it. Tell me what happened, Iris, I really need to know.'

'He found us. He killed Mary's friend, Hanna, and burned down her home, just to find out where we were hiding. It was my mother, Kathleen; she hit him with a claw-hammer, it was only to protect me.' She began to cry softly, 'we couldn't take anymore, David; but it was an accident, she never meant for him to die.'

So that was it, self-defence, a mother protecting her daughter, if they'd called the police surely the courts would have understood.

'Please, don't cry,' he whispered, 'I promise I won't tell anyone. He's gone now, no one will ever know. I'll stay until you're asleep; you can tell me the whole story in the morning. Lie down; I'll get you a blanket.'

It was gone midnight when he left and Iris had fallen into an exhausted sleep on the sofa; the room was warm in the glowing embers of the fire, but it would be cold by morning.

'Is that you, David?' called his mother when he closed the front door, 'Thank goodness, I've been so worried.'

'I'm fine, we just had to walk back; the roads were too dangerous to drive. I'll take some chains and fetch it when the snow stops. Go to sleep, woman; I'm much too old now for you to worry about me.'

He was worn out, but still he couldn't sleep; the wind howled outside his window. It blew the silent snow into deep drifts, covering the fields and obscuring the hills, until it was impossible to remember the way it was before. That was exactly how it was with Iris; she had changed everything.

CHAPTER 38

So, he'd known all along; he just hadn't been aware of it. Everything they'd done together, the conversations that seemed fresh and new, and full of hope, were now tainted by the knowledge that he'd seen the worst of her, the dark side, complicit in an act of violent murder. She'd ruined everything!
Mary was right, she attracted trouble, like wasps were attracted to jam; she brought it on herself because she lacked judgement. Why did she never stop to think? She was angry with herself, but her overriding emotion was sadness for the small boy who had watched while they buried Fin; and he'd told no one, preferring, somehow, to rationalise their strange, adult behaviour, before burying it deep in his subconscious where it wouldn't harm him; until now!

The room was freezing. She shook off the blanket and ran into the kitchen to turn on the stove; it was the quickest way to warm the place, provided the oven door was open. Mary always accused her of wasting money, but she wasn't around, she hadn't come back from Morgans Croft. The snow had blown into drifts, higher than the sills, muffling the sounds from outside and blocking the draughts, but it was melting slowly, dripping from the gutters, and blowing from the branches of the trees in damp flurries.

Would David ever speak to her again? She doubted it. The last few months had reminded her that life wasn't just about surviving from day to day. How could she have forgotten how important it was to have people around who laughed, and made the best of things, even when they had problems of their own? Her thoughts turned back to Mary, who was always content with life the way things were, though she could never be described as optimistic, or frivolous, but maybe she was different when she was with Megan. Was she up at Megan's now? Or had she suffered one of her 'dizzy spells' and slid into a ditch? She'd have to walk up to Morgans Croft later to check.

She went back into the sitting room and lit the fire. Would David go back to move his car, she wondered. It had been fun going into town with him; she often went with Mary, mainly to post her packages, but she was boring by comparison.

Someone was tapping on the window. 'David…' she cried,' and rushed to open the door, 'I'm so pleased to see you! I wasn't sure how things would be between us, after yesterday.'
'Forget it, Iris; we'll pretend it never happened. I imagined all of it! Come on, we've got to pick up the car, before the farmer decides to move it into a muddy field, or someone steals it. I'm not sure I should have

left the keys. Honestly, Iris, why on earth do I listen to you? I should know better!'

The tarmac on the road shone wet and black against the whiteness of the snow. It was melting now, but it still lay thick upon the high pastures. They walked in comfortable silence, stopping occasionally to watch a soaring buzzard, or a fox running from hedge to hedge across the white fields. The car was still where they'd left it the night before. They brushed the snow from the roof and the windscreen, and climbed in.

'Where shall we go?' he asked, 'I'll take you anywhere, Iris. If you were to leave now, you'd be free. There'd be no secrets between us, unless there are other skeletons in your past that you haven't told me about.'

'Actually, I'd rather you didn't mention skeletons again, if you don't mind. And no, there aren't, I can assure you of that.'

He smiled, 'Well that's a relief; so, where shall we run to? I've always fancied Australia.'

'Australia…! Your mother would love that, it was bad enough that you went to London!'

'I'm serious, Iris, we could just take off. We'll start again somewhere completely different.'

It seemed like an offer too good to refuse, she looked out of the window to her left, where the fields stretched as far as she could see. On the other side, the land climbed steadily, punctuated by grey streams and pools till it reached the high mountain peaks. She loved it here, it had sheltered her, and kept her safe, but it confined her too.

'I can't leave,' she said at last, 'Angelica will never find me.'

'Why do you think she'll find you here, Iris?' he asked, 'She's just as likely to find you somewhere else.'

'And Mary needs me,' she added.

'Really… does she? I'm not convinced; she has Megan, and you annoy her.'

'Oh, so I'm annoying now, am I?' he nodded; then squeezed her knee to show he didn't mean it. 'She's given up her life for me, David. I can't desert her. Anyway, you're being ridiculous, I'm much too old for you, it's unfortunate, but it's a fact, and nothing can change that!'

'There's something I have to tell you...' he said quietly, and her heart sank. 'Don't worry, nothing of epic proportions, just that you can't do that test I told you about. You see, everyone assumes that the bones belong to some poor, old tramp who took a wrong turn and finished up dead, in a ditch; no one would connect him to two middle-aged women living in a nearby cottage.'

'Middle aged… thanks, David! A few minutes ago, you wanted us to run off together!'

He laughed, 'Oh… shut up…! Anyway, it's a cold case, and no one was reported missing; whatever the circumstances it isn't being taken too seriously, however, if Angelica shows up, the police will put two and two together.'

'I don't know what you're talking about, David. We buried Fin,' she shuddered, 'my daughter had nothing whatsoever to do with it.'

'She shares your DNA, yours, and Fin's. She is the link between the two of you.'

'But how would they know, unless they tested the three of us?'

'Can you risk it, Iris? They'll already have his DNA on record.'

'I hadn't thought of that.'

A slew of icy snow fell across the road in front of them and David swerved to avoid it. Iris hardly noticed, she was thinking; perhaps she should get away, if it came out they knew Fin they could still be prosecuted, and, even if they were given suspended sentences, the publicity might reveal their whereabouts to Fin's brother, Declan. She still feared Declan, though she wasn't sure why after so many years. Perhaps David was right, she needed to escape, and so did Mary, while they still could, but it couldn't be with David, he'd get tired of her and that would be too much to bear; imagine, when he was only sixty she'd be ancient!

They didn't stop in the village; Mary's car wasn't outside the cottage, so she still wasn't home. Instead, they drove straight up to Morgans Croft. The tall hedges cast long shadows, and deep drifts, blown by the wind, were high against the banks, but Iris was reassured, because it explained why Mary hadn't returned. It was high on the tops of the gateposts too, sharp-angled cubes of snow, like sugar icing, and the lawn was a pristine, white carpet, except for where the sun had melted it to a vibrant green. Iris got out and knocked at the door. 'Mary, there's a car stopped outside, are we expecting visitors?' cried a voice from inside, and Mary bustled to open the door. Her face fell when she saw Iris.

'What's wrong, Iris, that you need to come looking for me?' She pointed at David, and he waved at her through the car window, 'And why have you brought him?' she asked.

'He drove me, I wanted to make sure you were safe. The roads are bad.'

'I know they're bad, it's why I'm still here, but it's melting now so I'll be coming back soon.'

'I don't know why I bother!' exclaimed Iris, when she was back in the car, 'She might just as well stay here.'

'Let her, it's the perfect solution, come away with me, Iris,' he took her hand, 'I'll look after you. I mean it; please, promise me you'll consider it at least.'

'Yes, alright, I'll consider it, I promise.' She pulled her hand away, 'I suppose it's time I went home now, I've got to get on with my knitting, after all, it's what we middle-aged ladies do.'

The snow had turned into rain and it was nearly dark when Mary returned. She was angry. 'That boy is too young for you; I've said it before, and I'll say it again. He reminds me of that half-wit who used to follow you home from school, hanging around when it was obvious you weren't interested.'

Iris smiled, remembering, 'You mean Ronan, Mary; and I'd have done well to stick with him.'

'You've half a brain, Iris Malone; I hope you've not been telling David all our business.'

'He saw us, Mary!' She wasn't sure why she said it.

'Saw what?' she asked, 'What did he see?'

'He saw us burying Fin.'

Mary's face paled and she grasped the edge of the table to stay upright.

'He was just five years old, that poor little boy. He was hiding in the bushes and he saw us.'

'Did he tell you that,' she asked, 'or was it you that put the idea in his head?'

'Why would I do that, Mary? I've as much to lose as you. He says we should leave, that if the police connect him to us we could be in trouble. He's promised me he won't tell anyone.'

'Well, that's nice of him,' she murmured, but there was a note of sarcasm in her voice. 'Think, Iris, just for a change! It can't be true, he'd have told someone at the time, it's just a lucky guess; he wants you to be beholden to him. Now why would that be, I wonder?

Anyway, they'd never believe him. Why would the police connect us to some nameless drifter who went missing all those years ago?'

'I want to find Angelica, Mary. I really want to find her, but David says…'

'Oh… David says… well, he's certainly got you fooled.'

'David says there's a test I can do, a DNA test, and if there's even the smallest chance that it means I can trace her, I want to do it.'

'Listen to me, Iris, and try to understand. If Angelica turns up it will be because she shares your DNA, and his! What if the police find out? He won't be some nameless tramp then, will he? They'll know exactly who he is; Finbar Delaney! He's sure to be on some missing list somewhere, in Ireland if not here, and then they'll be round here asking questions. Do you fancy the inside of a prison cell, Iris? No…! You didn't think of that did you? You never think; we wouldn't be in this situation if you did.'

'I'm a step ahead of you, Mary, I've already thought of that, it's why I think we should move away from here, then we won't need to worry. It's time we went; we've been here too long already.'

'I suppose he wants you to go away with him; is that what this is all about? And why would I leave? My life is here, how would Megan manage if I wasn't around, she's an old woman. Give up, Iris; you won't find your daughter now; she's grown, she doesn't need you anymore.'

'You're talking nonsense, Mary, and you're cruel. Of course, she needs me. You can stay here with Megan if you like, but does she know what you're growing out there in her greenhouse?'

'That's none of your business, Iris. Perhaps it's time we went our separate ways, we were always different, you and I.'

'Yes, I know that, Mary, we are very different, but we're used to each other after all this time and I'd probably miss you if you weren't around.'

'Don't worry, Iris,' she sighed, 'everything will be fine. I'll sort it out, I always have, and I always will.'

CHAPTER 39

BRISTOL

2019

Angelica

I decided to bring forward my trip to Bristol. It didn't feel right leaving Maura in the dark about my parentage, nor was it fair to inform her by email. I needed to see her, to explain, face to face, that her brother wasn't my father, and to ask her if she'd break the news to Don and apologise on my behalf for the trouble I'd caused.

Carolyn tried, frequently, to coax me out of it. 'They're nothing to you,' she said, 'so why are you bothered what they think?'

I didn't argue, I was certain she'd be the same in similar circumstances; not that she'd given any real thought to my problems as she was totally preoccupied with whether Jono's family would like her when she met them.

Roisin was even more opposed to my insistence that I visit Maura.

'Give it a rest, Angela,' she'd replied, when I told her I

was going, 'You've found your da, why can't you leave it at that?'

But I couldn't, not while Iris was out there; and maybe still looking for me.

Maura emailed to say that she'd be happy to meet me when I landed. It filled me anew with overwhelming feelings of guilt, as if I'd been responsible for everyone else's behaviour, when I was clearly the victim. I rehearsed the words I'd use when I told her, but it didn't help at all, and I began to wish I'd taken Carolyn's and Roisin's advice and just written.

Mr O'Donnell had managed to get me some last-minute tickets and I was leaving Dublin for Bristol at some ungodly hour. They were very cheap. He'd obviously considered that price was my main concern; after all, I didn't have a job, did I? And how was he to know about my nest-egg, tucked away in the bank? I was determined to get a taxi, Carolyn objected at first, insisting that they would drive me to the airport; she was less keen when she found out that I needed to be there before five in the morning.

I was leaving Ireland, for the first time in my life, and I couldn't decide whether I was excited, or terrified; both I suppose. The roar of the plane when we took off chilled me to the bone, and every thump, or sudden change in the engine noise, had me hanging on to the arms of my seat till my fingers started to cramp. I was terrified at the thought of all that space between me and the ground; it felt unnatural to be so high in the sky above snowfields of clouds, looking down over tiny green fields, and the Irish Sea, flat and calm, belying its currents and depths. We hit the runway with a bump that lifted me slightly from my seat and half frightened me to death, but I was there, and I could hardly believe any of us had made it in one piece.

The air felt fresh after the muggy warmth of the plane. I was one of the first in the queue and, before I knew it, I was out of the terminal and standing by the main doors, where Maura and I had agreed to meet. A small woman was waiting just outside, she looked up when she saw me and came straight over and kissed me on the cheek. 'You look just like your mother!' she exclaimed. I was starting to believe it!

I had a strong sense of déjà-vu as we drove off; just the week before it had been Neve driving me down the lanes of Cork, but this was England, and Maura wasn't Neve. Maura was small and well into her fifties, and the long black hair she'd sported in Don's photograph, was now short and grey. 'I'm sorry I haven't been able to help much,' she said, 'Fin was always a mystery, and if Iris was trying to hide from him, she'd never have told me where she was going for fear he'd find out.'
Tell her, tell her now! I said to myself, but I couldn't, it wasn't the right time; would there ever be a right time?
'It's good to meet you at last,' she added, in a soft Irish lilt that she'd never lost, 'I've waited twenty-five years,

and here you are, fit and well. At least they looked after you! When you went missing, we thought you'd gone for good! Children disappear all the time, it's depressing when you realise how often it happens!'

'Tell her now!' instructed the small voice in my head, and I opened my mouth to speak, but Maura picked up where she'd left off. 'I spoke to Don a few days back. He said he was happy you were coming to see me. He seems to have really taken to you, and your visits have perked up Mam no end. He said you looked just like Iris, but perhaps he could see something of Fin in you. I'm not sure that's a good thing, but maybe it's inevitable. He was your da, after all...'

I was beginning to feel sick. Why had I come? All I'd done was make things worse, more difficult than ever; and I'd given this woman some sort of hope that her family might be reunited. No, maybe that bit wasn't true; Don had never made the effort to keep in touch with his remaining brothers, so what difference would my unexpected appearance make to anyone?

'He says he spoke to the lads, Tommy and Declan, and James. You've brought us back together Angela. We've all been apart for far too long!'

I shut my mouth. Maybe I could escape, go missing again? I was panicking; I really needed to get out of the car!

We turned into a narrow cul-de-sac, lined with rows of modern detached houses. They looked quite new and were all identical, apart from small minor features, the addition of tiny porches, or doors and window frames painted in a variety of colours. Maura's house had a cherry-red door and a large tree in the front garden that was just showing signs of bursting back into life. 'Magnolia,' she announced when she saw me looking at it, 'it's gorgeous when it's in flower. Come in, would you like a cheese sandwich, Angelica, and a cup of tea?'

'Yes, I'd love a cup,' I replied, 'just one sugar, please; and a cheese sandwich would go down a treat.'

She set to work, cutting slices from a giant block of cheddar, and then the bread, until enough for half a dozen sandwiches formed a pile on the counter. 'Can I help you, Maura?' I asked, as she started on the lettuce, running it under the tap and separating the leaves. 'No, you just stay there,' she said, 'you'll be needing a rest after your early start.'

I sat in silence, should I break the news now, or wait until she'd put herself out even more? Would she be angry with me, and ask me why the hell I'd bothered to come? It couldn't go on, I knew that. The whole purpose of coming to see Maura was to tell her, to explain that we weren't related at all and, so far, I had failed abysmally.

'Maura,' I began, and she turned to smile at me. 'Have you something to say, Angie,' she said quietly, as if she half expected some important revelation.

I paused, trying to collect my thoughts, and she looked at me expectantly, 'Are you about to tell me that you've found Fin? Or Iris…?'

'No, it's nothing like that…' I took a deep breath, 'I have found my father, but… I'm sorry Maura, it's turned out that it wasn't Fin at all. It was a man called Ronan Kelly, I only found out myself this past week or I'd never have contacted you.'

Maura left the lettuce in the sink and came to sit down next to me; she didn't seem upset, or angry. She took my hand, 'Don't worry darlin', I can't say that I'm surprised; the saddest thing of all is that Iris ran off, and somehow, in all the violence and confusion, they managed to lose you. You could have written to tell me, I wouldn't have minded, but I'm glad you didn't because it's grand to see that you've survived it all and turned into a lovely young woman. I remember Ronan as a boy; he never looked as though he had it in him to father a child.'

'He's a good-looking man now,' I told her, 'and very rich, and successful. He has two daughters, so I've got two sisters; can you imagine what it's like to suddenly discover you have sisters?'

Maura got up and went back to washing the lettuce, 'I always resented the fact that I just had brothers, you're very lucky it's turned out so well for you. Thank you for coming to tell me, I'd have been disappointed not to see you.'

There, it was done, and I felt better immediately. 'It's the first time I've been out of Ireland,' I said conversationally, 'I never had a passport before. Where I'd come from was always a secret. I didn't find out who I was until Patrick died.'

She handed me a mug of tea and a plate of tiny cheese sandwiches with the crusts cut off. 'Oh, how silly of me, I'm so sorry, I wasn't thinking,' she burst into peals of laughter, 'my granddaughter prefers her bread without crusts. Lucy says I spoil her, but that's what you do when you're a grandmother.'

'Will you see your mam soon?' I asked, 'Only, I don't think she'll be around much longer.'

She nodded, 'Yes, I will, she looked so poorly in the photo you sent, and Don says I need to go before she forgets who I am completely.'

'It's Fin she really wants to see,' I said, and immediately regretted it. How could I have been so insensitive? 'She wants to see you too,' I added quickly, 'it's just that Fin has disappeared... and she worries about him; he was her youngest, her baby.'

'I know; don't worry, Angie, I'm not offended... she always was protective of him, it destroyed her when she lost him. I don't think it really matters how old they are, they're always your children. You'll find that out soon enough.'

Well, at least some good had come from my meddling. I'd brought Maura and her mother back together, before it was too late.

She shook her head, 'So you're Ronan Kelly's girl...! You know, I wondered why there were no little Fin Delaneys running around Dublin. He was always after chasing the girls, and they couldn't resist him. He broke their hearts, though he didn't really deserve the attention; he was my brother, but he wasn't a nice man and, I hate to say it, but he was cruel and selfish; you were protected from that, at least. Perhaps I'm being unfair; he might have been entirely different if he'd had a child of his own.'

We got on well, me and Maura, and it disappointed me in a way that we weren't related, but then maybe that wasn't necessary, we could still be friends. How many relatives does anyone actually need? And I already had a long list, even if most of them were third, fourth and distant. She said that her husband, Peter, would be in from work early because he was anxious to meet me, the long-lost niece, but that she would explain about the confusion so I wouldn't have to go through it all again. I was grateful for that. Her children were called Mark, Lucy and Siobhan, and Lucy would be coming over later for tea, with little Deirdre who was just three, and named for her mother.

Her mother, the old woman, wrapped in blankets, who relied on an over-friendly cat for company, and Mrs Shaunessy, who came in once a week to give her a bath. Why hadn't Don told me her name was Deirdre, reputedly the most beautiful princess in ancient Ireland? I supposed it was because she'd become old and of no consequence, and therefore no longer worthy of even a name.

'I hope you'll visit Ireland soon,' I said, 'she'd love to see you, and I know Don would.'

'I will do, it's been too long…' she stopped fussing with the pots and sat down again, 'thank you, Angie for reminding me. I'd like to see her, it's just… well, you know how it is; time goes by so fast…'

Her words reminded me of Aileen's. You think you have all the time in the world, but you don't realise how little you have until it's almost gone… 'It's not your fault, Maura,' I murmured, 'it's the same for us all, there's just never enough time. You just can't get off the carousel.'

She laughed, but I wasn't sure if she knew what I meant. 'It's from a song,' I explained, 'about how we've no choice, time passes, we get old, and all we can do is make the best of the time we have.'

I was starting to depress myself; when did I get to be so philosophical?

Lucy and Deirdre arrived soon after and we went to play in the garden. The sun was out but it was still cold, though Deirdre didn't appear to notice at all, she careered up and down after the ball with not a care in the world and I ran after her. Lucy couldn't, she was heavily pregnant. Did I need a child, I wondered, to show me how to enjoy life again?

CHAPTER 40

I was worn out when I went to bed. It was warm and comfortable, and deadly quiet, yet still I was awake until the early hours. My brain stubbornly refused to shut down, preferring instead to replay my life, and particularly the last few months, in fast forward, until I pressed the pause button; then it would shoot off at a tangent and I'd be more agitated than ever. Fin dominated my thoughts. It seemed that, despite his good looks and numerous girlfriends, there were no little 'accidents'; perhaps he'd realised, and that was that why he was so angry with Iris? Or maybe he was just desperate to hang onto me because I was the only child he truly believed was his. Only they would be able to tell me, but I wasn't looking for Fin, just Iris; maybe, one day, Iris would tell me.

In the end, I got up, what was the point of lying there tormenting myself? I looked in the mirror; my hair was a dirty yellow in the lamplight, and it needed a cut. I was neglecting myself, getting up every day and putting on the same old clothes, alternating between two pairs of jeans, wondering whether to wear the blue pair or the black, but not really caring either way. I went to the window and drew back the curtains; the houses on the opposite side were dark monoliths in the orange streetlights; it seemed strangely familiar somehow, I could be in any light polluted street. Did any of it really matter in the scheme of things, who you were, or where you were?

I could hear Peter snoring in his bed next to Maura, it reminded me of home when Patrick and Aileen were alive before everything became so complicated. When was that? I wasn't sure; before I'd started to ask questions, I supposed, before I met Conor, and long before Patrick died prematurely in the middle of the road. I thought back over the day, how Maura had welcomed me, and my reluctance to tell her the truth. She hadn't minded in the end; it was almost as if she expected it.

I was starting to shiver, so I went back to bed. Tomorrow I'd move on, it was always the plan. I'd stay the one night and then take the train down to Somerset, or Devon; I might even get as far as Cornwall. I'd have four whole days before making my way back to Bristol for the late flight.

Maura had invited me to stay longer but I didn't want to impose further. She was nothing to me and I really shouldn't have been there at all, according to Carolyn and Roisin. They were wrong as it turned out, because I liked her, and her family. My purpose had been to discover where I belonged and felt truly welcome, and I'd succeeded. I had a family, a father, and two sisters, and, if I wanted, a home in County Cork. I could stop this now and take up their offer of a normal family life; why was I even hesitating? What did Carolyn call it, 'a goose-chase'? It was true, I was on a goose-chase for a woman I didn't remember and would probably never find, and it had to end now.

It was raining; I could hear it pattering on the roof, gentle at first and then louder, flooding the gutters until they overflowed. I left the curtains open and watched the fat droplets running down the glass; it was soothing, hypnotic, almost. I made the decision to leave in the morning. On Tuesday I would fly back to Dublin and get my life in order. I slept then.

Roisin rang me at seven. I wasn't pleased; it felt as though I'd just dropped off.

'Is everything alright,' was my immediate response. I'd become accustomed to catastrophe, and surely a phone call so early in the morning indicated that something was amiss.

'No, all fine, more than fine actually…' she said, 'I had to call, I'm sorry if I woke you. The postman has just been.'

She woke me up to tell me the postman had just been!

'I got a letter, from Christy, in Canada… Angela, I think that Iris might be in Wales! …Angie, are you still there…?'

I was shaking. 'Yes, still here, Roisin… just in shock; tell me, where is she? Is it definitely her?'

'Don't get your hopes up, Angela, not yet. It might not be her… Are you there, Angie…?'

'Yes, yes, of course I am, I'm listening, don't stop, what did Christy say?'

'She said she found the blanket online. She was going to ask them to send it direct to Ireland, which would have made the most sense; then she decided to order one for another friend in Canada, so she asked if they'd send them directly to her. She said she needed to see it first anyway before it came to William.'

I'd calmed down slightly by the time she'd finished her long, drawn-out, and largely irrelevant, explanation. At least it had given my heart the chance to slow to about a hundred beats a minute, and my adrenalin surge was no longer threatening to give me a stroke.

'So, Roisin,' I managed to gasp, 'is her name Iris, and where exactly is she?'

The line began to crackle, and I panicked anew at the prospect of being cut off, but she was still there; 'Christy says there's a website. I haven't had the chance to look at it myself, not yet. I've got a job, so I'm a bit rushed; sorry about the unnecessary details… are you having a good time in England, Angela?'

I was beginning to lose patience, 'Yes, Roisin, it's great… but where will I find the website? What's it under?'

'It's under 'Morgans Croft Baby Gifts'. There's a photograph, of a large house, and a woman, she looks like you, only older, and her name is Iris. I've got to go; Google it!' And she was gone!

I turned on the search engine and in just a few seconds the information was at my fingertips, informing me that, 'the perfect gift for a new arrival, hand-knitted and lovingly embroidered...' was there to be purchased at just the click of a switch. I skipped to the bottom of the page and studied the images. There were several different versions in various colours, some were more intricately knitted and included birthdates and well as names, but basically, they were just baby shawls and I was amazed at their popularity. Other pictures were of an exquisite country house, surrounded by clipped hedges and perfectly pruned roses, Morgans Croft. Iris must certainly have come up in the world if that was where she lived. Lastly, there was a photograph of a woman who resembled me, though I doubted she was old enough to be my mother. She looked a great deal younger than Aileen in her latter years, but then Iris had been little more than a girl when she gave birth to me, so I suppose she was.

'Iris has been creating her perfect gifts for new-borns for more than twenty years', read the blurb, and it went on at length about how the wool was garnered from happy Welsh sheep, and the silk from organically-fed silkworms. It was all predictable stuff, dreamed up to persuade the customer to part with their money.

It had to be her! The contact details gave only an

email address and an order form. I wondered briefly if I should email, but how would it sound? 'Hi, Iris, I think I might be your daughter', what if it wasn't her? No, emailing wasn't an option, I'd go; I'd turn up on the doorstep and surprise her, there'd be no doubt in my mind then, and if it wasn't her, I'd order a knitted blanket for Maura's forthcoming grandchild.

Maura and Peter were already up. 'Did y' sleep well?' she queried when I staggered in. Her expression changed from smiles to concern when she saw my crumpled white face, as it was evident I hadn't. 'Eggs and bacon?' she asked cheerfully. 'You look like you could do with feeding up; she does, doesn't she, Peter? Why don't you stay a bit longer, let me look after you?' He raised his eyebrows, 'Leave her alone, Maura, she's old enough to have children of her own to care for. She should have had ten kids, Angie, or a farmyard, she's never happier than when she's feeding strays!'

'I think I might have found Iris, in Wales,' said the stray, 'some remote village in the mountains. Thanks for everything, Maura; I'd love to stay longer, maybe another time if that's okay?'

She stopped frying and turned to look at me, suddenly oblivious to the splattering fat in the pan, 'You've found her? Well, you'll still need a decent breakfast before you go, and I'll do you a packed lunch. It's wonderful news, Angelica! I really hope it's her. Will you let me know as soon as you find out? Here you eat this now, and then I'll drop you at the station.'

CHAPTER 41

We left soon after. I hadn't managed to eat any breakfast; my nerves were too ragged to even contemplate eating. We waited a while to allow a black car to pass; it slowed when it reached the end of the cul-de-sac, and I watched as it reversed and circled, before coming to rest at the kerb. Maura pulled out into the road and turned left. 'It's been great having you here, Angie,' she murmured, 'and good luck with finding this place; Peter reckons it's in the middle of nowhere.'

It was, I'd studied the Google map and discovered that Morgans Croft was at the edge of a tiny village, tucked between Snowdonia and the coast. I could hardly contain my excitement; had I really found Iris? It seemed likely, but lingering doubts remained. In an odd way I was pleased that they did, because then I wouldn't be too disappointed, too hurt, if Roisin was wrong. What if it was a coincidence, and there was another woman called Iris, who looked like me, and who made identical shawls to the one I was found in? But it seemed unlikely and I brushed my fears aside; surely it was fine for me to be optimistic, just for a change.

Maura stopped in a spot near the entrance to the station. She got out of the car and wished me a tearful goodbye, insisting that I stay in touch, and to contact her if I needed help at any time. I hugged her tight and waved until she was out of sight. Almost immediately, a black car turned into the car park and reversed into the space she'd just vacated; it looked like the car I'd seen earlier. A man got out, he was wearing sunglasses, yet there was something vaguely familiar about him. He smiled and nodded when I let him go ahead of me, then murmured politely, 'please, after you…' when we reached the front of the queue.

I'd written the address on a piece of paper, so I took it out of my bag and held it up against the glass of the ticket window.

'Can you tell me the best way to get to here?' I asked, 'I'm not sure how you pronounce it.'

The booking clerk laughed politely and squinted at it, and me, through the security glass and her wire framed spectacles. 'I'll have a look for you, dear… Bear with me… Right, you need to go to Pwllheli, change in Birmingham. Not sure after that, taxi, I suppose; must say, I've never heard of it! If you hurry, you'll catch the ten thirty. Do you want a single, or a return?'

'Single, please;' I said, 'I'm not sure when I'll be coming back.'

I paid and turned to make my way to the platform; about five or six people were waiting in the line behind me, but he was nowhere to be seen and I felt relieved, though I wasn't sure why.

The train was almost empty; I sat down next to a window and opened my bag to investigate Maura's packed lunch. Rather unsurprisingly, there were cheese and lettuce sandwiches, along with some biscuits and a couple of apples; I took one out and bit into it. I was feeling more relaxed, I was on my way, I just had to quash my expectations, the disappointment would be too much to bear if I was wrong. I consoled myself with the thought that soon I would know for sure; in just over an hour I'd be in Birmingham and nearly there. My mobile rang, it was Maura, and her voice was shaking. 'I've got to warn you, Angie, I saw Declan; he was driving into the car park as I left. He looked straight at me or I wouldn't have noticed him. At first, I thought I'd imagined it, but I just spoke to Don and he said they'd been in contact and he told him you were coming to visit me. He must have arrived here just as we were leaving and followed us to the station. Did you see him? Is he on the train?'

I peered around, taking care that no one noticed. 'Yes, I did; it was him in the black car, wasn't it?'

Maura's voice faltered, 'Yes, that was him.'

'Well he's not in this carriage, Maura. Are you sure it was Declan?'

'Yes, I've no doubt. I'd know him anywhere, he's hardly changed.'

I slid down further into my seat and my apple fell to the floor and rolled away. 'What shall I do?' I asked her.

'Oh my God, Angie, I'm afraid for you! Just watch out; hopefully, you've lost him.'

I lowered my voice to a whisper, 'Maybe he just wants to meet me? Look, don't worry, I'll let you know if he turns up, but I doubt he will…'

I put my lunch back in my bag and zipped it up, surely if he only wanted to meet me, he'd have introduced himself. I considered walking the length of the train, wouldn't it be better to confront him, to ask him why he was following me, if indeed he was? I was shaking, I stood up and walked to the connecting doors on unsteady feet, jolting and swaying with the motion of the speeding train. My head was spinning, what was I thinking? I couldn't confront this man, far better to keep a low profile, and no wonder he'd looked familiar, he reminded me of Don; they were both good looking men, even though they were no longer young. I sat down again and took a magazine out of my bag, burying my face in its pages, peering over the top from time to time, and jumping out of my skin every time someone came through from another carriage. I was on the verge of collapse by the time we rattled into Birmingham.

I let everyone get off in front of me and finally alighted, glancing warily up and down, before scuttling to hide behind a kiosk. I peeped out, quickly pulling my head back when I saw the figure standing at the far end of the platform, it was him. I looked again to be certain, and then, slinging my bag over one shoulder, I made my way to where he was standing. Nothing would happen to me in a busy station, there were too many people around. I'd ask him why he was following me, wasn't it possible that he just wanted to question me, to ask me if I'd managed to find his brother, or Iris? Maybe he did just want to meet me, but that seemed unlikely, he'd already had that opportunity and let it pass.

He was reading a newspaper, so he didn't notice when I came up behind him. I hovered, reluctant to stand between him and the train line, a furtive shove and I'd be under a train, though why he'd want to harm me I couldn't fathom. I cleared my throat, and he swung round to look at me. I took a step back, it wasn't him, I'd been mistaken; relief flooded through me, making me light-headed all over again. This man was younger, though of a similar build. 'Can I help you,' he asked, 'you look worried.' He had a nice face. 'I'm sorry,' I replied, 'it's just that…' he smiled at me, encouragingly, 'I thought you were someone else, from a distance. I'm really sorry I've bothered you.'

'Seriously, I'm not bothered,' he had a Welsh accent, 'you can bother me any time. Are you waiting for the train to Pwllheli?'

I nodded, somehow unable to find my voice, and walked quickly away, painfully aware that my cheeks were red with embarrassment, and relief. He must have thought I was trying to pick him up. He'd seemed okay, and company would have been reassuring, especially if Declan was following me, but I'd felt too agitated, and confused, to continue the conversation.

I saw him again when we arrived at Pwllheli; not Declan, just his younger look-a-like, he waved at me and went off towards the car park, and I regretted the way I'd reacted when he asked me where I was going. So what if he thought I found him attractive, he was, and he obviously thought I was too, the journey would have been far more enjoyable if I'd been friendlier.
Was I in the early stages of paranoia? I hadn't seen Declan on the train, or on the platform, so maybe he'd given up. I went back into the station and sat down on a bench to eat my lunch, I hadn't eaten since the night before and I was starting to get palpitations. I needed to prepare myself for the last lap of my journey, and for whatever lay ahead at my final destination.

CHAPTER 42
WALES
2019

'No, I don't go as far as that,' said the first taxi driver, when I showed him the address, 'it's not worth my while, it's too far out, and I won't get a fare back. You need Evan, he lives out that way, and he's just come in. See, he's over there, in that blue Honda.'

Evan seized my tiny case and threw it onto the back seat of the car, then he opened the door to the front passenger seat and indicated that I should get in.

'You were lucky to find me,' he muttered, in an accent I could barely comprehend, 'most of the drivers prefer short runs, and I don't blame them, but there aren't many people about, not yet, so I'm glad of the fare. Come Easter they'll be here, they like the beaches. Did you say it's Morgans Croft, you're wanting? That'll be old Megan; she's been up here all her life. Is she a friend of yours?'

'Yes,' I replied, it was easier to agree, 'but it's Iris I'm here to see.'

'Oh yes, Iris... must be a relative of yours, you look

very alike.'

My hopes soared, 'Everyone says so. She's my mother.' The words seemed strange, unnatural, I hoped I was right.'

'Daughter… well that's news to me, I never knew there was a daughter. She'll be pleased to see you. What's your name?'

'I'm Angelica,' I murmured, and suddenly it seemed real.

'I am Angelica.' I said it again, quietly, just to see how it sounded.

Is that what I'd say when I met her?

'And Mary would be your aunt, I suppose?'

'Yes, I suppose she would. Is she here too?'

'She's been here for as long as I can remember...'

We travelled along empty roads, under a sky that was purple and forbidding. Evan drove fast, with a confidence borne out of familiarity, and I cringed at his cavalier attitude towards the sharp bends, and the way the road sometimes seemed to drop off into oblivion.

It would be nearly dark when I arrived. To my right the fields stretched away into the distance, where lights from isolated homesteads glinted out of the gathering gloom. On my left, the land rose, a mass of oppressive, irregular shapes and sharp, ridges of slate. We climbed higher still, until the land rose on both sides and the road began to wind and twist, and I was just wondering whether to ask if I could move into the back with my case, where I might feel less vulnerable, when I saw ahead of us, a row of tiny, grey cottages, huddled against the hillside like snails upon a wall. Further along, bigger houses, with long hedges and driveways, occupied a small plateau and dominated the lane with their presence. 'Holiday homes,' said my all-knowing chauffeur, 'though not many people live up here when the weather's bad. Iris and Mary are at the other end of the village, just before the lane up to Megan's. We'll be there soon.'

The light had gone now, disappeared early, behind the glowering peaks. He stopped outside a small cottage; it looked welcoming, as if it were waiting for me, Angelica, to saunter up the path. We got out of the car and he reached into the back for my bag and handed it to me.

'Let me know if you need a ride back,' he said, then he got in, and drove away.

I stood by the gate, reluctant to open it, suddenly terrified. What if it wasn't her? Or worse, what if she didn't want me? But I had to find out. What else could I do, short of running down the lane after Evan? And at the speed he drove, he'd be miles away already. I was rooted to the spot, unable to move, but my heart was galloping, and I couldn't catch my breath. A spot of rain fell on my head, followed by several more, then the wind lifted, shaking me from my torpor and I ran down the narrow path and banged on the door. A woman opened it and peeped out, 'Mary, is that you?' she murmured. She clung to the door for support when she saw me, and the mug she was holding fell to the floor and broke, splashing the contents down her front and over her shoes.

I wasn't sure why I noticed these details; they weren't important. I couldn't speak, I just watched as she buried her face in her hands; Iris, who was my height, and slender, though thinner than me, and with hair that was the same colour as mine, piled on top of her head in an untidy knot.

'Hello, Mam, I'm Angelica...' They were the words I'd practiced countless times, but now they seemed out of place, presumptuous even.

'Angelica...' she said it so quietly that it barely registered in my confused brain. 'Angelica, is it really you?'

Tears were running down my cheeks, 'Yes, Mam, it's really me.'

We hugged then, and it was just as I imagined it would be. I was home, the stolen baby returned to its mother.

It had only taken twenty-five years.

CHAPTER 43

We were in the kitchen when Mary came home.
'Iris...!' she yelled, 'Why is there tea all over the floor and up the wall?'
'Never mind the tea, Mary, it doesn't matter...' replied Iris, 'and close your eyes, I've a surprise for you. Are they closed yet?'
'What nonsense is this, Iris? Have you lost your mind?'
'Just close your eyes...'
'Alright, they're closed; get on with it, it's late, and I haven't eaten!'
Iris took my hand and led me out of the kitchen. 'You can open them now, Mary.'
I was stunned by her reaction; her overriding expression was one of shock, as if I'd materialised, ghostlike, from the walls; perhaps she thought I had.
'Mother of God...!' she cried as soon as she'd recovered enough to speak, 'Angelica, is it you?' She reached forward to stroke my arm and then pulled it away again, as if she'd been scalded.
'How did you find her, Iris?' she asked, 'Didn't we agree to let things be?'
'I didn't find her, Mary; she found us. Isn't it amazing?'
'I suppose it is,' she answered grudgingly, 'if it stops

you making a fool of yourself with that boy next door.'

'What's the matter?' I asked her, 'Aren't you pleased that I'm here?'

Iris put her arms around me protectively. 'You should be happier than any of us, Mary, since you were the one that lost her in the first place.'

'That's unfair, Iris, I was only trying to hide her. Have you told her yet, how he tried to take her from you, and how he'd beat you as soon as look at you?' She turned her attention away from Iris and looked at me, 'Ask her, about the evil man that was your father, and the way he treated her; and why we left Ireland.' Her face softened, 'I'm sorry, Angelica, what kind of a welcome is this? I'm relieved that you're alive and well, I've often doubted it.'

'Fin wasn't my father…' I waited for a reaction, but neither of them spoke. It was as if the world had stopped. I could still hear the rain, hammering down on the roof, but we were enveloped in a smothering silence, while my words were considered, and rejected.

Mary broke the silence. 'You must be as mad as your mother, girl! Of course he was your father, though I've always wished he wasn't. There was no one else, was there, Iris?'

'I always, thought he was…' she whispered.

'You thought! What do you mean you thought? Surely you know?'

'I assumed he was,' she looked at me, 'what makes you

think he wasn't?'

'Because I've met my father; his name is Ronan. He remembers you fondly, Iris.'

'Ronan...' her voice was barely audible and as soft as a sigh, 'you're Ronan's child, not... his? I'm so sorry, Angelica...'

Then I told them about Roisin's baby blanket, and how it had led me to Morgans Croft, and Iris; and the story of my life, about Aileen, and Patrick, and how I'd found Fin's brother and sister, and the old woman that I'd believed, erroneously, to be my grandmother. Lastly, I described how I had found Ronan, and how kind he was, and how happy I'd been to discover that I had two sisters, after always being an only child.

To say that they were overjoyed by the news would be an understatement. For some reason, Mary seemed particularly delighted that I wasn't related to Fin Delaney. I would find out why before too long.

They had very little to tell me, only that Mary had left me in the field so that Fin couldn't take me, and when she went back, I'd gone. Other than that, I learned that Kathleen had died and was buried nearby, but I knew there would be more to come; so many years had passed so it was inevitable that there would be. As it was, we were all beyond exhausted, and I was shown to Kathleen's room, where I fell into a deep sleep as soon as my head touched the pillow.

CHAPTER 44

I couldn't work out where I was, not straight away. The window was small, and misted over, and I was too hot. I sat up and kicked off the covers, gazing around in disbelief. Was I really here, deep in some remote Welsh valley? How could this be happening? Had I really found Iris, or was I in the middle of some lucid dream, come as a salve to my troubled mind, to protect me from insanity? I shook myself, still unsure, and gazed around me. A long table stood under the window, covered in a mishmash of coloured wools and threads and assorted paraphernalia. A sewing machine sat at one end, and a pile of newly made blankets at the other, no doubt waiting to be completed. My mobile pinged, it was Maura, and I realised I had forgotten to let her know I'd arrived.

'Angie, are you there yet?' it asked, somewhat impatiently, and 'Have you any news?' I returned her text straight away, feeling incredibly guilty that it had slipped my mind the previous evening.

'I'm really sorry, Maura, I should have let you know as soon as I got here, it's unforgiveable of me. It's just that it's all been so overwhelming. Iris IS my mother, I can't believe it, and she's amazing! No sign of Declan, so all well. More soon…'

Unfortunately, my optimism would turn out to be misplaced, though I didn't know that at the time. Then I dashed off three identical texts, to Ronan, Carolyn, and Roisin, 'Have found Iris!!! She's wonderful!!! All well, speak soon! Angie.'

I went downstairs. Mary was already up and dressed, and I wondered if she'd been to bed. Her eyelids were heavy, as if she wasn't quite awake, and her pupils were over-large. She was cheerful enough though.

'You seemed concerned that I'd found you,' I said, 'why was that, Mary? Aren't you happy that I'm back?'

'Oh, I am, Angelica, I'm very pleased; it was the shock, sure it was. It's grand that you're here. Your mother never got over your loss, it ruined her life, and mine because I've always blamed myself, though when I left you it was with the best of intentions. I thought you'd be safe, how could I know…?' she stopped mid-sentence, as if she couldn't bear to continue.

Her Dublin accent hadn't diminished over the years, but I wondered if listening to me had revitalised it. It suited her; she reminded me a lot of old Mrs Shaunessy, big, and rather overbearing, but capable, and soft-hearted beneath her bossy exterior. 'Help y'self to breakfast,' she added, 'Iris only gets up when she feels like it.' Then she made her excuses and went upstairs.

Almost as soon as she'd gone, Iris wafted down. Her steps were delicate; the stairs didn't creak and complain, like they did when Mary went up them.

'Megan must have had visitors,' she exclaimed, 'how strange.'

I turned to look as a large, black car went past the cottage, then reversed to stop outside. 'Declan…!' I gasped, 'Quick, Iris, we've got to hide!'

'Declan...?' Her face changed at the mention of his name, only her lips moved, and her hand as it reached for mine. 'Declan...' she murmured again; then she turned to stare at me, accusingly, as if I'd betrayed her.

I shook my head frantically, 'I didn't tell him, Iris, you have to believe me!'

I glanced back at the front door, and reached for the lock, but Iris was gripping my arm, and pulling me across the room towards the kitchen, and I wondered how she had managed to recover so quickly when just moments before she'd seemed on the verge of collapse. Declan was on the path, and then he was turning the door handle, tentatively, as though testing to see if it would open.

'Quick, the back door,' she cried, 'David will help us!' She fumbled with the key, 'Get the bolt, undo the bolt…!' but it was too late, he was there, standing in the doorway.

Iris glared at him insolently, defiantly, her arms folded across her chest, almost as if she were daring him to threaten her in some way, and he glared back.

'How did you find me, Declan?' she asked.

'I was at the station, and there she was, waving her little bit of paper around, asking how to get here.'

He smiled at me, creepily, and a shudder ran down my back.

'Why do you think I let you go in front of me? Morgans Croft, I read it when you took it from your bag; it was easy to find, even if it is at the arse-end of nowhere. You should have been more careful, Angie; or is it Angelica, now that you've found your ma? Do y' know, I thought I'd have to force it out of Maura, but it wasn't necessary, I didn't have to bother, what with you being so obliging. Oh, and by the way, I never laid a finger on Hanna; fire was Fin's speciality, I had nothing to do with that, and Megan, was more than happy to tell me where to find you, when I explained how you were my long lost, and much missed, sister-in-law, our little Iris...' he wiped a fake tear from his eye,

Iris smiled, 'Fin isn't here, Declan, and I was never your sister-in-law, as if I'd have married the bastard! Don't you think I'd tell you if I knew where he was?'

'Oh, y' would, would you? You'll tell me now, Iris, or I'll make sure you do.' His voice was quiet... menacing... 'Fin would never have left without telling his mother where he was going. You're not as innocent as you look, Iris, you never were; so, where is he? What have you done with my brother?'

'Leave her alone!' I screamed, 'She's told you; she doesn't know where he is! Anyway, he wasn't my father!'

I saw a flash of uncertainty cross his face, then his eyes narrowed, and he laughed. 'Who is your father, Angelica, if not Fin?'

I could see Mary through the open kitchen door, she was just rounding the bottom stair, creeping silently, stealthily, closer, and closer, with an agility that denied her bulk, until she was standing behind Declan. She held a claw-hammer, and I watched as she lifted it, slowly, gathering her strength, so as to make the maximum impact.

I covered my eyes, dreading the blood, and the cracking of bone, but there was nothing; just a surprised gasp from Mary as someone caught her raised arm and wrestled the hammer from her grip.

'David…' cried Iris, and she pushed past Declan, and threw herself into his arms.

'Fin, wasn't my father,' I shouted again, 'and we don't know where he is, or what became of him.'

'Really, is that so?' said Declan softly, 'Well, I don't believe you, or them! You're a violent woman, Mary. I always said you were; attacking me with a hammer indeed. You'll not get away with it; I'll see that you don't.'

She stood next to him, and I noticed how shrunken and pathetic he seemed, compared to her. 'Enough of your threats, Declan. You're lucky that David came in when he did, or I'd have made sure you couldn't come back. You don't frighten me; you don't frighten me at all; now just go while you still can, before I change my mind.'

We heard the roar of the engine as he drove off. He was going too fast for the narrow lane, and part of me hoped he would miscalculate on one of the sharper bends and soar down to the bottom of the valley.

Iris was shaking, 'He'll be back,' she whispered, 'he's only pretending to be gone. He'll come back when we're sleeping, we should never have concealed Fin's death. We should never have buried him, Mary.'

'Be quiet, Iris,' hissed Mary, she glanced at David, and then at me, and laughed, 'as if we'd conceal a death; no one knows where Fin is.'

'Stop lying,' said David, 'we know where he is! He's in the morgue awaiting burial. You can't hide the truth, Mary; not any longer, it's time you confessed.'

'There's nothing to connect us to him... He wasn't even her father; he was just a tramp who fell in the ditch, and anyway, he's gone now!'

I was confused, what were they saying? Who was lying in the morgue awaiting burial, surely not Fin?

David spoke first, 'You have to tell her Iris, you have to tell Angelica.'

'What...? What must you tell me?' I asked. I looked at Mary, then Iris, and finally David.

It was David who answered. 'They buried him here, in the garden, but they didn't kill him; at least, I don't think they did.'

Mary shook her head, 'We didn't kill him; it was Kathleen, God rest her soul, and she didn't mean it, she was defending Iris. He found us. He killed Megan's sister to find out where we were hiding; burnt her bookshop to the ground, with her in it! And now she turns up, after all these years, and informs us that he wasn't her father! You might at least have told me, Iris, even if there was only the slightest doubt.'

I felt numb, I'd found my mother but, in the process, I'd stumbled into a morass of fear, and deception, and... murder...

'Ronan was there for me when I needed someone,' murmured Iris, 'someone who wouldn't judge me.'

'Oh, and I suppose I would...'

'You always judge me, Mary; you're judging me now!'

'But what about Fin,' I asked, 'how did he come to be buried in the garden? Wouldn't it have been easier just to explain how he'd killed Megan's sister, and made you fear for your lives? You should have told them the whole story when it happened; no one would have blamed you.'

Mary sighed, 'Don't you understand? We were still afraid of Declan. He would have made sure we suffered if he'd found out we'd murdered his brother.'

My head was spinning, if they'd killed and buried Fin

then why was he in the morgue?'

'We hid ourselves away here, hoping no one would find us...' explained Iris, 'and Fin was gone for good, buried in the copse. We worried for a while that he might have told one of his brothers where we were, but time passed, and we accepted that we were safe, until...'

'Until he rose from the earth entwined in the roots of a tree...' finished Mary, and I recoiled at her words, 'they didn't know who he was; and no one had reported him missing, no one cared... us least of all!'

I realised then why Mary had been so shocked by my arrival. There had been nothing to connect them to the dead man, until I arrived and provided them with the link, because I would have shared DNA with both Fin and Iris; except I didn't, because Fin wasn't my father. They would have got away with it if I hadn't stupidly led Declan to them. Declan, who would go to the police and insist that the bones belonged to his brother, and that Iris was his common-law wife.

'You have to go to the police first,' I said, 'to explain, before Declan gives his side of the story. They'll be lenient with you; it was Kathleen who killed him, not you, Mary, or Iris. You were just trying to protect your elderly mother from prosecution.'

I'd said the wrong thing.

'Elderly...!' she glared at me accusingly, 'She wasn't much older than I am now so how would her age have been any excuse?'

'Then what's your excuse, Mary?' I asked her, 'If David hadn't arrived, we'd likely be burying Declan in the garden, at this very moment.'

'I'll put the kettle on,' said Iris.

'Yes,' I murmured, 'let's have a nice cup of tea and then we can forget that any of it happened.' I looked at David; he'd hardly said a word, 'David, you tell them, please. It's time to end this. We can't be party to murder, or concealment.'

Mary glared at me, 'You should never have come here; all you've done is dredge up the past. Declan wouldn't have found us if you hadn't led him here.'

'No, Mary, I knew,' he said quietly, 'didn't Iris tell you? I was watching when you buried him.'

'She did, but I didn't believe her. So, it was never a secret after all, not really, I got that wrong. It's time I left, I've work to do in the greenhouse, Megan is expecting me. Iris, you'd better decide where we go from here, I'm over making the decisions, and tired of taking the blame for your stupidity, I've better things to occupy me. Just let me know what you decide.'

We stood in silence in the kitchen, me, Iris, and David, the person whom Mary had referred to as 'that boy next door', although he wasn't a boy, he was older than me. Maybe Mary was jealous; perhaps she'd always been jealous. I had nothing to add; everything I said would be superfluous, or damaging, if that were at all possible; though how could I make it worse than it already was?

I felt in the way.

'I'm going upstairs to cancel my flight,' I said finally, 'in case I need to give evidence.' The idea terrified me.

When I went downstairs an hour, or so, later, they'd gone. I'd heard Iris climbing the ladder to her attic room, but she'd come down again almost immediately. They must have left by the back door, Iris and David, heading over the fields, to narrow paths that led high into the hills. I wondered if Iris might decide to finish it there, one last dramatic finale to her troubled life. I doubted it though, because I suspected that, despite her fragile exterior, she was a survivor, and she would fight to the end in any way she could.

I called Maura after that, to tell her that Declan had found us. I couldn't believe how naïve I'd been to think I'd managed to shake him off in Bristol; and how idiotic not to realise he was standing behind me when I bought my ticket. 'You're not to blame yourself,' she said, 'I'm surprised he went to so much trouble. Why would anyone keep all that anger inside them for so long?'

'Maybe he was right to be angry,' I replied. I wondered then if I should tell her the whole story. I'd almost forgotten that Fin was her brother, because she was so different to the rest of them, although I hadn't met Tommy and James, and now I'd never need to.

'Fin is dead though, isn't he?' she asked. It was as if, in some way, she already knew.

'Yes, Maura, I'm sorry, Fin has been dead for a long while, and I need to tell you everything because he was your brother, I owe you that.'

I told her then, how he'd torched Hanna's house to find out where Iris had gone, and how Kathleen had killed him with a hammer, just as Mary would have killed Declan, had David not intervened. She seemed to take it remarkably well, but then I suppose she'd separated herself from them all long ago, because they frightened her too. 'I'm sad for you, Angelica,' she murmured, when I'd finished, 'you must have longed for a normal life, to be re-united with your mother, and your father, though it's turned out to be anything but normal, and perhaps you're wishing you'd let things be.'

'No Maura, quite the opposite. I had no choice. Aileen and Patrick were loving parents, but they stole me from Iris, and I didn't even exist until recently, not officially; and I'd never have found out that Ronan was my real father. And I'd never have met you! I'm happy to have found Iris; whatever happens we'll have closure.'

I said goodbye then, promising to get back to her as things progressed. After that I called Ronan, but he was at work, so I told Neve instead, and she said how excited she was that I'd found my mother, and she'd ask him to call me when he got home.

I needed to talk, to hear the voices of others who would sympathise, and reassure me that all would be well.

Iris was still out with David. He'd be consoling her with calm words, telling her over and over, how it was nothing to do with her, she was simply a victim of circumstance. She was, but so was I. As for Mary, would she be relating the entire saga to Megan? Or ensconced in the greenhouse, smoking weed? For I'd guessed why her pupils were so dilated, and recognised the aroma pervading the cottage with its musky sweetness.

Then I called Roisin, but she didn't answer her mobile. She was probably at work too; her new job, I couldn't remember what it was, or if she had even told me. Carolyn answered straightaway. She was at work too, but I knew that wouldn't stop her, if she felt like talking.

'They buried him in the garden?' she shrieked, and I just knew that anyone within hearing range would, instantly, have stopped whatever they were doing to listen to my revelations. 'He was hanging from the roots of a tree?' Her voiced dropped to a whisper, 'Oh, you poor thing. Would you like me to come and rescue you? I can get some time off.' I laughed, 'No, Carolyn, thanks for the offer though. I'll stay and sort it out. Iris is lovely, by the way; it's just all the other stuff.'

'Yes, Fin Delaney, the dead man in the tree… sure, you've given me the shivers, Angelica. I must get on, but I'm here anytime you need to talk, and just say if you need me to fly over.'

Someone was banging on the front door, I sat quietly, hoping they'd go away, but they weren't giving up, and I wondered if Declan had come back looking for Iris.

Mary's room overlooked the lane, so I opened her door and tiptoed across to the window. Two people were standing on the step, a man, and a woman; I breathed a deep sigh of relief, and nearly passed out from the reek of cannabis clinging to her curtains and blankets. I'd come uninvited into her little nest, her haven from reality, and I wondered why Iris hadn't been tempted to try it.

I opened the door. A young police officer flashed his badge at me, and my legs turned to jelly.

He smiled reassuringly, 'We're looking for Mary; is she here? Or Iris…?'

'Mary is up at Morgans Croft,' I replied, 'I'm not sure about Iris, she went out a while ago. She should be back soon if you want to wait. Or I could give them a message?'

'We've a few questions relating to the disappearance of a man named Fin Delaney. Do you know him?'

'No, I'm sorry but I don't,' I replied, and it was the truth, I didn't know him.

'Who are you?' asked the younger of the two, 'do you live here?'

'I'm Angelica; Iris is my mother…' it still surprised me when I said it, 'and I'm just visiting. Who are you?'

'Can you tell them the police came from the local constabulary; they'll know who we are. We've had cause to speak to Mary before.'

It was a cryptic reply and I wondered why they knew Mary; I could make a guess.

I watched them walk away; they looked back at me from the gate and smiled again. I could tell they were trying to be friendly, but I was worried. Why were they here? Had Declan carried out his threat and told the police that Mary had tried to attack him? Maybe he'd told them that he believed she was responsible for the murder of his brother. I ran back upstairs to Kathleen's room and sat on the bed. I was quaking with fear; it was over. They'd inform Declan about the body that had recently come to light, and then they would all know that Mary and Iris, and Kathleen had buried him.

CHAPTER 45

Mary didn't return that evening, or the next, so I wasn't able to tell her that the police needed to speak to her. In the end, we went to the police station without her, and Iris explained how Kathleen had killed Fin, and how they'd buried him in the garden because they were afraid that she would be imprisoned. She went on to explain how Fin would have killed her if Kathleen hadn't stepped in prevent it. He had mistakenly thought he was my father, and they'd had to hide themselves away. Tears ran down her face when she related the story of her life; how Mary was innocent, and had always been there to protect her, which was how I'd come to be left in the field. They sat on the other side of the desk looking completely dumbfounded, as if we'd invented the whole thing.
'And how do you fit into all of this?' asked the inspector when she had finished. He was obviously trying to decide if I was as mad as my mother.
'I was stolen at the age of three months, from a field in Kilkenny,' I said, 'and I arrived here just a few days ago. Declan followed me.'
'From Ireland, I suppose?' he queried.
'Yes, and from Bristol; I was visiting my aunt, who

turned out not to be my aunt at all. He nodded, and then turned to look at his stunned colleague, who raised his eyebrows. 'Will Iris and Mary be charged as accessories to murder?' I asked them.

'We'll have to check the facts, but I doubt the Crown Prosecution Service will want to pursue it. Declan Delaney has a number of unanswered charges against him in the Irish Republic, and Fin was being sought for suspected arson and murder before he disappeared.' He turned back to face Iris, 'We'll let you know where you stand as soon as we've looked into it. Don't leave the country, will you? And, Angelica, if you'd be good enough to stick around; we might need evidence from you. One more thing, if you'd mention to Mary that we're keeping an eye on her. We think she's been supplying some of her clients with something stronger than mint and parsley. I'd hate to have to arrest her.'

David was waiting outside the police station. 'Well,' he asked, 'will they be locking you up?' Iris shook her head, 'I'm not sure.'

'I reckon they'll do all they can to avoid it,' I replied, 'they were both violent criminals, you did everyone a favour when you buried Fin.'

'There, I told you so!' said David, 'This could all have been sorted out years ago.'

CHAPTER 46
Iris

Mary was back from Morgans Croft when we got home. I don't think she'd ever considered, not for a single moment, that I'd be able to stand on my own two feet. To begin with, I thought of all the years we'd wasted, hiding away, when we should have admitted it from the start and accepted the consequences. No one would have mourned Fin's passing, except his mother, and perhaps Declan; but then, maybe, some good had come from our life in Wales. Mary had been content, and she told us she had no intention of leaving, that we could go, and she would be happy to live up at the big house with old Megan until she passed away, and then she'd stay there, since Megan had promised it to her. I hoped she wouldn't turn it into a giant, weed factory; it would be ironic if she were arrested for supplying drugs when she'd escaped a charge of accessory to murder. Best of all, I'd met David, he was my friend, and I was certain we would remain friends whatever happened, even when I went back to Dublin. I spoke to Ronan; it took a while to explain everything, and he told me about the loss of his wife, who wasn't dead, though she might as well have been, and he said he couldn't wait to see me, just as soon as the police allowed me to leave.

Angelica is the best thing that has ever happened to me. I'd begun to believe that I'd never see her again, but she proved me wrong, turning up out of the blue the way she did. It was odd, almost as if she'd just come back after a few weeks away, as if we were linked by some invisible strand that had never been broken; and there was no denying she was my daughter because she looked exactly like me when I was young, as if I'd turned up out of nowhere to confront an older version of me, to see what I'd become.

I used to wonder what it would be like when she came, how I'd react, but I never realised I would feel this sense of closeness, as if, in some way, we'd never been apart. She wasn't the child I'd lost, a baby of three months, already taken for granted, and even slightly resented for the amount of time I had to give her. I'd fed her, and changed her, and we'd all marvelled at the small changes every day, and the way she recognised us and smiled. She looked like me from the start, and she was calm, and sweet natured; there was nothing of Fin; of course, now I know why.

Ronan was sweet, and kind, and we'd known each other for most of our lives, but I was captivated by Fin's good looks; he was exciting, and attractive; people noticed us when we walked into a room. Mary was jealous, she always was, and she is now, it shows in her sarcastic remarks when David calls, and in the way she looks at him; except that now I know she was only trying to protect me, in her own heavy-handed way.

I remember every second of that afternoon, all those years ago. I was washing dishes in the kitchen, and Kathleen was dozing on the couch by the back door, with Angelica, fast asleep on her lap. It was a warm autumn day of dappled sunlight, a palette of red and gold, and green, and all around us the countryside lay undisturbed for miles. A blackbird was singing just outside the window, it stopped when Fin's rusty, old van roared up the lane; and suddenly, he was there, demanding his child.

Angelica had gone, and I thought about her every waking second of every single day, worrying about her, convinced she would be missing me, wherever she was. Even if someone else were caring for her, it would never match the love that I could give her... Why did this woman think it acceptable to steal another woman's child? How could she justify causing such pain, and anguish? The burden of guilt must have been unbearable, and yet she'd continued with the deception for twenty-five years!

I'm sad that I wasn't there when she was growing, and for all that I missed, and I regret the sadness I've caused her because of my stupidity, but she's here now... at last.

We walked up into the mountains today and she told me about her life, and I was comforted to know that she'd been loved and cherished. I even felt a twinge of sympathy for Aileen and Patrick, though God knows why.

And I showed her our secret paths and the sheep on the hillside, and the way the earth sometimes falls away revealing perilous drops to the valley below us, and the blue of the sea in the distance.

I'll miss it when I leave…

Epilogue

Angelica

We said our goodbyes just a month later. It had taken that long for the police to liaise with the courts, and they'd concluded that Iris and Mary had no case to answer and were free to continue their lives. Mary had already moved out and was living on the upper floors at Morgans Croft. It had been her second home for many years, and Megan appeared more than happy with the arrangement. I'm sure Mary would have moved in before had it not been for her commitment to Iris. We went to see them before we left, and Megan told us how much she missed her sister, and that her grief had become more acute in later years when old memories were clearer, and more vivid, than those of yesterday. I don't think Mary had ever explained to her why Hanna's shop burned down, and it was probably better that she didn't now.

Iris found it harder to leave David. They'd become attached, and I'm certain that he was hoping their relationship would evolve into something else over time, but she told me she was glad they'd only ever been friends, because it meant that their friendship would continue from afar.

His mother asked us to dinner on the evening before our departure, and I was amazed that it was the first time Iris had been inside their home, despite the fact they'd been neighbours for so long. I couldn't help wondering if we were only being invited now because she was leaving. It was as if his mother was afraid; maybe she'd decided that Iris was a threat and she didn't want to risk losing him again; but what about before then, when they first arrived in Wales? Was that because of an instinctive dislike of people who didn't belong, or who were different in some way? Though the same criticism could be levelled at Iris and Mary; why had they kept their distance? Were they afraid of being noticed? Or was it because their mother had murdered Finbar Delaney?

Either way, I made up my mind that if I ever had a son, I'd accept he would, one day, leave, and I'd never resent it. David's sister had moved away a few years earlier, and she seemed able to accept that readily enough. It made me think of Don's mother, still hoping that her youngest boy would come back to her before she died. I knew now that it would never happen, and I wondered if Don, or Maura, would tell her. I hoped not, better that she went on hoping; perhaps I'd pay her a visit one day soon.

Iris was looking forward to returning to Dublin;

we'd find somewhere to live; just the two of us to begin with, though I knew she couldn't wait to meet up with Ronan, her old friend, and my father. My heart practically stopped beating every time I thought of it.

Was it too much to hope for a fairy-tale ending? All five of us, Iris, Neve, Rose, and me, living together in Ronan's big house in Cork; I could already picture it in my mind, and perhaps, if I thought about it hard enough, it would become a reality.

We were just leaving when I noticed a photograph propped against the clock on the mantelpiece. There was David, in cap and gown, accompanied by a young woman, whom I presumed was his sister as they looked so similar, but it was the smiling person standing between them, arms casually draped around their shoulders, who interested me the most.

It was Jono!

I couldn't believe it, not even six degrees of separation; Iris, David, and Jono, and myself, only three, or four if I included Carolyn, so, maybe, we'd been destined to meet all along.

David drove us to Holyhead the next morning, my mother Iris, and me, Angelica Mary Malone.

We were going home, at last.

Made in the USA
Columbia, SC
25 August 2020